THE DEAD DON'T DANCE

Also by John Enright
Pago Pago Tango
Fire Knife Dancing

THE DEAD DON'T DANCE

BY JOHN ENRIGHT

THOMAS & MERCER

Text copyright © 2014 John Enright
All rights reserved.

Published by Thomas & Mercer, Seattle

www.apub.com

ISBN-13: 9781612185026
ISBN-10: 1612185029

Cover design by Sue Walsh

Library of Congress Control Number: 2013909766

Printed in the United States of America

This one is for Liam, my one and only son

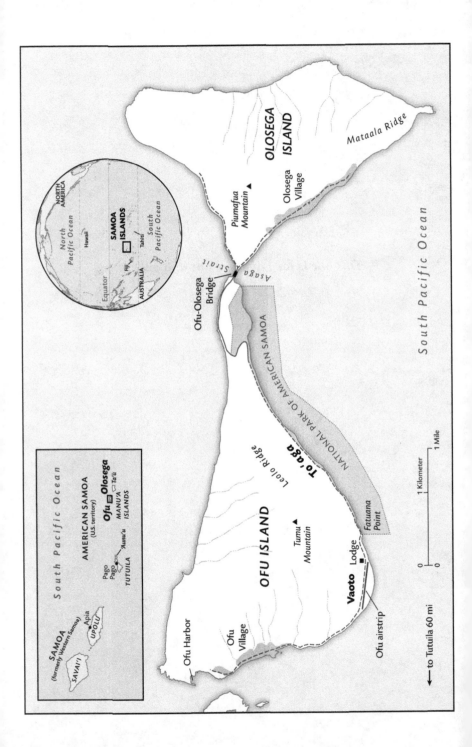

CHAPTER 1

———— o ————

W HAT APELU LIKED ABOUT WALKING DOWN THE ROAD
through To`aga was that nothing much ever changed. One
end of the road looked pretty much like the other end, and both
ends were like the middle, if you didn't pay particular attention
and didn't know the names and stories of each separate piece of
land along the way. There were no visual hints as to where one
place name ended and the next began, no boundaries. It was all
just one long straight stretch of two-lane packed-sand road bordered by plantation bush—no buildings, fences, hedges—just jungle that for thousands of years had been briefly used then allowed
to return to altered wildness, briefly planted with bananas and
taro and breadfruit then abandoned, made briefly useful then
allowed to become enriched again by being ignored, generation
after generation. The names on the land stretched back beyond
memory. But knowing all that, he could ignore all that and just
watch his feet precede one another down the sandy road. It was a
dry hot day and each flip-flop step produced a little puff of dust.

The name To`aga referred to the entire narrow strip of bush
and beach and reef along the eastern end of the tiny island of Ofu.
The road led at its eastern end to a two-lane bridge across a

narrow channel to the neighboring island of Olosega. As usual, today Apelu had the road to himself, all three miles of it from his shack at Va'oto to the Olosega bridge, then back. No one had lived here in To'aga for generations. The spirits had driven all the living away. Maybe one or two old pickup trucks would rattle past him as he walked. Off to the south side of the road beyond a shallow strip of trees and bush was the beach and the reef and the ocean. On the north side of the road the green curtain of Le'olo Ridge rose abruptly to fifteen hundred feet. In some places the distance between the cliff base and the beach was only a couple of hundred yards. It was too hot for birds today down here in the sun, but up in the shadow of the ridge he could see the ghost-white pairs of fairy terns and long-tailed tropicbirds busy at what looked like play across the cliff face. This was what he did for his hangovers— he hiked the six-mile round-trip from Va'oto to the Olosega bridge and back. He sweated last night's beer and vodka out of his body. He took his pounding head out for punishment.

Of course, sometimes he didn't make it all the way to the bridge before turning back and sometimes he might flag down a pickup truck for a ride home and sometimes he would just go sit on the beach, but it all was a form of punishment. He deserved it. He had no idea how long his sentence would run. He didn't care. What he yearned for was exile, exile from himself.

Fewer than three hundred people now lived on Ofu's volcanically precipitous and largely uninhabitable seven square miles, and Apelu wasn't really one of them. He wasn't really from there. He didn't count himself among them. And he really wasn't living. There were ten vehicles on the island—nine pickup trucks, only six of which were running, and the school bus, which also wasn't running. The road was fairly safe walking for someone not into paying attention. The only new pickup truck belonged to the *pulenu'u*, the island's mayor—a government truck. The mayor drove it too fast over the washboard road. It would soon enough be old, but it didn't yet rattle a distant warning of its approach as all the other trucks did. So Apelu was surprised, awakened from his walk, when it pulled up beside him.

"Making your daily road inspection, Detective?" The *pulenu`u* was a big man. He even looked big sitting behind the wheel of his F-150. He spoke in Samoan, friendly enough.

"It's still here," Apelu said.

"And so are you, Pelu. I don't think you've met my nephews. They just came in on this morning's plane from Pago. Ace and Danny Po`o." There were two younger Samoan men, much thinner than the *pulenu`u*, seated beside him in the front of the pickup truck who nodded and smiled. "Danny, Ace, meet Detective Apelu Soifua."

The *pulenu`u* was much too big a man to reach across to shake hands. The usual polite Samoan expressions of greeting were exchanged. Apelu asked where they had come from, and one of the brothers said Carson, California, as if Apelu might not know where Carson was.

"Your mother's name was Elisapeta Mata`alii, wasn't it?" Apelu asked.

"Yes, that's right. How did you know?"

"Her mother was my father's cousin, Filemu, from this island," Apelu said.

"You can't have many secrets from the inspector here, boys." The *pulenu`u* put the truck back into gear. "Just wanted you to meet."

"Then we're family," the brother who looked to be younger said, leaning forward to look at Apelu. "Let's get together."

The truck bounced away down the road.

———————— o ————————

When Sarah died, Apelu had lost it, even though, toward the end, her death had come as no surprise, almost a relief, for her. Acute lymphoblastic leukemia the *palangi*—Caucasian—doctors

9

finally called it, almost after the fact, when his little eleven-year-old angel was already in a coma from which she would never come back to him. During the endless hours of the endless days of watching Sarah die in the children's ward of the hospital on Tutuila that word—acute, a cute, so cute—had bounced around inside his brain, scrambling it the way a twenty-two slug behind the ear ricocheting around inside the skull made mush out of what once had pretended to sort it all out.

He blamed himself. In the end, too late, it had been just a simple blood count test that led the MDs to give her disease a name—a disease not uncommon among children elsewhere and curable with a timely bone marrow transplant somewhere else, always somewhere else. Why had no one thought to give her that test earlier? Why had he not insisted on more tests or a trip away from this primitive facility to a better diagnostic hospital in Hawaii? How could he have been so stupid, so uncaring, so trusting in the so-called medical authorities? Instead, early on, he had just picked on her for her growing laziness and lethargy, blamed her bruises on her being clumsy, and tried to get her to get more exercise and eat less junk food. And then it had all come crashing down—the first collapse, complications, organ failures, his inability to get the hospital board to take her case seriously enough for a medical evacuation up to Honolulu—the funneling black hole of defeats, each of which he had now to pass every day through his guilt-stained fingers like an endless string of worn prayer beads. And always her face before him, filled with innocence, pain, and trust. And so he drank and wandered the road and paths and untrailed bush of Ofu. Seventy miles of open ocean separated him from his home island of Tutuila, the scene of his crimes—but it was not buffer enough.

Although Apelu did not think of himself as a resident of Ofu, part of him was—a quarter of him if you fractionalized people that way. His grandmother, his father's mother, had been from here. And Apelu himself in the first dozen years of his life had spent many summers in his grandmother's *fale* near the center of the island's sole village. So he still held a certain connection to the island, including the use of several small parcels of mainly useless communal land that had been associated with the lesser, largely honorary title that his father had been given before he died. After his father's death, Apelu—at the urging of his brothers and sisters, now all back in the States—had come over to Ofu and had cleared part of one parcel of their land at Va`oto and built a rudimentary *fale* there in order to insure that the family's claim to their father's land was maintained even in their absence. Several times a year he would take the half-hour twin-prop flight from Tutuila to Ofu and spend a few days clearing the land again, repairing the shack at Va`oto, and reinserting his family's existence into the island's consciousness.

There were no land-use pressures on Ofu. The island's population had been slowly decreasing ever since the Americans had set up shop over on Tutuila a hundred years before. Whenever Apelu visited Ofu he made sure to pass out gifts—mainly money—to the holders of the island's other chiefly titles on behalf of his father's title, now unoccupied but still real even without a body to give it presence. Their family's parcels of land were outside the village of Ofu proper and insignificant. Aside from the place with the shack on a small level piece of cliff face above the landing strip in Va`oto there were several plots in To`aga and one on a stretch of the wild, uninhabited, and unvisited north shore. Nobody else really wanted them, so no one went to the political trouble of trying to claim that Apelu's family had deserted them. Many families were in the same situation. Besides, the shack was now Apelu's home.

Although Apelu thought he remembered most of what had happened at Sarah's funeral and afterward, he still couldn't make much sense out of why everything had turned out the way it did. Within a couple of weeks Apelu was on extended leave with pay from the Department of Public Safety. His eldest son,

Sanele, sixteen, had moved to his cousins' house in Aua, at the other end of Tutuila. Apelu's wife Sina had taken the two other younger kids, Isabel and Toby, and left for her mother's home in Apia in her native Western Samoa at the other end of the archipelago. And Apelu found himself clearing the bush from around the shack in Va'oto, cleaning out rats' nests in the walls, and suffering through the twilights alone.

Dusk was always the toughest time of day, when the ghosts in his brain argued the loudest—the accusers, the survivalists, the prosecutors, and the mute defendant. That was when Apelu really started to drink. If he could get all those voices inside his head drunk maybe one of them could find a song to sing or at the very least find some other topic to pick to death.

———————— o ————————

Apelu woke up in the morning to the smell of smoke, wood smoke. It was already light. In his drunken dream battles he had pulled the mosquito net above his sleeping mat down on top of him, where it was useless beyond holding him entangled in place for the mosquitoes to feast on him. There was a voice outside speaking to itself, a mumbled Samoan chant punctuated with rhythmic interjections of the English word "motherfucker" voiced as sort of a neutral observation. Then he smelled the roasting cacao seeds. Nu'upo. He was back.

Squatting beside a low fire in the lean-to cook shed behind the shack was a long stork-like old man dressed in a dirty dark lava lava and a torn Manu Samoa rugby shirt from which the sleeves had been torn off. Rail thin and white haired, he had skin the color of tree bark and limbs like outer branches. On a stray piece of roofing iron he was rolling and roasting a small basketful of dried cacao seeds. At the side of the fire Apelu's old cook pot was sending up the steam of almost boiling water. The old man stopped his roasting chant as Apelu came to the shack's screen door.

"Resurrection," the old man said in English. Then in Samoan, "You do a bad job of killing yourself."

"Bad work is what I'm best at," Apelu said, trying to get his mouth to work.

"Ah, but you have done fine work aging yourself in the past few weeks." The old man hadn't looked up from his roasting nuts.

"Thanks," Apelu said, then he wandered off to a place in the bush to take an urgent piss. Nu'upo returned to his little ditty.

Apelu had running water here at the shack—a hose he had run up through the bush from the rear of the lodge down by the airstrip—but no plumbing to speak of. A fifty-five-gallon drum at the end of the shack served both to catch rain runoff from the roof irons and to absorb the dribble that came through the low-pressure, sometimes no-pressure hose. He bathed and cooked with that water. He seldom drank it. There was still the faint taste of gasoline to it in spite of the old barrel's inner skin of green moss. He washed in an enamel basin there, splashed water over his head and upper body, rubbed the worst mosquito bites with a crumbled handful of ti leaves to numb them.

He had no electricity there so his refrigerator was really just a food locker. From it Apelu took a breadfruit he had cooked in an earth oven *umu* two days before and a can of *pilikaki* mackerel. At the side of the shack he cut two fresh banana leaves and placed the breadfruit and tinned fish on top of them on the ground near the cook shed, where Nu'upo was now grinding the roasted seeds on a flat rock, using another rock as a grinder. He was just humming now.

"*Fa'i uma*," Nu'upo said, nodding toward the fire where two leaf-wrapped bundles of green bananas had been lodged among the coals. They were cooked, and Apelu retrieved them with a green branch folded into tongs. As Nu'upo stirred the cocoa into the boiling water, Apelu opened the tinned fish with a cooking knife. They worked in silence. Apelu fetched two chipped enamel mugs from the shack for the cocoa, which Nu`upo drank straight. Apelu preferred his with milk and sugar, but he only had sugar. There were ants in the sugar container, but that didn't matter. Apelu stirred two big spoonfuls of it into the thick steaming brew in his mug. It was still bitter with scorched caffeine.

"Leai se miti?" Nu`upo asked. He wanted some coconut cream to dip his bananas in. There was none. "Motherfucker," he said calmly and dipped his banana into the mackerel can instead to soak up some juice. Otherwise they ate in silence.

It had been a week or so since Apelu had last seen Nu`upo. Nu`upo did that. He just went away, disappeared, and he never seemed different when he reappeared or said anything about where he had been. Not that he was one of the ghosts, an *aitu*, who populated most of the island. Everyone knew Nu`upo. For more than a few locals he was all too real, a sort of civic embarrassment. A lot of people would have liked to be able to pretend that Nu`upo was just another ghost story, but he wouldn't let them.

Apelu didn't have much appetite. He took his mug into the shack and added a shot of cheap vodka to the brew to steady his nerves and to see if it would improve the burnt taste. It didn't.

"I've got something to show you," Nu`upo said.

"So show me," Apelu said, tearing off a piece of breadfruit.

"It's not here," Nu`upo said, in disgust. "If you want to look at something here, you can look up my ass."

"I'm not an astronomer," Apelu said through a mouthful of breadfruit.

Nu`upo spat out a mouthful of cocoa with an explosive laugh. "I agree—seen one black hole, seen them all. What I want to show you is back on your title's land in To`aga."

——— o ———

It was the usual walk for Apelu except that Nu`upo was along. Nu`upo had insisted on bringing along plenty of water, so Apelu had slowly filled four one-liter plastic bottles from the hose while Nu'upo had cleaned up after their meal. Apelu watched Nu'upo wrap with leaves the leftover breadfruit and bananas and stash them. Where he stashed them was one of the incongruities of Nu'upo. In his nomaderings Nu'upo carried a single piece of luggage—a stained but still sturdy Lands' End fanny pack with zippers and Velcro and quick-release plastic clasps. It had once been yellow. The old man didn't wear shoes, not even flip flops, much less underwear, but he had his yuppie equipage. Apelu carried the bottles of water in a string bag hung over his shoulder, where they bounced like a well needed massage against the small of his back as he walked.

It was a gray morning. The bottom of the cloud sky had sunk to halfway down the face of Le'olo Ridge. Mist spies crept like fingers down the cliff's crevices. The sand road was spotted with khaki-colored puddles. There were no birds. The only sound was of them walking, and even that sound seemed muffled, absorbed by the air, as if no noise was to be suffered here. Even the sea was silent. So was Nu'upo—no chatter, no chants.

Apelu knew about Nu'upo about as much as anyone else knew about Nu'upo, except Nu'upo himself, of course. Nu'upo was notorious for his refusal to supply any additional information about his past. He had been born in Ofu and had spent his first sixteen years here as perhaps the most privileged child in the village—the only child of the island's only *faifeau*, the Samoan Christian minister. The oldest villagers remembered him as slight, polite, quiet—the *faifeau*'s kid. His contemporaries—like the fat *pulenu'u*—remembered him as the wild kid who never got caught while someone else—one of them—would always end up being blamed.

When Nu'upo was sixteen, his father the *faifeau* accepted a more lucrative offer to head a larger congregation over in Pago Pago, and the family left the island with the villagers' bad feelings trailing after them, because they saw the departure as a desertion.

End of part one of Nu'upo on Ofu story. Flash forward thirty years. Nu'upo returned and took to the bush, alone. He set himself up in a minimal camp in a back valley up the mountain and basically disappeared. It spooked the shit out of everyone—Samoans don't do things like that—but after a while other things happened in the village and people got used to him being up there and just wished he would stay up there. He'd come down to the village every so often to pick up his mail—all from the mainland—and buy a few things. After a while, somehow, the *taulasea*, the women curers, were getting much of their jungle herbs and roots and berries and bark squeezings from Nu'upo. But nobody liked him. He spoke rudely to the men and lewdly to the women. He wanted no part of their gossip and politics. He never came to church. He lived out there with the *aitu* and not even the spirits could hurt him. He had been in the bush now for almost twenty years. Apelu wasn't sure how he felt about him. Nu'upo seemed unknowable, but Apelu found his presence calming.

Apelu broke the silence of their steps. "Say, Gramps, why did you come back here?" he asked, not expecting a response.

"They elected Ronald Reagan President of the United States," Nu'upo answered matter-of-factly, in English. Their conversations had a way of bouncing back and forth from Samoan to English depending on the topic. Sometimes a sentence would start in Samoan and end in English or English words would pop in.

"Took it personally, huh?"

"No. It was just a sign—everything spinning too fast in the wrong direction. Time to retreat."

"Forever?"

"What else is there?" Nu'upo said with a shrug and picked up the pace.

Nu'upo was maybe ten yards in front of Apelu when he cut off the road into the bush on the ridge side. Apelu followed. There wasn't much of a trail, just the path through lush weeds that Nu'upo was making. Nu'upo could be right. One of Apelu's family parcels, a wedge-shaped piece along the bottom of the cliff, was in the direction they were headed. It had a weird name that sounded more Fijian than Samoan to Apelu, and it was the only parcel Apelu didn't know the story of. It was wet as they walked. The morning hadn't warmed up enough to dry the dew from the greenery. When the high canopy trees closed over them it was almost chilly—the atmosphere, not the temperature. Nu'upo finally stopped at a small clearing where a partly visible Samoan house foundation—a circle of raised stones maybe ten yards across filled with broken coral—held its own against the jungle.

"*Vai, fa'amolemole*," Nu'upo said, sticking his hand out for a bottle of water. Apelu unslung the net bag from his back, opened it, and handed a bottle to Nu'upo, who wouldn't take it. "*Fa'amolemole*," he said, raising his eyebrows at the bottle. Apelu opened the bottle. Keeping the cap, he passed the bottle to the old man. "*Fa'afetai lava*," he said as he took it then drank. When he finished drinking, half the bottle had been drained.

"This yours?" Nu'upo said, nodding toward the earth and handing the bottle back to Apelu.

"Yes, this is Nandiaka."

"Yes, this is where your Rotuman blood comes from."

Apelu was not aware that he had any Rotuman blood in him.

"You don't know the story, do you?" Nu'upo asked as if uninterested in the answer.

"No."

"Good," Nu'upo said. And he stuck his hand out again for the water bottle, took it, finished it, and handed the empty bottle back to Apelu. "Come," he said and started off toward the base of the cliff. "Walk this way," and he started doing a clownish monkey walk, then cackled and resumed his normal gait. Every so often after that to try to make Apelu laugh he would break into a few ape steps, cackle, and then walk right again. Apelu realized he hadn't thought about Sarah all morning, until just then, of course. Sarah would have loved Nu'upo's antics, mimicked him.

Nu'upo stopped at a boulder about the size of a compact car. The boulder was obviously newly arrived on the scene. The bush and trees behind it to the base of the cliff were all crushed, and a small talus slope of fresh earth pointed to its path down the sheer face.

"Your new tenant," Nu'upo said in English. There was no word in Samoan for tenant.

Apelu again unslung the net bag and took out another bottle of water, unscrewed its top, and offered it to Nu'upo, who shook his head and made a disdainful face as if Apelu was offering him a drink of warm piss. Apelu drank.

"She's just moved in with her family," Apelu said. The bush here was erratically strewn with similar, earlier visitors from above.

"But this sister brought a message," Nu'upo said, moving around to the back of the rock. Apelu joined him. There on a particularly flat rock face were chiseled patterns of human design. Apelu emptied what was left of his bottle of water over the careful incisions and wiped it with his hand to remove the surface dirt.

There was a large sea turtle, seen from above, in the middle of the composition, carefully rendered. Above it and below it were tattoo-perfect representations of western square-rigged sailing ships with just bare masts and spars as if anchored in small covens around the turtle. Outside of that things got a little wild. There were randomly placed closing spirals and a repeated design that looked distinctly like a woman's genitalia.

"Nice cunts, huh?" Nu'upo said.

"I especially like the big one on the upper left," Apelu said, gesturing with his eyes. Then, caressing the turtle's back, "Kind of nice."

"If you've got a thing for Stone Age art, I guess."

"Let's keep it."

"Let's."

"Nu'upo, which is your favorite pussy?"

"My favorite's not up there. She never made the top ten."

"The top ten being the ones that get engraved in stone?"

"Stone Pussies. Leaves me cold."

"A country and western lesbian band?"

"Whatever gets you there," Nu'upo said, wandering off.

Apelu stood there for a while, transfixed, running his hand over the design, picking gravel out of cracks. He found Nu'upo back at the house foundation, sitting on a rock, eating the leftover breadfruit. "*Vai,*" he said, dispensing with the polite *fa'amolemole,* and stuck out his hand. Apelu handed him the third bottle of water.

"I think we better keep this a secret," Nu'upo said. "Maybe even cover it up with dirt."

"Okay by me, but why?" Apelu said, reaching over for a piece of breadfruit.

Nu'upo slapped his hand away. "Because of those park people," he said. "They'll make a big stink about it, probably try to take your land." Nu'upo reached into his fanny pack, which was on the ground next to him, and pulled out a very dry baked banana and handed it to Apelu. After a few bites Apelu had to open the fourth bottle of water in order to wash the banana down.

The park people were the American *palangis* who managed the National Park of American Samoa. Part of the park was here on Ofu—the beach and the reef that ran for two miles along To'aga's oceanfront. It had to be the most unvisited National Park in the world. Ofu was at the end of nowhere. The only way out was to go back. There were no stores besides three tiny bush stores in the village, no restaurants, no bars. The only accommodations were at the lodge beside the airstrip, and its ten cabins were almost always empty. There was the pristine beach and the reef and the scenery—all of which could be found at places much closer to a fresh tube of sunscreen or a piña colada and much easier to get to. There were marine scientists sometimes and *palangis* from Tutuila over on a weekend getaway. Samoans would never come here, to the most famously haunted island in the archipelago, to bask on a beach—which is not a Samoan pastime anyway—fronting the capital of bad juju, To'aga. All of which was just fine with the locals. The village got yearly lease payments from the National Park Service for the beach and the reef. No one ever went there anyway.

Apelu didn't share Nu'upo's distrust of the park people. In the abstract, the idea of the park made him uncomfortable, but the park people themselves seemed pretty harmless. In most cases they were polite and well meaning, sort of childlike really. Over the years he had gotten to know a few of them. They were always changing—be here a few years then get transferred out. Most of the time there were no park people here on Ofu. They just came over from the park headquarters on Tutuila, stayed at the lodge a few days, and conducted their wildlife studies. But Nu'upo and others seemed to see their presence as the feds making a beachhead in a campaign to take the whole island away from them. It was an emotional issue.

"So why don't we just ignore the rock?" Apelu said. "Pretend it's still hidden up at the top of the cliff."

"You don't think we should try and cover it?"

"If we walk in here one more time, someone is going to wonder where that newly beaten path goes." Besides, it's too much trouble, Apelu thought.

"Good point. We'll go out another way."

Nu'upo led the way out. They walked parallel to the cliff a ways until they were off of Apelu's land, then found a path leading out from a grove of coconut trees. As they approached the road, they heard voices speaking in Samoan and stopped. Nu'upo left the trail and motioned for Apelu to follow. A bit further up the road away from the village, they could see the metallic glint of a truck parked at the side of the road, then a couple of yellow hard hats at the edge of the bush, one close, one farther away.

"Whose truck is that?" Nu'upo whispered.

"The *pulenu'u*'s, I think. It's the only one still that shiny."

"What do you think they're doing?"

"Looks like they may be surveying, from the way those hard hats haven't moved."

"Surveying! It's those park assholes, and on this side of the road, too, not on their side, and the *pulenu'u*, that prick, is helping them out surveying our land."

"I don't know any of that, old man."

"Come on, we'll deal with this. Give me this," Nu'upo said, pulling on Apelu's net bag that now held just four empty plastic bottles. Apelu slipped it off and gave it to him. "Now, go further back in the jungle and when you hear something funny, start shaking some trees."

Apelu did as he was told. He remembered a stand of bamboo they had just passed on the trail and headed back there.

It was a funny sound. Knowing what was making it, he almost laughed. But if you didn't know what was making it, it could be spooky, especially if you were a Samoan intruding into a place you knew was deserted because of its history of spooks and possessions. Nu'upo had obviously taken one of the bottles out of the bag and was making it whistle by blowing over its mouth, but the weird part of the sound was the rest of the bottles inside the net bag being used as an arrhythmic rhythm instrument bouncing together inside the net bag. They made an unearthly, unidentifiable hollow sound. Apelu started shaking the bamboo, which being tall and slender kept up a swaying motion as he worked his way through the stand, getting as many as he could in motion. The morning being so profoundly still and silent made all the noises more surprising. Nu'upo was getting into it. He would stop, move, and start again. He began throwing in little inhuman grunts and moans. Apelu moved forward in the bamboo, getting into it too. Then they heard the truck doors slam and the truck take off a little too fast, as usual for the *pulenu'u*.

Nu'upo was pleased. He had incorporated his monkey walk into a little dance that he was doing in the trail as Apelu came back toward the road, smiling. Nu'upo was improvising another "motherfucker" chant. But when Apelu clapped him on the shoulder, Nu'upo stopped his chant and his dance and jumped away. "Best be going," he said abstractly as if suddenly bored with being there. "Not on the road though. Someone might see us. On the beach. No one will see us there." And he dropped the bottles on the trail for Apelu to pick up and left. Apelu never caught up with him. He had the feeling he wasn't supposed to.

CHAPTER 2

———————— o ————————

A DOG WAS DYING SOMEWHERE IN THE BUSH OFF TOWARD To`aga. In the dark Apelu could hear its panicky whine in the distance. The sound went on much too long, long enough for Apelu to begin to understand the pain the animal was describing.

Apelu was drinking, watching the darkness beyond the screens and the yellow light of the kerosene lantern on the table in front of him. There were also two tin mugs on the table and a big green bottle of Vailima beer and an even bigger clear plastic bottle of vodka. One mug was for the beer, the other was for the vodka. He missed having the beer cold and ice cubes in the vodka, but that was part of the punishment.

It had been several days since his outing with Nu`upo, who had disappeared again. On his way home along the beach that day, Apelu had realized that it had been many weeks since the last time he had touched another human being—he had been surprised by the skeletal hardness of the old man's shoulder— then wondered how much longer it must have been since Nu`upo had felt the touch of a human hand. It was as if that sort of thing—human contact, the feeling of your skin on someone else's skin—was a thing of the past, a memory like passion or laughter or dreams without nightmares. He took a drink of vodka, winced, and washed it down with a gulp of jungle-temperature Vailima. He lit another cigarette. Another night in paradise. He watched big coconut beetles banging into the screen door, trying to get in to visit his lantern. Then he saw the fairy lights dancing on the leaves. Just like Tinker Bell—one of Sarah's favorites. Fairy lights?

"Yo, Apelu." It was a man's voice, *palangi* flat, friendly. Apelu got up and went to the screen door and opened it, leaned out. The disembodied beams of two flashlights were bouncing up the overgrown ruts of his lane from the road. "*Talofa*, Apelu. It's me, Martin."

"And me, Bobbie."

Park people. It figured. Only *palangis* would dare come out at night in this neighborhood. Apelu went back inside, recinched his lava lava around his waist and found a cleanish T-shirt to slip on.

"Come in, come in," Apelu said as the pair of *palangis* came under the eaves of the shack. He splashed his vodka cup full of vodka, then stuck the bottle out of sight.

"We brought you some cold beers," Martin said as he opened the screen door. He handed Apelu a plastic bag with a six-pack in it. "We're not interrupting anything, are we?"

Apelu knew that Martin was just being polite, but the question sounded almost like an insult to him—like, of course you're not doing anything up here in the dark alone, are you, you solitary, useless piece of shit?

"Just memorizing the Koran," Apelu said, accepting the bag of beer. "When did you guys get in?"

"On this morning's plane," Bobbie said, following Martin into the shack. "How are you?" She gave Apelu a peck on the cheek and a squeeze on his arm. For a moment Apelu felt the panic Nu'upo must have felt when he touched him on the trail.

There was a muscle impulse to flee, but the scent of her—soap, health, spearmint gum—quelled it.

"Hey, terrific. Pretty soon I will totally understand the Islamic mindset," he said, still frozen.

Apelu knew Martin and Bobbie mainly from seeing them around Tutuila, but they had been up to the shack a number of times before, in happier times. They were both marine biologists with the Park Service and had been around longer than most park people because their specialty was the reef, the likes of which existed in no other National Park. They were among the harmless ones. They weren't a couple, just co-workers. Martin Berm was Apelu's age, maybe a little older, slight and sandy haired, with thick glasses. A precise, undemonstrative type, a man who seemed to care more about reef fish, their habits, habitats, and happiness than about people.

Bobbie Wentworth was much younger, not long out of graduate school. She was a stretch of lanky bone covered with finely formed tanned flesh basted with a delicate fuzz of golden sunburned hair. She carried herself like an NBA player, had eyes the color of the sea inside the reef and a slightly crooked-tooth smile, suggesting that she had fallen off a bike more than once when she was a kid. Her hair was cut short like a boy's. Bobbie had once told Apelu that in graduate school she had decided to do her dissertation studies on a certain type of shrimp because it lived only in tropical waters. She had grown up in Wisconsin or Minnesota or one of those places and had had enough of that. She had told him that the first time they met, standing next to each other in a random group gathered around the back of a pickup truck in the dark outside a party. They had been drinking beers, and someone passed a joint around. They had gotten stoned together and talked. Bobbie hadn't known then that Apelu was a cop.

Apelu opened three of the beers, and they all found seats at the table. Apelu moved the kerosene lantern to the far end so it wouldn't be between them. They toasted each other—*Manuia*—and clinked bottles.

"Good to see you back," Apelu said. "How long you here for?"

"Just four or five days," Martin said, "to check our reef transects."

"You've been over longer than usual this time, Apelu," Bobbie said, watching him take a drink from his vodka mug. "Tired of commuting?"

"I've given up commuting for communing." Apelu got up and emptied the ashtray.

"I was sorry to hear about your daughter," Bobbie said, going exactly where Apelu didn't want her to go. "It must be tough."

"Kids shouldn't go first," was all Apelu could manage. "So, Martin, what's new?"

"Well, we've gotten some exciting new sea turtle data. Some of the species may not be as close to extinction as we previously feared, and some new international protocols about protecting them are closer to being in place . . ." Martin went on about what was new, for him. Apelu was still feeling frozen inside from Bobbie's touch. He didn't have it in him to say that he didn't give a shit about fucking sea turtles. Bobbie was watching him closely.

"Apelu," Bobbie broke into Martin's monologue, "are you eating well?"

"You know us Samoans, we just laze around all day and eat whatever falls out of God's green trees, like canned mackerel and cabin biscuits."

"You've lost weight."

"The Shack Diet Plan. You've discovered my secret." That must have sounded a little harsh, because both Martin and Bobbie went silent and just sipped their beers.

Martin came back unfazed. "Say, we heard down at the lodge that there were some surveyors from Tutuila over here recently. Know what that's about? They were taking surveys down by the park, we were told."

"I heard about it," Apelu said. "I thought they were with you guys."

"No," Martin said, "we don't need any surveyors."

The howls of the dying dog had stopped with their arrival. Now they resumed, weaker, more hopeless, even farther away.

"Poor thing," Martin said matter-of-factly, like a scientist taking a reading.

"I wonder what could have happened to it?" Bobbie said. "It probably wasn't hit by a car."

"Probably had a hunting run-in with a feral pig," Martin said in that tone that had no "probably" about it.

"Ghosts got it," Apelu said. "A slow death because they're incorporeal. It takes a while for them to suck the soul out of something." Sometimes empirical answers bothered him, especially when they were based on guesses.

The evening's visit didn't last much longer. Martin and Bobbie left the remaining three cold beers, which Apelu drank quickly, savoring their lingering coolness. As they were leaving, Bobbie invited Apelu down to dinner at the lodge the next night, as their guest.

───────── o ─────────

They sat with their cups of coffee at the lodge's long dining table after the dishes of the communal meal had been cleared away. Apelu switched seats so that he was downwind from the fan and from Martin and Bobbie. He was going to have a cigarette with his coffee and he knew that Martin would make a little scene if his smoke got anywhere near him. It was one of those new gestures of cordiality these people expected. That he would smoke at all in front of them was already a social imposition almost as bad as whacking off. First he went out the front screen door and picked out a blackened shell that some previous sinner had used as an ashtray.

Apelu had arrived for dinner half drunk, but the hot meal had eroded the edge of his high. He decided to have a beer—all there was—with his coffee and cigarette, and he got himself one from the cooler. For some reason the mashed potatoes—Sarah's favorite real food—had almost reduced him to tears. He was all right now. In control. He'd have a smoke, a cold beer or two, then get back to the safety of his shack.

As if she had learned the previous day, Bobbie had not given Apelu a welcoming hug and kiss—just a big hello from across the room—nor gotten close to him all evening. He appreciated her giving him that comfort distance. Ironically, it made him feel closer to her. Martin was Martin. His consistency in being Martin was one of his endearing qualities. You could rely upon Martin to be Martin.

Bobbie wanted to know about To'aga being haunted. "I mean everybody says it is, but no one's told me why, or how."

"Oh, pooh," Martin said. "That's because it isn't, and there is no why or how. People had to come up with some reason why no one wants to live there, so they invented some spirits to blame it on. The real reason was probably something as simple as they got tired of having their houses flattened by boulders coming off that cliff, so they moved their village around the corner of the island to where that doesn't happen."

"I guess there are just places that stories get stuck to," Apelu said. "Some places—like Lourdes, say—good stories get stuck to. Other places—like To'aga—only the scary stories stick. It's one of those self-feeding, self-fulfilling phenomena."

"Like what other self-feeding, self-fulfilling phenomena?" Martin asked.

"I can't think of a single one." Apelu paused. "Maybe the Chicago Cubs?"

Bobbie laughed. Martin either didn't see it or didn't care to acknowledge seeing it.

"I mean a reputation isn't a cause and effect thing," Apelu went on. "It's an accumulative thing. When you see a stranger having a cigarette and a beer, you don't necessarily conclude he's a good-for-nothing. That reputation takes diligence and repetition."

Bobbie looked at Apelu and said nothing.

"Let's get back to the point," Martin said. He took off his glasses and wiped them with a corner of a napkin. He looked decades younger without the glasses on, like a graying Boy Scout. "We do have an effect—To'aga's reputation. Ockham's Razor leads us to posit first a simple cause, not a complex series of causes."

"Whose razor?" Apelu asked. "I don't know what tradition you're talking from. I do know that if you're going to try to explain something that's alive—like To'aga's rep—then you have got to study it where it is at and not lob it off and take it to some lab somewhere. You got to study the scene of the crime. Look for clues, not causes." Apelu got up to get himself another beer. He offered to get one for Martin and Bobbie. Martin accepted.

"We don't call them clues," Martin said. "We call that data." He hadn't put his glasses back on, which was strange. He was looking at Bobbie. Ah, that inclusive "we." There was a soft look on his boyish face. Bobbie didn't notice.

"What clues?" Bobbie asked Apelu.

"Let's say all your rapes occur in the same neighborhood. Wouldn't you conclude that your rapist lived in that neighborhood?"

Bobbie blanched a little at the example, but Martin went with it. "A serially successful criminal would be bright enough not to soil his own nest." His glasses were back on.

"We're not talking bright here, Martin. We're talking dark, like in the dark."

Bobbie said, "We heard that the survey crew that was here refused to go back to To'aga after something that happened to them in broad daylight."

"Goldbrickers," Martin said.

"They left on the next plane, right?" Bobbie looked to Martin for confirmation, but Martin was no longer looking at her.

"You are not going to attempt to defend a superstitious position, are you, Apelu?" Martin had taken on a little glow.

"You're the scientist, pal," Apelu said. "You want some data?"

"That's what I was talking about," Bobbie said, tucking her long legs up under her on her chair, "the skinny."

"The blarney, you mean." Martin leaned forward, his elbows on the table, slowly turning his bottle of beer back and forth between his palms.

"Okay," Apelu said, "in your mind make three columns, label them P, S, and WS and give them each a distinctive symbol. Now draw a mental map of To`aga. I could cover that map with those symbols where stuff happened and fill the columns with incidents. P stands for possession, S for seduction, and WS for weird shit. Possession is when the unresolved issues of a dead person are strong enough for them to take over a living agent. Seduction is when an unhappy spirit with sexual issues convinces someone, somehow, that it is materially and erotically available, and the seduced human almost always dies. And weird shit is other unexplainable stuff that happens."

"You used the word spirit," Martin interjected. "Can you define it?"

"Nope, can't. Why don't we call it X, the unknown we are trying to solve for."

"Give me an example of possession," Bobbie said.

"Let's call them case studies." Apelu lit another cigarette. "Confirmed and agreed to by all witnesses."

"And only orally documented, I presume," Martin said.

"Just because knowledge is communally owned doesn't make it false," Apelu said, turning on him. "All you have is a belief system for a certain method. There are other methods of knowing things."

"I like things measurable," Martin said.

"That's your basic problem. You can't stick a thermometer up an apparition's ass."

"Because it is an illusion."

"Anything you can't measure is automatically an illusion? How many teeth do you still have, Martin?"

"Why, I'm not sure. I could count them later."

"I guess until then your teeth are an illusion. I wouldn't eat anything if I were you, Martin, until you have counted them, and I wouldn't accept your conclusion that they aren't an illusion until you could have that data affirmed by an independent study."

"I am not counting Martin's teeth, and he seemed to do all right with dinner," Bobbie said. "Besides, I thought we were going to hear some bedtime ghost stories."

"Bobbie, have you ever experienced anything here that you can't explain?"

"You mean aside from that constant feeling that I'm being watched? Yeah, a number of nights, lying awake in my cabin, I could swear I heard a party going on down at the beach—songs and people laughing, loud conversations. I only went down to check the first time I heard it and there was nobody there. I sort of knew there wouldn't be, but I had to check. After that I just figured it was. . . well, an illusion, or delusion, I guess. I was just wrong."

"Martin?" Apelu asked.

"My experiences have nothing to do with your proving your hypothesis, whatever it is. What is it, by the way?"

"That shit goes on that you can't measure or explain, Martin. That there is a reason why no one has lived in To'aga for so long. There is a cause for that effect, and that by calling it superstition or native voodoo or whatever doesn't cut it as an explanation. That dismissal is both racist and willfully ignorant. You just don't want to know, that's all. Maybe if you found some haunted reef fish you'd get involved in all those things your scientific method likes to ignore."

JOHN ENRIGHT

"How would I know if they were haunted?"

"Precisely."

"Oh, pooh."

"Bobbie, I'll give you a possession case study that you can check up on because it happened just a couple of years ago here in the village, but it is similar to other older stories I could pinpoint on our To'aga map. A perfectly normal twelve-year-old girl—I can give you her name—one night after dark, out of nowhere starts speaking in an older woman's voice and acting strange. She starts yelling out swear words and snatches of accusation loud enough to get the neighbors' attention. She marches out of her house and down the road through the village, sounding all the while angrier and older. A crowd has formed, following her, keeping their distance. The girl stops outside the house of an elder chief and in this now fully adapted role and voice calls out the chief's wife to upbraid the old lady over an affair she was having with 'my husband,' whom she names and who has been dead a dozen years. The real wife of the dead man had recently died. No one knew anything about an affair between the chief's wife and the dead man. The possessed young girl screeched out where and when it had happened, not in the village, but over in Pago. The chief's wife denied nothing, collapsed, left for Pago, and died in the hospital there a month later. The whole village witnessed it."

"My god. How was the girl afterward?" Bobbie asked.

"It took her about six months to get back to normal. She couldn't remember any of it. She's still a little strange. The weird thing was that she wasn't closely related to any of the parties involved, but, it turned out, she had been in To'aga earlier that day, had snuck off there with her boyfriend. I could put where they went on the map, right in the middle of a crowd of our other symbols."

"So, it's like a village of the unhappy dead," Bobbie said.

"Think of it as a retirement community. We do." Apelu went suddenly silent.

"Now how about a sample case study for seduction and one for weird shit?" Bobbie asked.

"Another time," Apelu said as he got up and stuck his cigarettes and lighter into his pocket. "I gotta go." As he had told the story the young possessed girl had taken on in his storyteller's eye the shape and form not of the actual girl but of Sarah. It was Sarah he saw screaming the words of the dead woman. It was all too confusing. He felt cold inside again. He needed a real drink. He turned and left without saying goodnight.

———————— o ————————

It was that time of year. Technically it was the dead of austral winter, mid-July, but "winter" gave the wrong impression. The temperature was, on average, several degrees below what it reached in the opposite season, and there were no endless days of solid rain nor the threat of cyclones, but winter it wasn't. Apelu had spent enough years in Northern California to know that the islands' minimal climatic shifts from solstice to solstice would hardly be noticed by a visitor. It was still eighty degrees when the sun went down. That didn't mean that the weather was nice. When the trades stopped, the wind could shift around into any direction it chose. For a bunch of days now it blew from the south, which was not nice. It was squally, unfriendly weather, especially if you lived in a shack with no windows over the screens and a roof that was better at keeping the sun out of the place than the rain.

It was depressing inside the shack, so Apelu hiked a lot. Even soaked to the skin there was no threat of hypothermia, unless it was from the glacier he'd managed to become inside. He was back into his prisoner-of-himself routine. He was beginning to loathe it. So he started working on his plantations just to do something else besides sulk. One rainy afternoon, hiking back on the road to Va`oto from another parcel of his father's land in To`aga, carrying a bush knife and a shoulder pole with bunches of coconuts tied to either end, he saw something move in the beachside bush a hundred yards ahead. He stopped and watched. A minute or two later Bobbie limped out onto the road. She had on a turquoise swimming suit top and a wet green lava lava tied around her waist. White zinc oxide cream on the bridge of her nose and her cheekbones gave her a weird painted warrior look. She was carrying an orange net dive bag with her snorkel and fins and other gear in it. She was favoring her right foot to the extent that she was moving slowly. It didn't take long for Apelu to catch up with her. She didn't hear him coming. She was looking down at her foot as she hobbled along. His "Yo, Bobbie" startled her.

"Oh, it's you," she said, regaining her composure. "I thought I was about to be possessed, seduced, or exposed to other weird shit."

"What did you do to yourself, girl?" They had stopped and Apelu stooped down to unburden himself.

"Occupational hazard. I was resetting one of our transect markers on the outer edge of the reef when a big wave hit me, slammed me into some fire coral."

"Hate that."

"Me too, but I've got some goop in a tube back in the room that takes the sting out, after a while."

"Where's Martin?"

"Still out there working."

"How gallant."

"I can and do take care of myself, Apelu."

"You bleed well, anyway." The T-shirt Bobbie had wrapped around her right ankle was red with blood. Apelu picked up his pole with the coconuts and hid them and the bush knife a couple of yards into the bush. He came back and took Bobbie's dive bag and slung it over his right shoulder. "Come on. I'll be your crutch." She hung her right arm over Apelu's shoulder and lifted her injured foot off the ground. Apelu put his left arm around Bobbie's back to help her hop along. This meant his skin was touching hers across her back and his hand was in her left armpit, but this time his core did not get colder. It began to warm up a little.

They walked and hopped along in silence a while. The rain started up again in earnest. Apelu broke the silence, "So you work even on shitty days like this?"

"It's better on sunny days, but if you're underwater anyway it really doesn't make that much difference if it rains, as long as the seas aren't rough."

"Weren't you supposed to leave like a couple of days ago?"

"No planes."

"Yeah, they can't land with the wind from the south like this."

Another hundred yards of silence. This time Bobbie broke the silence. "Since we're talking about work, I'll ask. So now you're just a recluse farmer and no longer the star detective of the Department of Public Safety?"

"Star detective?"

"I was just being flattering. I don't know anything about what you do, or did."

"I'm on leave."

"Leave from what?"

Another hundred yards of silence. They came to the curve in the road where the base of the ridge jutted out toward the beach marking the end of To'aga.

"Apelu, let's rest. I'm getting tired of hopping." They sat down on a boulder by the side of the road. Bobbie fussed with the T-shirt around her ankle. Still bent over she asked, "What are you doing tonight? Still studying Islam?"

"No, gave up on it. Realized that it was just another religion that doesn't make any more sense than any other religion."

"That's a rather bizarre conclusion, coming from a Samoan. I thought everyone here was a hundred and fifty percent religious."

"Exactly. How possible is that?" Apelu started tossing pebbles at a puddle out in the middle of the road.

"So, you bring down the average by being zero percent?"

"It's just the churchy thing, the holier than thou competition, the money rip-off. It sucks. Let's not go there. Why? What are you doing tonight?"

"I heard there was going to be a song and dance performance over in Olosega tonight. I thought I'd like to go. I thought you might take me."

"It's a church fundraiser."

"So, don't give them any money."

"What about Martin? Can't he take you?"

"Come on, Apelu. Martin doesn't do things like that—people, crowds, culture—and he has to be in bed by nine or some unspecified disturbance would upset his life cycle."

"You've got cabin fever, huh?"

"Everyone's not a hermit like you." Bobbie stood up. "Okay, let's get on with it." They resumed their traveling position. "So what do you say? We can take the park pickup truck to get over there and back."

"What about your foot?"

"Between my goop and a palmful of pain killers I'll be fine but not danceable."

"What time?"

"Come down for dinner again. We'll go after that."

"Okay, I guess."

"You guess?"

"We'll see, sure."

"This is not boosting my ego any here, Apelu."

"No. Sorry. It should be fun. It's just that . . ."

"What?"

"I need a haircut and I don't have anything to wear."

"So who cares?"

They walked on pretty much in silence from there to the lodge. The rain let up some. When Apelu got back to his shack there was a surprise waiting for him—hanging on a hook under the eaves there was the cleanly severed right rear shank of a wild pig with flies all over it. There was no way he could build a fire and cook it now, what with the rain, the lateness of the day, and the fact that he had a date tonight. So he left it there. The flies could tenderize it for him overnight. God knows these wild pigs needed all the tenderizing they could get.

○

The twin islands of Ofu and Olosega were separated by a narrow, swift and deep channel. About thirty years before the US Army Corps of Engineers had come and built a two-lane concrete bridge across the channel. It seemed the natural thing to do for them, and sure enough after a while vehicles and then roads began to appear. Build a bridge and things will come. Olosega was relatively the same size, population, and mainly uninhabitable geography as Ofu, meaning that between the two islands there were fewer than seven hundred men, women, and children.

Apelu didn't get to Olosega often. No reason to. The people from Olosega had to cross the bridge and come to Ofu to get to the only airstrip and the only boat harbor, both on Ofu. But the people from Ofu had little reason to cross the bridge the other way and visit Olosega. Cricket games maybe. And the only elementary school was there. Each island had its own Christian

Congregationalist church. The kids all left at high school age and seldom returned, so there were few inter-island marriages anymore. In the old days the islands had occasionally been bitter enemies, in the hate-your-neighbors tradition of human settlements everywhere. All was harmonious now. The two villages just sort of ignored each other as much as they could, being connected by a concrete bridge.

Dinner at the lodge that night before Apelu and Bobbie left for Olosega was subdued. There was a Swedish family of snorkelers visiting—mom, dad, and three kids, each as blond as the next—but only the father spoke English, and they were a glum group. Maybe that was because they hadn't come halfway around the world to sit in the lodge and watch the rain and not be able to leave. Martin was quiet in front of strangers.

Apelu had forgotten to count the park ranger's pickup truck in his census of vehicles because it was almost never used. It spent most of its time parked in a tent beside the lodge's most removed cabin, which the Park Service kept as its sole—and usually vacant—presence on island. No one had said anything, but Apelu could tell that Martin was not pleased with Bobbie's taking the truck to Olosega to see the *fiafia* performance—not official park business—but he wasn't about to try and stop her. It wasn't like she'd be stopped by the police. There were no police, much less a police car. It was just against the regs that's all, and he was her boss and was supposed to enforce the regs.

Even though nobody asked him and the topic hadn't been raised, Apelu decided to help Martin out. "Martin, isn't part of your official duties here to maintain a good relationship with the natives?"

"Yes, goal number four in the park's mission statement."

"So, will Bobbie get overtime for fulfilling that goal by being the Park Service's representative at the community fundraiser tonight?"

"We don't get overtime."

"Comp time then?"

"Oh, all right. Take the truck," Martin said like a dad letting his daughter go out on a date.

It was well after dark by the time Bobbie and Apelu left for Olosega. Apelu had snagged a couple of cold beers from the cooler then made an excuse to go back up to his shack, where he quickly downed both of them along with as much vodka as he could. He changed his shirt and put on a dress lava lava. Bobbie was waiting for him when he got back down to the Park Service cabin. She asked him to drive. Because it was after dark, they would be the only people going over to Olosega tonight for the *fiafia*. No one else would pass through To'aga after dark. Whoever from Ofu wanted to see the performance would have gone over to Olosega before sunset and would stay there for the night. The rain had stopped. The wind had shifted back toward the east, and the cloud cover was breaking up. There was a drier feeling to the evening air. Bobbie had changed into a *puletasi*, the Samoan woman's formal wear—your basic Mother Hubbard muumuu, but more tailored, trimmed, cinched at the waist and with a fancy neckline. It came down to her ankles, the right one swollen and bandaged.

"All powered up on pain killers?" Apelu asked as he backed the Park Service truck onto the road and headed toward To'aga.

"I'm fine. How about you?"

"Good for an hour or two. You look nice all dressed up." Bobbie's *puletasi* had a wide square-cut neck that showed off her tanned collarbones and throat.

"Why thank you, Apelu. You look good, too, clean shirt and all."

The ride through To'aga was dark and peaceful, not a soul, not a light. When they crossed the bridge to Olosega some moonlight was struggling out of the clouds and spangled the ocean on both sides of them. The village was another half mile further on. Most of the villagers had already gathered at the church hall.

Apelu parked the truck by the side of the road well before they reached the hall, so as not to be too conspicuous, and Bobbie and he walked from there. As they approached the hall, the people in front of them parted to give them passage. In the outer ring were the adolescents, separate groups of girls and boys, then the younger kids gathered like moths around the hall's lights. When they got to the hall it was full, but a space was quickly cleared for them on some mats near the front, and they sat down on the floor to a wave of murmurs through the crowd.

"Looks like you're the sole Caucasian presence here tonight," Apelu said. Bobbie was blushing deeply. She sat up very straight and was looking straight ahead. "Relax. Everyone is here to enjoy the show, and your entry was just a little warm-up act."

Apelu was happy to see that Bobbie had not brought a camera. All she carried was a heart-shaped woven fan, which she now put to use. Apelu greeted the people seated around them by raising his eyebrows and nodding and exchanging quiet expressions of polite greeting. Off to one side he saw the Ofu mayor and his two nephews, the younger of whom gave Apelu a little wave and a smile.

Then the speeches began—a welcome from a high chief church elder, a five minute invocation from the village *faifeau* minister, then another, joking introduction in which the presence of special guests was acknowledged, including the Ofu mayor and his nephews and Bobbie.

"What did he say about me?" Bobbie asked Apelu from behind her fan as the crowd laughed.

"He said you were here representing Uncle Sam."

"And?"

"And that Uncle Sam must be having a hard time of it these days, a famine, if even his young lady chiefs looked so starved for food. Smile."

Bobbie smiled on command and even gave a little bow of acknowledgment. This was well received, and a ripple of smiles and applause passed through the crowd.

"You're going to be very uncomfortable sitting cross-legged like a Samoan for very long on that ankle," Apelu said and he gestured for another *laufala* mat to be passed to him. "Here, you can stretch your legs out under this and still be chaste."

She did. "Thanks," she said, resting a hand on his forearm and giving him a quick smile. "You're sweet."

CHAPTER 3

———— o ————

THE *SIVA MA PESE* SHOW THAT FOLLOWED WAS GOOD, VERY good. In this small village out on the very oldest edge of the culture, there was still a purity of identity in the dances and songs. These were not performances. These were not performers, no matter how perfectly rehearsed they seemed. These were expressions of something so shared it seemed seamless. The dancers were just the kinetic enactment of the audience's will. The songs were sung in a harmonic voice that sang for everyone within hearing. The words were as well-worn and familiar as the sound of the surf on the broken coral beach.

Apelu watched Bobbie becoming cocooned within the weaving sounds and movements, a painless possession. If the singers and dancers were performing for anyone, they were performing for her, the one outsider there, the one whom they wished to enthrall into joining them. It was working.

The next-to-last song was sung by a group of the eldest villagers, who took their time finding their places to sit cross-legged facing the audience. Time was on their side as they settled in and made their flower *ulas* comfortable around their shoulders. The old men started slapping their bare knees, old bones shifting to find the place of least pain. The rhythm established itself, skin on skin, slow. The oldest woman in the group, eyes closed behind a web of wrinkles, called out the first refrain in a high nasal falsetto. The line was repeated by those behind her, who were now nodding in unison with the beat. The leader again led the call and response, voices louder, the beat a little faster. The next line they all sang together in old half-tone harmony, and Apelu felt the hair on the back of his neck, the hair on his forearms and calves, even his pubic hair rise up. They were singing a war song that had not been sung for years, an `o le pese a le taua. It was the story of a war fought long ago between Olosega and Ofu. The old woman knew all the words and—her obsidian-irised eyes now open and drilling the crowd—she led the chorus through the gruesome details of Olosega's victory. As a woman her role was to incite the young men to take as many heads as they could and bring them back to her. She did it well. As the song went on, others inside and outside the hall were caught up in the ancient inherent rhythm. A primal moment washed down off the moonlit mountain behind them and out to the sea. The old lady's cracked voice of victory and revenge held them all together as within a net. Bobbie, not knowing what was transpiring, was transfixed. The old woman's eyes held her. Her ancient voice rose, pleading for more blood. Bobbie didn't understand a word of it. She didn't have to.

The final dance was the money-maker, the *tauluga,* where the high chief's most eligible daughter did a solo *siva* as the virginal personification of the village's continuing image of its essential purity. One by one, then in droves, members of the audience rose from the floor and approached, bowed, and threw dollar bills at the dancer's feet or slapped them onto the coconut oil–glistening skin of her bare shoulders and arms. The dancer's expression never changed—a Mona Lisa smile focused on some distant middle vision. The Ofu *pulenu`u* and his nephews threw lots of money at her, too much really. There was something unseemly about their excess. Bobbie got up to lay money at the dancer's feet; then she joined the other women now standing who swayed in their own supporting *siva* in a wide circle around the dancer. Bobbie did well. She was limping but she wasn't blushing.

Outside the hall as they were leaving, the younger nephew of the *pulenu'u* came up to them and shook hands with Apelu. "Detective Soifua, good to see you again."

"I'm sorry. I never did determine if you were Ace or Danny."

"Danny," he said and turned to Bobbie.

"Danny Po'o, Bobbie Wentworth," Apelu introduced them. "Doctor Wentworth works for the National Park."

"Quite a performance, wasn't it?" Danny said, shaking Bobbie's hand.

"Yes, it was," she said, still smiling.

"Staying here in Olosega tonight?" Danny asked Bobbie.

"No, we're going back to Ofu," Apelu answered.

"Oh," Danny seemed surprised. "My uncle wanted me to invite you to the guest *fale* where we are staying for some refreshments, but if you must get back."

"And what do you do here, Danny?" Bobbie asked, freeing her hand from his.

"Oh, here on family business, trying to finalize a few old legal matters. Just visiting, really. It's been almost twenty years since I've been back here. Sure you won't stop by for something before you head back?"

"Thank you. Maybe some other time," Bobbie said.

A hand landed on Apelu's shoulder, and he jerked his shoulder instinctively away. It was Danny's brother Ace. "Detective, good evening," he said, taking his hand away.

"Yes, good evening," Apelu answered. "And how are you tonight?" Apelu didn't like the man. Physically, he was bigger, thicker, and coarser than his brother. A gold chain around his neck, a certain swagger that Apelu's cop mind had instantly typed as perp. Apelu now noticed that there was even a crude jailhouse tattoo on the back of his left hand; predictably it was the ace of spades. The sort of guy who should carry his rap sheet folded up in his back pocket to save both of you the time and trouble of looking it up. Southern California ghetto thug, standard model.

"You guys coming over to the *fale* for a little food and drink?" He spoke LA street Samoan.

"No, thank you, Ace," Apelu said in English. "We'll take a raincheck. Thanks."

"But, ah, but I thought we could have a little talk."

"That would be nice. Another time, though."

Bobbie and Danny had drifted away from them in the moving crowd. Danny had said something that made Bobbie laugh.

"Uncle says you're with the Police Department," Ace persisted. "I was just wondering if you were over here working on something. Just curious."

As if I would tell you if I were, Apelu thought. "No, just a little break from duty to take care of our land over here. And you? You here working on something?"

"No, no, just, you know, visiting the family, getting back to the roots. So, are you still a cop, or what?"

There was a reason why this guy had done jail time. It had to do with mental development. "When did you get out?" Apelu asked casually.

"A while ago. Hey, what do you mean?" Ace was now on his guard and turned to face Apelu. "I ought to pop you one."

"Just curious, Ace. Have a pleasant rest of the evening, and give your uncle my respects and thanks and regrets." Apelu walked through the thinning crowd to where Bobbie and Danny were talking at the side of the now moonlit sandy road. They made a nice couple—blonde and brown, slim, almost the same height. Bobbie was laughing again. She'd had a nice night out. That was good.

"Well, sorry you guys can't stay," Danny said as Apelu joined them. "Maybe I'll swing by the lodge tomorrow and see what you're doing."

"I hope I'm flying out tomorrow, if the wind holds like this," Bobbie said.

"Well, whatever," Danny said cheerfully. "Goodnight."

———————— o ————————

Apelu drove slowly out of the village and out onto the bridge back to Ofu, never getting out of second gear. In the middle of the bridge he stopped. The night was suddenly very bright, not a human light in sight. The just past full moon was high, and the ocean bounced its glow all around them.

"It is peace, isn't it?" Bobbie said.

"It's where peace comes from anyway."

"You looking for peace, Apelu?"

"A piece of what?"

"A piece of your past?"

"No, I'm not looking for anything." Apelu put the truck back in gear and rolled softly ahead.

"You know," Bobbie said, "that guy Danny went to the same school I did, Cal State Fullerton. He played baseball for them, so of course I didn't know him. Isn't that weird, though? I mean, all the way out here running into someone from way back there?"

They drove up over the ridge at the bridge end of Ofu and then down into To'aga.

"Same years?" Apelu asked.

"Pretty much, though he was an undergrad and I was in graduate school then. He seemed nice."

"You know that song the old lady sang tonight?"

"That was heavy, wasn't it? Wow."

"Well, she was singing about a battle that once took place between Ofu and Olosega."

"So that's what it was all about."

"And that battle took place right here in To`aga."

"That was what her song was about?"

"Part of it."

Apelu was still driving slow, in second gear. He had the high beams on, when out at the edge of the headlights he saw a figure come onto the edge of the road, stop, then quickly cross the road into the ridge side bush. "Did you see that?" he asked.

"No, what?"

"It looked like Nu`upo."

"Who? Where? There's no one out there."

Apelu stopped the truck near where he thought he had seen the figure go into the bush. "Wait here," he said. He got out of the truck and walked to the side of the road. It was very close to the spot where Nu`upo and he had walked in to see the boulder. The truck's high beams were still on and the moon was still out, but it was perfectly black in the deep bush.

"Apelu?" Bobbie asked.

In the dark of the bush there was a motion, then a commotion. There was a whooshing sound, and Apelu instinctively ducked down. A large white owl flew out of the bush and close over Apelu's head, turned into the light of the head lamps and with a rower's muscular beat of its wings swept up the road into blackness.

"Just an owl," Apelu said as he got back into the driver's seat.

"Just an owl," Bobbie repeated.

Apelu continued to drive on slowly. At regular intervals through the rest of To`aga the owl would be waiting for them, then fly ahead in their headlights. Twice it came swooping over the truck from behind to scout the road ahead. Bobbie was silent.

"It's a good omen, you know," Apelu offered. "In all the old stories when owls appear it's before a battle. If the owl is flying in the same direction that you're marching, like this one is, it's a good omen—success in the coming fight. But if the owl is coming at you, you might as well just give up then and there and plead for a truce."

Bobbie was pretty much quiet the rest of the way home. It was late. Apelu parked the truck under its tent, got out, and handed Bobbie the keys.

"Thanks for the night out," she said.

"No, thank you," he said, "for getting me out. Goodnight, Sarah."

He was three steps away before he realized what he had said. She was still standing there, watching him. He turned and said, "I meant, goodnight, Bobbie."

———————— o ————————

Apelu was up and gathering firewood the next morning when he heard the Twin Otter land down at the airstrip just after dawn. Martin and Bobbie would leave on that plane back to Pago. He heard the plane take off as he headed back to his shack with the wood. As he chopped and stacked, then started his cook fire, he tried to count back how long it had been since he had been back on Tutuila, but he had hopelessly lost track of days and weeks with no markers. A month maybe? No, longer. He had no idea what day of the week it was or of the date. He could always go down to the lodge and ask, but he could see how silly that would make him look in their eyes, and besides, what did it matter?

He whacked the shank of pig still hanging under the eaves with the flat of his bush knife a couple of times to knock the flies and maggots off of it. He started the *umu* fire and filled his big pot with water to boil. The fire took a while to get going. They always did here for some reason. It was just hard to get a fire properly started on Ofu. Even Nu'upo complained about it. "Maybe our less visible neighbors don't like fires," he had suggested. "I guess to them it's all second hand smoke." Then Apelu washed the meat in a basin and cleaned it as best he could. He submerged the meat in the boiling water for a while then skinned it. He packed the meat with mango leaves and wrapped it securely with green taro and banana leaves.

Could it be that he had been here six weeks? There had been no messages for him, no contact. He shredded some dry coconut husks to spread on the fire and hurry it up. The sun was high now, and the air was still. The smoke didn't want to leave the lean-to cook shed. He had to walk away to clear his eyes. He went inside the shack, pulled up a floor board, reached his arm through the hole, and pulled out a big zip-lock freezer bag. Inside the bag were his passport, his wallet, his badge and ID case and handcuff case, a ring of keys, a return plane ticket to Pago, and a small photo album of pictures of Sarah and the family. He counted the money left in the wallet—only thirty-some dollars. He left the bag on the table.

The fire was finally hot enough for him to pile on the stones to heat. He was dripping with sooty sweat. He fetched a couple of breadfruit to bake in the earth oven *umu* with the pig. At home Sanele always helped him with the *umu*, and Apelu would let his son prepare the fire while he fixed what was to go in it. Here he had to do it all himself and get the timing right. Apelu wondered how Sanele was doing, and a fresh wave of guilt crashed over him. He knew that Sanele had taken his sister's death almost as hard as Apelu had, and then he had been deserted by his family, shipped off to live at his cousins' house, and expected to just continue with his life, go to school, deal with it. Apelu had been so wrapped up in his own loss and self-loathing that he hadn't fully considered his eldest son's feelings. All he knew was that when he had come to Ofu he was not fit for human companionship and that he did not want his son to see him as a wasted drunk.

Apelu finished preparing the *umu,* making a space in the middle of the hot rocks for the leaf-wrapped meat and breadfruit, covering it all with more banana leaves and then a couple of pieces of rusted roofing iron to hold in the heat. Then he went down to the beach to wash the soot and sweat off his body and take a long float. On the way back to the shack he stopped at the one-room office at the airstrip and booked himself a seat on the afternoon flight to Pago. When he left the shack to catch the plane he stuck a note on the screen door—"Nu'upo, thanks for the pig. Dinner is in the oven."

Apelu didn't go right home. He wasn't ready for the empty house. He had the cab he had caught at Pago airport drop him off down in the middle of his village of Leone, on the edge of the bay, and he sat there for a while. It was getting on sundown. He walked to Sarah's grave in the old family plot back in the village. No one was around. There was still no gravestone, just the humped earth already crawled with runner weeds, some tubs of plastic flowers tipped onto their sides. He left them as they were. The grave meant nothing to him. He never could understand the thing about graves. He had wanted Sarah's body to be buried at sea, like he thought all islanders should be buried, but of course Sina and her church would have none of it.

It was only a ten minute walk to his house. He got there just as darkness fell and the cicada chorus was rising. The porch light above the front door was still burning, but the rest of the house was dark. His old pickup truck was still parked in the side yard. The first thing he did was call Sanele. It was an emotional call. They had to cut it short because they both were close to tears of relief. Apelu would pick him up the next morning. Get his stuff together, screw school. Then Apelu called Sina at her mother's in Apia and told her he was taking Sanele back to Ofu with him for a while. The distance on the line wasn't just long distance. It was cold long distance. Sarah's sickness and death had opened a chasm between him and Sina that was a mystery to Apelu. Sina seemed to blame it all on him. She had seemed offended even by the strength of his grief. It was like she didn't want to know him, didn't want to hear what he felt or thought. She didn't like the idea of Apelu pulling Sanele out of school, but Apelu knew in his bones that what he and his boy needed was time together just to themselves, and in Ofu they could have that. He had to tell Sina that she had nothing to say about it. She hung up before he could ask about Isabel and Toby, and every time he called back after that all he got was the busy signal, its foreign *erp erp erp* sounding like the warning siren at the end of an emotional highway—bridge permanently out.

Apelu and Sanele had breakfast in town the next morning. Sanele could not stop talking. He was like a released spring. He was thrilled with the idea of going to Ofu. He was thrilled with the idea of giving high school the finger. They could fish. No one would be looking at him funny. He could help his dad on the plantations. He wouldn't have to wear a uniform. Breakfast was great. He loved the food. Could he have another glass of passion fruit juice? He sort of bounced around in the booth. There was a kid in him coming out that Apelu had thought he would never see again. It was infectious. They talked and talked, knitting over the weeks and months of pain. They even laughed.

Apelu dropped Sanele at home where he was reunited with his room, his PlayStation, and his cable TV, then Apelu went back to town to take care of business. There were three paychecks waiting for him at headquarters, so he had been gone at least six weeks. When the captain saw that he was back on island, he declared that Apelu's leave was now over, but Apelu went to see the commissioner. According to the Department's internal staffing orders there was supposed to be an officer permanently assigned to Ofu and Olosega. But there hadn't been one for a number of years. Apelu pointed this out to the commissioner and then said something which he had no idea was true or not—that the people there felt slighted because they weren't being given their due protection. Who knew? Maybe somebody felt that way, although Apelu had never heard anyone actually complain about it. The commissioner put him back on active duty with the Ofu assignment. The problem had been that no one else would take that duty. Apelu asked for a four-wheel drive black-and-white SUV. What the hell? The look the commissioner gave him said, *Don't push your luck.*

Apelu shopped on his way home, stopping in half a dozen stores. He had money in his pocket now. He spent it. For dinner he fixed Sanele's favorite meal—a big pot of spaghetti and meatballs with garlic bread and a Caesar salad. He bought himself a bottle of Zinfandel, but no vodka. Sanele went to bed soon after eating dinner and doing the dishes. Apelu sat up late, sipping his wine at the kitchen table. There were too many ghosts still in this house. He and Sanele would be going to Ofu as soon as he could get done what he needed to get done. The phone rang once. He didn't answer it. It had to be a wrong number. Who would be calling a ghost number?

———— o ————

It took three more days. Apelu paid bills and arranged to have a bunch of household stuff and building materials shipped to Ofu by boat at the Department's expense. He and Sanele went through their limited wardrobes and pooled what they thought they might need. Sanele at sixteen wore the same sizes Apelu wore, down to his flip-flops, and, as Sanele enjoyed pointing out, they were now the same height, an even six feet. By the fourth day, a Sunday, Apelu had checked just about everything off of his lists. It was strange to have lists again.

Manulele Airlines was the sole air connection between Tutuila and Ofu. It flew its one aging, short takeoff and landing Twin Otter air taxi back and forth between Pago Pago's huge airfield and Ofu's abbreviated airstrip twice a day, except on Sundays. On Sundays there was only the one flight to Ofu, the one at dawn, and there were usually seats available on it because it conflicted with church, but this flight was almost full. Danny

Po'o was there in line along with a bunch of *palangis* Apelu had never seen before. They had several large metallic yellow and black cases of equipment. Danny said hello, but he was busy negotiating charges for the extra luggage. Apelu had his own cache of boxes he wanted on the plane—cardboard boxes secured with yards of duct tape—and when he checked in he made sure the agent slapped Priority stickers on his boxes. Because Danny hadn't known enough to ask, there were no Priority stickers stuck on the *palangis'* equipment cases.

The flight was smooth. Sanele slept. The landing at Ofu was faultless. All of Apelu's and Sanele's luggage made it. The *palangi's* yellow and black equipment cases did not. The *palangis* were not happy. As Apelu and Sanele began the first of their three trips to haul their baggage and boxes up to the shack, the *palangis* were having a white-guy fit inside the one-room airline office. One of them got back on the plane to return to Pago to check on their precious cases and make sure that they got on the next day's flight. By the time Apelu and Sanele came back to the airstrip for their second uphill load the rest of the *palangis* were sitting at tables on the lodge's patio drinking beers, still complaining. They never noticed Apelu and Sanele walking past them, carrying their Samoan cardboard luggage. Danny wasn't there.

"Who are those guys, Dad?" Sanele asked.

"Don't know them, but my guess is that they're surveyors."

"That was their equipment that didn't make it, huh?"

"Tough break."

At the shack, two words had been scratched in charcoal at the bottom of Apelu's note to Nu'upo, which was still stuck to the screen door—"Yummy umu."

——— o ———

Apelu and Sanele spent the rest of that day and much of the next making the place more livable for two. Apelu disliked having to acknowledge that his teenage son was basically a neater person than he was, so of course he didn't acknowledge it, but it was true. He couldn't say it was his mother's influence, because Sina wasn't an especially orderly person either. Their house had always remained in a state of semi-something, never tidy—except for Sanele's room. Now Sanele wanted to use some of their precious water to wash the screens, and Apelu had to stop him. No need. A new roll of screening was among the things coming on the boat.

Monday afternoon they knocked off when it got too hot and went down to the beach for a swim. On the way back they stopped at the lodge so that Sanele could get a cold soda and Apelu could get a cold beer. The place was deserted, not even the kitchen help was around. It was that sleepy time of day. Apelu ran a tab at the lodge and after they got their drinks—both taking an extra for later—he flipped to his page in the green accounts ledger on the counter beside the cooler to enter his purchase. He noticed that there was a new page in the ledger with the *pulenu'u*'s name at the top. He flipped it open. The mayor had run up a nice little party tab the day before. He would've been hosting the group of *palangi* surveyors, since as far as Apelu knew they were the only people staying at the lodge.

Apelu and Sanele took their drinks back up to the shack, which Sanele now insisted he not call the shack but their *fale*, Samoan for house. Okay, fine, *fale*. Nu'upo was sitting on the steps of their *fale* when they got there. He was rolling tobacco in a piece of dried banana leaf, scowling at it as it failed to cooperate. Then he scowled at them. "This your kid?" he said.

"Yes, this is Sanele. Sanele, Nu'upo. Nu'upo, Sanele."

They both leaned forward for a quick handshake.

"Good. We need all the help we can get. They're back."

"The *palangi* surveyors? Yes, they came in on the plane with us."

"They're back in the same area. I don't like it."

"They're not park people, according to the park people."

"I still don't like it." Nu'upo finally got his unwilling cigarette lit. He spotted the plastic bag that Sanele was carrying their extra drinks in. "*Vai*," he snapped.

Apelu took the bag from Sanele, pulled out the second bottle of beer, and was about to open it with the butt of his cigarette lighter when Nu'upo said angrily, "No, no. Not that one, the other one." Apelu looked to Sanele, but Sanele was fixated on Nu'upo. Apelu handed Nu'upo the sweating plastic bottle of Pepsi, which he opened and drained, dropping both the cap and the bottle on the ground beside him. His cigarette had gone out and was again falling apart. He flung it aside. "Motherfucker." Apelu offered him a cigarette from his pack, Nu'upo refused it with a wave of his hand.

"Sanele, your father is a drunken jungle bum. What do you think about that?"

"I think you're wrong," Sanele said softly.

"You think I'm wrong? Everybody thinks I'm wrong about everything, but I know they can't all be right, can they?"

Sanele didn't say anything.

"Can they?" Nu'upo persisted.

"Who is everybody?" Sanele asked.

"Precisely. Who counts as part of everybody? Just the ones that get to gossip? There are a lot of invisible heads behind you right now nodding in agreement with your young wisdom. God, that stuff is awful!" Nu'upo got up and kicked the Pepsi bottle with his bare foot. "Give me a cigarette. The *palangis* got guns. What do they need guns for? You can't shoot a ghost."

Apelu had decided not to publicly announce yet his appointment as island cop. He would let someone else do that—the commissioner, the *pulenu'u*, someone official—but *palangis* carrying guns might mean opening up for business early. The only legal guns in the Territory were twenty-two rifles and shotguns.

"What kind of guns?" Apelu asked.

"Sidearms is all I saw, *pistole*. Who knows what else they have?"

"You sure?"

"No, I made it up, just like I made up the fact that you're a jungle drunk. Motherfuckers. Big ones, hanging from their belts. Go look for yourself. They're down by your Rotuman land." Nu'upo motioned with his eyes toward the bottle of beer Apelu was still holding. He opened it and passed it to the old man, who took a mouthful, swirled it around in his mouth, than spat it out. "Pepsishit," he said, kicking the plastic bottle again and handing the rest of the beer back to Apelu. "Stop drinking Pepsishit, Sanele. It will turn you into a girl, and all the other boys will want to play with your tits." With that Nu'upo turned and walked into the bush beyond the cook shed, kicking the Pepsi bottle along in front of him.

"Neighbor," Apelu said.

"People these days," Sanele said, picking up the bottle cap.

Apelu laughed. Sanele went into the *fale* and put the bottle cap in the box for trash, then went to the room he had created for himself by hanging two of their lava lavas from a ceiling stud. Sanele had brought his iPod, and soon Apelu could hear the low bass thump of a hip-hop beat leaking out of the earphones. Apelu hitched himself up a young coconut tree beside the *fale* and knocked down a couple of drinking nuts that he quickly husked. He cracked the top of one open with his bush knife. He went into the *fale* and knocked on the wall by Sanele's curtain. The hip-hop beat stopped. Apelu pushed aside the lava lava and handed Sanele the *niu*. "The anti-Pepsishit," he said.

"Thanks, Dad." Sanele smiled and took the coconut. "*Manuia*," good luck, he toasted before he took a sip and Apelu let the curtain close again.

CHAPTER 4

———— o ————

THE NEXT MORNING THEY HAD A COLD BREAKFAST. THE REST
of his household stuff wasn't due to arrive for two days, but
Apelu already so anticipated their brand new two-burner kerosene cook stove that the thought of building a slow starting cooking fire just to warm something up repulsed him. Sanele didn't
say anything, but this time he fetched, husked, and delivered the
drinking *nius*.

Apelu sat cross-legged on the ground, sharpening his old
bush knife and a brand new one with a big rasp file. "Today we'll
work a piece of your grandfather's land I've not paid much attention to." He told Sanele to fill all their plastic water bottles from
the hose. "It will take some time. You may want your iPod for
company."

This time Sanele carried the net bag with the bottles bouncing against his back. He was alert but quiet as they walked down
the sand road and turned the rocky corner into To'aga. It was
still early. The jungle birds were still making their breakfast
sounds, or was it the morning bush news? Last night's events,
today's expectations. *News flash—two of the big ones coming
down the road on foot carrying knives.* They were headed for

Nandiaka. As they walked Apelu told Sanele the names—just the names, nothing else yet—of the parcels of land they passed. Sanele repeated them out loud, filing them away. Apelu walked past Nandiaka to the mouth of the trail he and Nu'upo had come out on.

"What's that?" Sanele asked. Up ahead a yellow plastic ribbon flapped listlessly in the off-shore breeze from a rusted stake hammered into the earth about a yard off the beach side of the road. Then they saw the others, further up the road, on both sides. A couple of coconut trees near the markers had white numbers newly spray-painted onto them.

"Our surveyors' work," Apelu said. "Nu'upo was right."

"Do you think he was right about the guns, too?"

"Uncle Nu'upo likes to expand upon things. It makes them more interesting for him. It's one of his sole sources of entertainment. Come on, let's go, son." And Apelu headed in on the trail then cut back toward Nandiaka.

As they worked at Nandiaka—clearing around the old house foundation first then working outward with their bush knives, ripping down vines and clearing the ground of any plants they didn't want, leaving the breadfruit and some young coconuts and ta'amu and ti and female papaya trees and a low patch of manioka—Apelu wondered about the surveyors. Maybe they were just from Public Works, planning road improvements, or working on some harmless federal research project. Then why would the mayor be buying their drinks? Apelu wondered what the people in the village knew about them that he didn't know. Had the fono, the village council of chiefs, been told why they were here? In the past six months—during Sarah's decline and his hermitage—Apelu had had nothing to do with the fono—on which, titleless, he did not sit—nor with any of its member chiefs. Maybe he should check that out first before playing an obvious hand.

They took regular breaks. There was no rush. The sun was above the ridgeline now. They drank their bottled water and re-sharpened their bush knives as they sat in the shade. Sanele cleared bush as meticulously as he kept his room. He liked his new bush knife once he got a proper edge on it. During their breaks Apelu would feed a little smoky fire he had gotten started to keep the mosquitoes at bay. As they took turns with the file, Apelu started telling his son the stories of To'aga, starting with the framework of its fame, the really old stories. Sanele listened. It was suddenly important to Apelu that Sanele learn it all. But for him to learn it well, Apelu had to tell him well. To do so, Apelu knew he had to cook them slowly, serve them with relish, enjoying them himself as he told them. These were not facts to be engorged and then disgorged. These weren't the multiplication tables or the names of the fifty state capitals. This was the land-scape of everything that surrounded them. This was the blanket of the past that sat upon them like the smoke of the first fire ever built here. It enclosed and protected them. This was like know-ing the rules of the road. These were the facts of life on Ofu that you ignored at your own peril. But there would be plenty of time. What else did they have to do but share what every father—or uncle or grandfather—had shared before them—the good, funny, scary, complex, sometimes sexy epic of their place—who they were? Sanele listened.

The bullet passed high over their heads. It ripped through the upper story leaves, but it was a gunshot in their direction nevertheless. Apelu grabbed Sanele by the back of the neck and pulled him down with him onto the earth. Sanele's eyes were wide.

"Grab and go time, son. Get that." Apelu gestured toward the water bottle bag as he gathered up their bush knives and the file. "Stay low, follow." Apelu headed, scrambling on his hands and knees, away from the direction the shot had come from toward the base of the cliff. Another warning shot rang out behind them, echoing wildly off the ridge face, raising all the birds.

"I don't know who the fuck you are, but you better get off this land," a *palangi* voice yelled out, followed by another high shot. It sounded like a large handgun, Apelu thought, and the voice was the voice of America—someone not from the South trying to sound as if they were from the South because somehow that made the threat sound more crazily authentic. The same way all pilots wanted to sound like Chuck Yeager, all thugs wanted to sound like they were with NASCAR or from Muscle Shoals, Alabama. Apelu and Sanele found themselves behind the carved-on boulder, closest to the cliff face.

"Dad?"

"Hush, son. They're not coming in. We'll wait and leave. It's okay." Listening hard, Apelu wasn't sure of that, but he could say it. "Just stay down." It must have been the smoke from the fire that let them know that they were there, but what gave them the right? Now Apelu could hear them crashing into Nandiaka, stomping out their little fire.

The same high-pitched honky voice yelled out again. "We don't believe in no stinking ghosts, nigger, so just keep away." Another shot into the air, then Apelu heard them walk back the way they'd come. Talking together, pumped up after combat. There was the smell of cordite captured in the still air inside the ridge's concave face. The jungle birds were still all on wing, confused.

"Assholes," Apelu said.

"People these days," Sanele answered.

They waited a while. There was no rush. They turned around and rested their backs against the boulder.

"You okay?" Apelu asked as calmly as he could.

"I thought it would be peaceful over here."

"Me too. This is new. Want to go back?"

"You want me out of here?"

"No, not especially. I like having you here. We got stuff to do. I'll straighten this shit out this afternoon. Hey, I never asked, did you leave a girlfriend back there?"

"Yeah, sort of, but it will keep."

"What's her name?" Apelu asked as he stood up and scoped out the silence around them.

"Filemu," Sanele answered. "She says we're related somehow. I hope it's not too close. Those guys gone?"

"Yeah, let's go home," Apelu said and he led Sanele back along the cliff face away from the bad guys and to another way out.

They went to the beach to bathe and swim, then washed off with fresh water at the *fale*. Apelu noticed that Sanele looked over his shoulder often. In the heat of the early afternoon they both took naps. The sun was already back behind the western limb of the ridge by the time Apelu headed off to the village. Sanele wanted to come along as far as the lodge.

"Do you think I could use their phone to call my girlfriend?"

"Sure, but keep it short."

There was a girl in the kitchen starting dinner at the lodge, but otherwise the main house was as deserted as before. Apelu left Sanele there with the phone. It was another mile and a half walk around to the village on the western shore of the island. About halfway there he caught a ride in the first pickup truck to pass. He was back in the sun again now, but it was the friendly sun of late afternoon, throwing green shadows onto the rocky lava road. He shared the back of the pickup with a load of firewood, several large bunches of green bananas, and a sullen young man who ignored Apelu as if it were his job. They bounced along in rattling silence.

In the village Apelu went to the house of the chief he knew best. Tiafatu was Apelu's age and like Apelu had put in his time stateside, in his case getting a degree in sociology. Now he ran the island's sole bakery. For a chief he was very frank. He was also very large.

"*Afio mai*, Apelu, come in, come in," Tiafatu greeted Apelu in Samoan as he came up to the steps into his *fale*. "Excuse me if I don't get up. But I have just gotten down and comfortable. Do so yourself. You are looking well." Tiafatu picked up a chunk of coral from the floor and tossed it toward the cook house in the back where several women were making dinner to bring their attention to the fact that he had a guest. "I am honored by your stopping by. Where are you off to?"

"I've just come to see you, chief. I have missed your talk and hospitality." Apelu waited for one of the women to bring him a mat to sit on, then he lowered himself onto it cross-legged with his back against a *fale* pole facing his host. "It is a good day."

"Any day you grace my house with your presence is a good day," Tiafatu said. Then in English, "What's up?"

"*Palangi* surveyors in To`aga?"

"Yes, I heard."

"Did they ask the *fono*'s permission?"

"It was more like we were told they would be here."

"And no one cares?"

"I believe the consensus feeling was that To`aga could take care of itself."

"They fired a gun at my son and me today."

"I heard that your son was here. This is good news."

"They fired a gun at my son and me."

The youngest woman from the kitchen bowed her way into the *fale* and placed on the mats in front of each of them a tall glass of Tang with ice cubes tinkling in it and a small plate of store-bought cookies. Still stooped over, she hurried out of the *fale*.

"Guns in To`aga is not good," Tiafatu said, selecting a cookie from his plate.

"It upset the birds," Apelu said, taking a sip of Tang, which would have benefited from a good splash of vodka.

"And your son?"

"He's fine, a little spooked, I think."

"And you want me to . . . ?"

"Tell me what's going on. They were surveying adjacent to my land."

"Your land? You mean Nandiaka? How is that your land?"

"My father's land."

"Your dead father's title's land."

"We were tending it."

"That does not necessarily make it your land."

"What are you saying?" Apelu finished his Tang, and the girl brought him a fresh glass as he and Tiafatu sat in silence waiting for her to leave.

"I think we should have a saofa`i for you, Apelu. Give you your father's vacant title. Then you can call it your land, at least until you die. Then maybe your son can tend it and in his turn vie for the title."

"The *fono* would let me take that title?"

"I think the *fono* would welcome your presence, as I do, both among its members and out there in To`aga. Would any member of your family object to your taking your father's title?" Tiafatu slipped another cookie delicately into his mouth.

"No," Apelu said. "They'd welcome it, I'd guess, if it meant maintaining claim to the land."

"Then it will be done, and let us do it quickly, so that we will have more say about whatever it is these *palangis* are scheming." As Tiafatu finished the final cookie on his plate Apelu had not yet touched his. Two flies figure-eighted above them.

"But what about the *palangi* surveyors and their guns?" Apelu said, waving the flies away.

"I think having your title investiture as quickly as possible is the best step we can take against them. Apelu," he said, gesturing without looking to the women in the cook house, "I also think you should stay for supper. Someone will drive you back, with a plate of food for your son. You must stay so that we can arrange the title ceremony. We will keep it simple."

The girl brought plates of fried reef fish and taro, bananas in coconut cream, and a salt-beef concoction of questionable age. They ate and talked as the sun set into the sea. Tiafatu had a messenger go to the *fales* of other chiefs to invite them over and bring some beers. When Apelu left with a plate piled high and wrapped in aluminum foil for Sanele, it was all but done. Apelu would take on his father's old title and claims. Sanele would get some real food for dinner.

Dawn was late the next day. The bottom of the sky was resting on the ridgetop again. On and off, it became a light rain. Apelu skipped breakfast. He woke Sanele long enough to give him some chores to do around the *fale* when he finally did get up. Apelu headed for To'aga. He was dressed in his town clothes—jeans and a polo shirt—not in his bush lava lava and T-shirt. He didn't bring his bush knife. Instead, his handcuff case was strapped to the back of his belt, and his badge and ID case was in his back pocket.

Apelu waited on the concrete steps where the US Navy dispensary had once stood in the center of To'aga. There were just the steps now and in the undergrowth behind him the remnants of concrete pedestals with rusted rebar sticking out of them like rotten teeth, and a concrete water catchment tank in the process of being reclaimed by ficus. This was the site of the sole Western landmark to To'aga's suprasensory powers. Some eighty years before, around twenty years after the US Navy had claimed the islands, the Naval governor in Pago Pago had decided to put a medical dispensary in Ofu and Olosega, staffed by a *palangi* pharmacist's mate and his wife. Of course, it was cheaper to build just one dispensary for both islands, situated halfway between the villages of Ofu and Olosega. Halfway between them was the old battleground beneath the mountain home of the oldest and most unpredictable ethereal creatures in all of the islands, To'aga. It would be just a short canoe ride across the channel for the Olosega people. So they built it there. Of course, no one from either Ofu or Olosega would go there. As if to draw attention to their stupidity the Navy had chosen a site adjacent to a set of graves whose stories took hours to tell. It didn't work out. Almost immediately the pharmacist's mate was complaining to his superiors back in Pago that invisible parties were occupying the place day and night, talking in loud Samoan voices and moving the furniture around. The capper came when the pharmacist's wife was home alone one day and answered a knock at the dispensary door to face—as it were—a headless naked man. The Navy moved the dispensary into the safety of Ofu village.

The last stake up the road with a strip of yellow plastic tape hanging from it was across from where Apelu sat. He lit a cigarette and waited. The rain came now only as a mist. The birds were silent. The *pulenu'u's* F-150 came up the road slowly, sensibly, so he wasn't driving. Only the *palangi* surveyors were in the truck. They stopped the truck in front of Apelu.

"Can we help you somehow?" the driver asked.

"Sure. So are you the surveyors doing this work?" Apelu didn't get up from the steps. "You got a permit to do this work? Permission from the National Park?"

At this all four of the *palangis* got out of the truck—the three in front and the one in the back.

"We don't need a permit to survey, nor do we need anyone's permission," one of them said.

"Surveying without permission is trespassing."

"We have all the permissions we need. Who are you?"

"One of the land title holders out here, whose permission you didn't get."

"Like I said, we got all the permission we need—the mayor's and the village council's." This was the fake Southern drawl voice Apelu had heard at Nandiaka. "So maybe you ought to take it up with them." He was a short round man, six inches shorter than Apelu, with beefy shoulders and a flushed complexion. Strapped to his khaki-covered right thigh was a large handgun in a flapped leather holster. He rested his hand on top of the holster. "What's your name?"

Apelu stood up and pulled his badge and ID case out of his pocket as he walked over to the man. "Detective Soifua, Criminal Investigation Division, American Samoa Department of Public Safety," Apelu said, opening his case in front of the man's face. "Yours?"

The short man looked at Apelu's badge and picture ID. He took his hand off his holster. "I don't think that this is any of your business, Sarge. Look, guys, they give these boys badges and they think they can ask anybody questions. Forget it, Sarge. You got nothing on us. Show me a warrant. You'll never get one."

"I don't need a warrant to arrest someone in the act of committing a crime. Your name, please."

"Criminal surveying? Yo, guys, doing our job is a crime over here, according to Sarge. Come on, man, move aside, we got work to do. If you go talk to what's his name the mayor, I'm sure he can make it worth your while to go look at some other crime over here, like why none of the girls will put out." He turned away from Apelu back toward the truck.

"No, you are under arrest for wearing that weapon. I'm sure it's not licensed, seeing as all handguns are prohibited here. So you are under arrest for having that firearm in the Territory and for wearing an unlicensed firearm."

The man turned back to him. "You ever hear about the Second Amendment, Sarge? I have the right as an American to defend myself, especially out here in the jungle. It's for snakes and spooks." One of the other men laughed. "Excuse me, Sarge, we have to get to work."

"There are no snakes here," Apelu said, stepping up close to him, "and you are under arrest. Please remove the weapon, in its holster, from your belt and hand it to me."

"No way, Jose. You want to take it from me?"

"Shall we include a charge of resisting arrest?"

One of the other men stepped forward. "Hold on, Edgar. The man is the law here. Officer, what do you say you just take Edgar's weapon there into custody, we finish up our work here, and we sort this out later back on Tutuila?"

"Thank you, sir. That would go a long ways toward resolving this."

The four of them walked around to the back of the truck, where Edgar was convinced he should give up his handgun. It happened so quickly Apelu suspected that he had another weapon in the truck. The man who had intervened brought the holstered gun to Apelu.

"There you are, Officer. I trust this will settle this little matter, for the time being at least. My colleague was unaware of your local rules about sidearms. No harm done."

"Thank you," Apelu said, taking the gun, "but I don't think this settles much." He unsnapped the leather holster grip guard and pulled the gun out of its case. It was a heavy Smith and Wesson. He sniffed the barrel. Edgar had failed to clean his gun since he had fired it the day before. "There is also the matter of a Class D felony of unlawful use of a weapon—aiming a weapon at another person in a threatening manner."

"I don't believe we saw anything like that happen here, Officer. Don't be ridiculous."

"Not here today, no, but here yesterday." Apelu walked over to where the short man was standing between the two other men. "Edgar whatever-your-last-name-is, you are under arrest on three charges—possession of an unlicensed firearm, wearing an unlicensed firearm, and unlawful use of a weapon. You have the right to remain silent . . ." As Apelu recited the Miranda spiel his natural impulse was to turn the perp around and handcuff him, but he decided not to. He was on foot. He had to get Edgar back to Tutuila somehow to formally charge him. He had no backup.

Edgar exploded. "What do you mean, unlawful use? Give me my gun back. All deals are off. What's he going to make up next? That I was hunting some endangered fucking species?"

"That's good. I'll add that too. Hunting ghosts, weren't you? They're so endangered they're all dead already. Edgar, you and I are going to be on this afternoon's flight back to Tutuila so that I can file formal charges against you at headquarters."

"Hold on, Officer." It was the other dude again. "What's this about aiming his gun at someone? Edgar may have fired his gun high up into the trees to scare off some poachers yesterday—the mayor had asked us to look out for poachers on his land—but they were just warning shots, not aimed at anyone."

"Those poachers were me and my son, and we weren't on the mayor's land, we were on our own land, and it is still against the law to fire a gun to threaten anyone—natives, niggers, poachers, spooks, whatever. Edgar, I'll keep your gun as evidence and book us on this afternoon's plane back to Pago. Be there. That plane is your only way out of here, and if you don't make today's plane, the police will be meeting every plane until you do return, and then you will also be charged with resisting arrest. See you there." Apelu stepped off the road and disappeared as quickly as he could into the bush. Not your standard arrest.

Apelu waited in the bush for the surveyors to get back in the *pulenu'u*'s truck and return toward the village before he stepped back onto the road. No other trucks passed him on his trek to the airstrip.

Apelu figured the *pulenu'u* would be there at the airstrip when he returned late in the afternoon to catch the flight. He was right, but the mayor was more subdued than Apelu had anticipated. He had expected some sort of power scene, the *pulenu`u* throwing his weight around, so Apelu had called his captain in Pago from the lodge's phone that morning to inform him of the charges, the arrest, and the arrangements for having a squad car meet them at the airport. He also asked the captain to have someone—the commissioner preferably—call the *pulenu`u* and inform him of Apelu's new assignment. Someone must have called him, because the big man had little to say at the airstrip. "I'm sure this can all be worked out, smoothed over," was about it.

Edgar—whose last name turned out to be Houston—was still pissed off but under control. He already had a lawyer lined up in Pago, he told Apelu, and would be seeing him before answering any more questions. Apelu told Edgar that he was supposed to handcuff him to take him onto the airplane, but wouldn't. Apelu had put Edgar's gun into his only luggage—a carry-on backpack—which he checked so that it wouldn't be in the cabin with them.

Apelu had tried to get a third seat on the plane for Sanele, but he couldn't. As it was he had to bounce two confirmed passengers for his and Edgar's seats. He didn't like the idea of leaving Sanele alone at the *fale* for the night, but Sanele insisted he would be fine. Apelu assured him that he would be back on the next afternoon's plane. Sanele was determined to be brave about the whole thing. "I mean, you arrested the guy, Dad, so he's out of here." Sanele had come down to the airstrip with him, "Just to see the guy," he said.

Getting off the plane from Pago was Bobbie Wentworth. She was coming back to finish the work she hadn't done because of her injured ankle. She was alone, no Martin. Apelu walked out to meet her on the tarmac. Edgar was having a final confab with the *pulenu`u*.

"Apelu, you're all dressed up. In honor of my arrival?" Bobbie was smiling. She wasn't limping.

"Of course, and in preparation for my departure. I'm glad to see you, Bobbie. You can do me a big favor, ease my conscience a bit."

"Whatever." Her smile tightened, became quizzical.

"I want you to meet my son, Sanele, who is over for a visit to help me out on the plantations." He nodded toward Sanele, who was standing back in the shade of the porch in front of the airstrip's one-room office. "I have to go back to Pago for a day on police business, and he'll be all alone up at the shack until I get back. Could you sort of check in on him for me, keep an eye on him until I get back? He's a big boy, sixteen, but he's not used to being alone in the bush."

"How dare you leave him here alone. That place you live in gives me the creeps even when you and Martin are around."

"It's a bind."

"Where is he?"

Apelu and Bobbie walked over to where Sanele was waiting to say goodbye, and Apelu introduced them. The departing passengers were boarding the plane.

"Son, I've got to run. Be back tomorrow. Love you. Look out for Bobbie here, would you?" He gave them both a quick hug. As he headed toward Edgar waiting for him at the plane's steps, he heard Sanele ask Bobbie, "Need some help with your stuff?"

"Sure," she said. "It's not far."

———— o ————

Apelu had hoped he could just deliver his prisoner and evidence, file his incident report and an affidavit in support of an arrest warrant, and get back to Ofu, but it wasn't going to happen that fast. The nature of the charges and their details were sufficiently strange for the Attorney General's Office to dither over drawing them up and the district court judge to delay signing off on the complaint and arrest warrant during business hours the next day. The AG wanted Detective Soifua present in court to answer any questions at the prelim hearing, so Apelu would have to stay an extra day. There was nothing he could do about it. The delay also meant that Edgar Houston was released from custody, as they couldn't keep him for more than thirty-six hours on just the suspicion holding, and his holding had technically started with his arrest in To`aga. The gun was in the police evidence locker.

So it was two days and nights before Apelu could return to Ofu, and he was lucky to get a seat on that flight. When he got back to their *fale* above Va`oto, Sanele wasn't there, but all of their boat-shipped stuff had arrived and the boxes were piled inside, almost filling the place. Apelu could see from the tracks up their lane that a four-wheel drive pickup truck had brought it all up. He did a quick search of Sanele's room and could not find his iPod. He found this encouraging and set about unpacking boxes and finding places to stash stuff.

His new two-burner kerosene stove was there and he was assembling it out in the cook shed when the park truck came up the lane. Sanele jumped out of the passenger side door.

"Dad, Dad, you're here, you're here! You gotta come. They're doing something weird. No one's going to stop them. They got a bulldozer. You gotta come, Dad. You gotta stop them."

Bobbie was behind the wheel, dressed the way Apelu had seen her the other day coming back from the beach, zinc oxided nose and all. "Get in. We'll explain on the way," she said, leaning out her door window. Apelu did, Sanele slipping between them. Bobbie backed down the lane then turned toward To`aga.

"We saw them this morning when we went to set Bobbie's transects." Sanele was looking straight ahead but talking to his dad. "They've been really busy since you left."

"They've been surveying off the road, on both sides," Bobbie said.

"They went in toward that place where we got shot at."

"Yesterday they went into the park lands on the beach side."

"Then when we came out from the beach today they had a bulldozer there."

"A front loader with a backhoe, belongs to Public Works," Bobbie added.

"And they had started cutting a road into Nandiaka. Isn't that our land?"

"Who is 'they'?" Apelu asked.

"Those *palangi* guys and a couple of Samoans."

"The *pulenu`u* and that guy Ace and a Public Works guy driving the front loader," Bobbie said. She was speeding over the washboard road, but slowed down for the curve into To`aga. All of her gear slid sideways in the bed of the truck. She honked the horn. A large foam-white owl rose out of the road in front of them, rising at their speed above the windshield, leading them on.

"Just an owl," Bobbie said.

"Just an owl," Apelu said.

Sanele said nothing. After a while the owl veered off into the cliffside bush.

About halfway through To`aga, short of the trail where Apelu and Nu`upo had encountered the first group of surveyors, the *pulenu`u's* truck was parked and there was a fresh slash of crushed vegetation and tread-torn earth heading in toward Nandiaka. They could hear the machine revving and crushing ahead deep in the bush. No one was by the truck, but further up the road Apelu could see one of the surveyors squinting into his surveyor's thing on top of its yellow tripod. He was looking into the bush.

Apelu figured it was pointless to tell Sanele and Bobbie to stay there, so he didn't. They followed him up the rough cut the dozer had made. The first person they encountered was Ace the thug carefully picking his way back out the dozer tracks, looking miserably out of place in his city shoes and trousers and aloha shirt.

"What are you doin' here?" he asked, surprised to see them.

Apelu didn't answer him, and the three of them kept going past him.

"Hey, I don't think—" Ace started.

"That's right, and don't start trying now," Apelu said.

The *pulenu`u* and the *palangi* surveyor didn't notice the three of them approaching. Their backs were to them and the machine made a lot of noise.

"What do you think you are doing?" Apelu called over the dozer, startling them.

"Apelu, back so soon from Pago?" the *pulenu`u* yelled, glancing at the surveyor and then ahead at the dozer.

"Stop the machine," Apelu shouted.

"Just cutting a little access road."

"Stop the machine."

"He's almost done. Besides, what's it to you?"

"To start with, you're on my family's land."

"That little piece your father claimed back here but never used? He never had that surveyed, did he?" The *pulenu`u* gestured with his head for the surveyor to go to where the dozer was clearing.

"You know that no one would stand for anyone to survey in here. Everyone knows what is what. The stories mark where the edges of the place names meet."

"Well, let's just say that these fellows," the *pulenu`u* motioned toward the *palangi* in the yellow hard hat walking away up the scar, "checked the story boundaries of our land out here and determined that this isn't your family's land but ours, and in a couple of days that will be registered as fact with the Territorial Registrar's Office back in Pago."

"Stop the machine. That's an order, not a request. Stop the machine now."

"On what basis are you giving me an order? I just told you that I can prove that I'm not the trespasser here, you are."

"You need a land use permit to cut a road like this no matter whose land it is. You're the *pulenu'u*. You know that. Got one?"

"No, but I'm the law here. I don't need a permit from Pago. You got a stop order?"

Apelu brushed past the *pulenu'u*. Bobbie and Sanele followed him. The dozer's trail of destruction cut through the center of Nandiaka, where Apelu and Sanele had been clearing. It had pretty much obliterated the old *fale* foundation and had flattened many of the fruit trees Apelu and Sanele had cleared around. It was cutting a fairly straight line toward the base of the cliff. Apelu caught up to the *palangi* in the yellow hard hat—the same guy who had interceded earlier for Edgar.

"You again," the *palangi* said as he turned to try and stop Apelu. Apelu knocked him aside with a forearm, backward over a tree trunk and onto his back. His hard hat bounced away. He went down hard.

Apelu could now see the back of the dozer, its backhoe tucked up like a rusted yellow scorpion's tail. It had stopped almost to the base of the cliff. It was idling.

"Turn off the machine," Apelu yelled as he came up behind it.

"No, no, keep going!" It was the *pulenu'u*, coming up behind him, sweating and breathing heavily.

"This is an order from a police officer—turn off the machine."

The dozer driver was paying them no attention but was staring straight ahead. The *pulenu'u* came huffing up behind Apelu and laid a heavy hand on his shoulder. Apelu shrugged it off. He found a foothold on the backhoe and climbed up onto the machine. When he got up behind the driver he could see what the man was staring at. Standing on top of a boulder not ten yards in front of the dozer's front blade was an apparition of weirdness, dancing a crazy dance, pointing a long crooked pointed and polished snakelike piece of driftwood at the driver's face, making a noise like a chorus chanting in tongues. Ferns grew out of the creature's head, and its face was powder white. There seemed to be an extra eyeball imbedded in each cheek. Its chest, from sternum to navel, was gashed crimson in what looked—in the crazy dance—like a huge open wound. It had tree bark legs. Now it started spitting blood at the driver, calling him by the worst Samoan swear words, the we-fight-now words. It even called the driver by name and insulted his mother.

Apelu had never seen Nu`upo naked before. What he noticed immediately was his rather lanky flaccid uncircumcised penis slapping back and forth against his thighs as he hopped from foot to foot. As he danced his member became more tumescent and rigid, like a second brown snake growing to point at the driver. The old man was hung like a horse. Finally the swear words and curses took their effect on the driver, who yelled *"Ufa!"* back at the old man and slammed his Cat into gear, lifted the front blade, and lurched the machine forward, almost knocking Apelu loose.

"No!" Apelu yelled as the dozer blade smacked into the boulder. For a moment Nu`upo looked airborne, his arms flapping, then he was upright again on top of the boulder. The blade's impact on the rock sent up a fine spray of dust, which a gust of wind caught and swept over the dozer, Nu`upo flapping his arms as if to direct it. At the impact Apelu fell forward over the driver. He reached out for the ignition key and turned off the engine. When he looked back up Nu`upo was gone, but off to the side at the edge of the bush Bobbie, Sanele, and the *pulenu`u* stood, frozen, staring at the space atop the boulder where he had just been. As Apelu got his bearings on his newly ravaged land, he realized that the boulder that the spirit warrior had chosen to defend, the one they had been going after, was the one with the petroglyphs.

CHAPTER 5

———— o ————

THE NATIONAL PARK ARCHAEOLOGIST'S NAME WAS DREW, Dr. Drew Dresden. Apelu had never met the man before, although he had been stationed at the park for several years. Dr. Dresden was on the next afternoon's flight from Pago, and Apelu, Bobbie, and Sanele were at the airstrip to meet him. Dr. Dresden—"Call me Drew"—gave a rather military first impression. Part of that, of course, was due to the fact that he deplaned in full park ranger uniform—albeit in shorts and hiking boots—including the Smokey Bear hat, but his carriage, his athletic trimness, and his short-cropped dark hair made the uniform look like something other than a disguise. He liked being in uniform. Even though Apelu had spent many years on the beat in uniform before becoming a detective, he had always kept his distance from the guys who actually liked wearing a uniform, the regalia, and gear.

Drew traveled light—a single small green duffel bag with the NPS logo on it and a laptop computer which never left his hand, like a lady's purse, Apelu thought. Sanele picked up the duffel bag, and the four of them walked off toward the Park Service cabin. Bobbie, with Sanele's help, had fixed a late lunch for them. As it turned out, Sanele had spent the two nights Apelu was gone at the NPS cabin rather than up in the *fale*. Bobbie's cabin had the amenities of fans, a phone, a hot plate, a TV set with a DVD player and a pile of DVDs, and—unspoken—company. Sanele had made himself quite at home. Bobbie didn't seem to mind. Sanele waited on them at lunch.

"The demolition has ceased?" Drew asked. They were seated in plastic lawn chairs under an awning in front of the NPS cabin.

"Yeah," Apelu said. "All quiet on that front. I took the keys to the dozer and rattled off a string of possible criminal charges to the driver, who was happy just to get out of there. The crime scene, such as it is, is intact. The *pulenu`u* and the rest of the surveyors got out of here on this morning's plane."

"Good. Well, I've got your stop order for you. Thank you, boy." Drew had asked for a cup of tea, and Sanele had fixed one for him. "In your request for the stop order you mentioned that there are carvings on this boulder, which is a major reason why I am here."

"I don't get it," Apelu said. "The boulder is on my family's land, not in the park."

"Your Territorial Historic Preservation Office requested that I come over and conduct an independent investigation of the situation. I was happy to accommodate them. Important archaeological sites adjacent to park lands are of great interest to us. Do you have some milk?" he asked Sanele.

"Just canned evaporated," Sanele said.

"That would be fine." Drew had taken off his Smokey hat. The circular imprint of its sweat band remained, like the ghost of a hat, around his head. Apelu was pleased to see that Bobbie, who could never hide much of what she was feeling, did not especially like Drew. She sat with her arms crossed and her head tilted slightly to one side as she watched him.

"His name is not 'boy,' it's Sanele," she said.

"Your boyfriend? Assistant?" Drew didn't seem to care.

"My son," Apelu said. "He likes to be helpful."

"Thank you, Sanele," Drew said as Sanele came out of the cabin and handed a can of evaporated milk to him—dried yellow crust around the two puncture holes. "You know, as a scientist I truly appreciate your layman's effort and concern in protecting your cultural resources." Drew was trying to decide which puncture hole to pour the milk out of. "With the speed at which your language, culture, and traditions are vanishing, such physical evidence as you have found may soon be all that is left of your *Fa'a Samoa*." He finally decided and poured an uneven stream of evaporated milk into his tea.

"Would you like some honey?" Sanele asked.

"No, the milk is sweet enough. Thank you."

In Samoan, Apelu told Sanele that he had done enough, that he should sit down and join them as he was as much of a witness to what had happened as any of them. Neither Bobbie nor Drew understood a word of what he said. Sanele sat down in a porch chair near the door, out of their circle.

"There is still enough daylight left to get out there today," Bobbie said, "if you want to see it."

"Where exactly am I staying tonight?" Drew asked, putting down his cup of tea.

"I booked you into cabin number seven," Bobbie said. "It gets the best breeze."

"I won't be staying here in the Park Service cabin?"

"I thought you'd be more comfortable in a space of your own. This place is a little crowded."

"And dinner at the lodge is when?"

"In an hour and a half or so."

"Then let's wait till tomorrow morning. I'll get settled in."

As Apelu and Sanele walked back up to their *fale* afterward, Sanele said, "You know, I've seen that guy Drew before."

"Oh yeah?"

"Yeah, he came to our history class last year and gave a talk."

"About what?"

"About how sad it was that none of us Samoan kids knew anything about our history."

"Was it a good talk?"

"I don't know. Nobody listened. He used a lot of big words. He's smart, I guess."

———— o ————

In the morning they drove Drew to Nandiaka, where he took a bunch of photographs and made some measurements. Apelu had him take photos of the dozer, the wrecked *fale* foundation, and the track of destruction. It was one of those digital cameras that Drew held about a foot in front of his face as he framed the shots. He was very serious in all this, making many notes in a fancy waterproof field notebook. Sanele and Bobbie got bored with Drew and took off for the beach. Apelu started up the dozer, found reverse, and very slowly backed it out over its tracks through the slash it had made. It would have been magically pleasing if all the damage undid itself as the dozer backed out, erasing its tracks and its presence, but that didn't happen. In fact, at points along the way back out, Apelu, fumbling with the unfamiliar controls, inadvertently widened the track or nicked a new tree. By the time he had backed the stinking and infernally noisy machine to the road he felt thoroughly sullied and headed for the beach to join Bobbie and Sanele for a swim. Screw Drew.

But when they all got back to the NPS cabin, Drew was excited. It was quite a discovery. A few Samoan petroglyphs had already been found on the other islands. Some of their motifs and execution—the turtle and the ships especially—were very similar to these. Drew had seen them. But none of them were as large as this one, none so complex. It was a major find. The bordering designs were similar to those found on Rapanui—an island thousands of miles and thousands of later migrational years to the east. Drew enthused and expanded.

"So, there's a scholarly article in it for you?" Bobbie asked.

"It needs to be reported fully."

"Why is that?" Apelu asked.

"Why, it's a major discovery."

"Of what?"

"Of your pre-history."

"What's so pre about it? It's there now," Apelu said.

"But can you tell me what it means?" Drew scoffed.

"I could make up a pretty good story for it. Want to hear it?"

"No."

"Why?"

"Because you are not the person who carved those images. You can't know what he meant by them, what the real story is."

"Why *he*?" Bobbie asked.

"Because women were not artisans."

"You know that?"

"Traditionally—" Drew started.

"Traditionally, I know the story the rock tells," Apelu interrupted. "How can you suppose one piece of tradition and reject what is offered?"

"You don't understand history. Things were different then. Whoever carved those images didn't think the way you think."

"But you think you can interpret the way he—or she—thought better than I can?"

"I can't say if anyone can interpret their actual original meaning." Drew was pacing, getting pissed.

"Then why is it an important find in my pre-history if you can't tell anything from it? What if it's not pre at all, but culturally continuous to the point of being current?"

"You don't know what you are talking about. You haven't read all the literature, haven't thought about it for a long time."

"I don't have to think about it a long time. To'aga's meanings are no stranger to me. How often have you been here?"

"This is just my third visit, but that's not the point."

At this point Sanele slipped from the room, and Bobbie found something to do over by the hot plate.

"It's still on my land," Apelu said.

"Is it?" Drew said.

Apelu shook his head and left. Sanele was waiting for him outside. They went home.

———————— o ————————

"Martin would kill me if he saw me doing this," Bobbie said, taking a puff on Apelu's Marlboro then putting it back into the tuna-fish can ashtray.

"Martin never struck me as the homicidal type."

"Okay, well he wouldn't talk to me for a couple of days anyway, and he would give me those weird sideways looks."

It was getting on toward sundown and Apelu and Bobbie were seated at the table in Apelu's *fale*. Drew was still on island, and Bobbie was hiding from him. Earlier, before Bobbie had come walking up the lane with a plastic bag of cold beers from the lodge, Sanele had taken his father's bamboo pole and gone off to do some reef fishing.

"Does Martin's opinion mean so much?" Apelu took a drag on the cigarette her lips had just touched.

"He likes to treat me like his daughter or niece or something. *In loco parentis.*"

"The *loco* part I understand."

They were stoned.

"I saw Sanele head out to the reef to fish," Bobbie had said when she showed up at the screen door, "and I thought, I want to get stoned with that cop again, take a mini vacation from being responsible." She had brought a tubby joint of local *pakalolo* with her, and they had smoked half of it and opened two beers.

"I only smoke tobacco when I get high," she said now. "Martin wouldn't understand that."

"Martin only wants the best for you."

"Right now I don't care what Martin wants. Martin only wants what only Martin wants."

"He wants you."

"Well, he can't have me. Excuse me for saying so, Apelu, but most men are about as one-dimensional as roadkill."

"No offense taken. I'm genderless here."

"What is it with you guys?"

"We're preprogrammed. We can't help it. We only want beautiful children, so we want to sleep with the most beautiful women. You should take it as a compliment."

"I can't take Drew as a compliment. This morning he told me it was an unwarranted expense for him to be paying for a room at the lodge when the Park Service maintained a cabin there, and he moved his stuff out of his room into the NPS cabin. I can't sleep in that place with him there." Bobbie took another drag on Apelu's Marlboro. "And what do you mean, Martin wants me? He just wants to be my father, and I had enough of that from my own dad, thank you."

Apelu wondered if there was some way to change the topic. He opened another beer.

Bobbie relit what was left of the joint. "I do like the way men smell, though," she said.

"Searching for positive things to say? Don't strain yourself."

"And I really don't enjoy the company of most other women, but then I have to work with guys like Drew and Martin and the superintendent. Ugh."

"Old man Ilmars on the roadkill list too?"

"That creep. He came on to me once right after he was assigned to be our boss. I couldn't believe it. I told him to keep his distance or I'd report him."

The thought of Ilmars sighting down his long blade of nose at Bobbie did something unpleasant to Apelu's stomach. "The direct approach. Did it work?"

"Like a charm. He immediately tried to make me take an involuntary drug test, but they don't do them here, and he backed off. We don't see him much. He's either off on leave or hiding in his office. I get talkative when I'm stoned, and I get the munchies."

Apelu got up and found a bag of unshelled peanuts. Now Bobbie shucked and chewed as she talked, making a neat pile of shells on the table beside her.

"Like I like the way you smell, Apelu, a nice honest smell. The first boy I fell for in school had hippie parents and smelled of patchouli oil. How about you? What smells do you like?" She glanced up at Apelu as she popped a couple of halves of shelled peanuts into her mouth. Her look was one of innocent buddy camaraderie. With her short hair, deep tan, small breasts, no makeup or jewelry, and simple sun-bleached T-shirt and shorts, plus the way she leaned forward, bare feet apart, elbows on knees as she shucked the next nut, someone who didn't know her might have to look twice at a photograph of her to see that she was a woman and not a thin teenage boy. Or maybe it was something about the almost horizontal sunlight. But in real rounded life, not in black and white, there was no missing her unpolished femininity.

"You got any brothers?" Apelu asked.

"Two, one older, one younger. Why? Do you like the smell of brothers?"

Apelu had to laugh. He picked the end of the joint out of the tuna-fish can ashtray and lit it. "Where are they at?"

"Home still in Beaver Dam. You want some peanuts? So, where are your other kids?"

"With their mom in Apia."

"Is she pissed at you or something?"

"None of your business."

"I can't imagine being married. What's it like? I mean, I see it like some sort of game show. You know, two people who have to perform all the normal things that people do—like brush their teeth—only they are tied together, hand and foot, waist to waist."

"It's something like that. You better like the way the other person smells anyway."

"I got pregnant once. Had an abortion. Boyfriend insisted. I had liked the way he smelled up till then. Then I didn't like it anymore. Love tricks your senses, puts like a filter on them." Bobbie took a pull on her bottle of Steinlager.

"The suspension of disgust."

"What's that?"

"Being in love requires the suspension of disgust. If you had had the baby, you would have discovered that things that would normally disgust you—like shit and piss and vomit—didn't disgust you if it's your baby's. It works like that in love affairs too. Sorry about the baby. Yeah, I'll have some peanuts."

"Maybe you're right," she said, staring at her bare feet, turning her ankle to look at the new scars there, "but I miss that good smell. And why don't I just shut up now?"

"I like the smell of the reef at real low tide," Apelu said.

"I like that too," Bobbie said, smiling, looking up, "and I always sniff the inside of surgical gloves before I put them on in the lab."

"And the smell of someone else peeling an orange."

"Yeah, oranges," Bobbie said, the munchies still on her.

"Oranges? Who's got oranges?" It was Sanele's voice from outside the screen. Only the high clouds held the last light.

"Got fish?" Bobbie asked.

"Got fish," Sanele answered. "Let's eat." And they started arguing over who was going to do what to fix dinner. Apelu finished his beer and emptied the ashtray. He lit the kerosene lantern. Both of his kids were home now. He could relax.

CHAPTER 6

———— o ————

"NO, NO, SHUT UP. AND USE A CUP. WHERE'S YOUR CUP?"
Apelu grabbed the bottle of vodka from Nu`upo's grip and
splashed some into his own metal cup. Nu`upo had been taking
swigs straight from the bottle.

"Cup?"

"Find another one. Over there." Apelu gestured with the
bottle abstractly. "Now listen. I'm on to something here." They
were sitting alone at the kitchen table in Apelu's *fale*. The kerosene lantern was lit on the counter. Sanele was still down with
Bobbie at the party in the village. Apelu's *saofa`i*, his title investi-
ture that morning, had gone well. The whole village had been
there. The official stuff had ended hours before, but the village
had been ripe for a good excuse to party. After the formal feast
that followed the investiture ceremony, Apelu had taken aside
the owner of the best-stocked bush store in the village, given him
three hundred dollars cash, and told him to keep the beer and
sodas flowing until the money ran out.

Getting drunk had been Nu`upo's idea. He had come to the
saofa`i. Apelu had seen him in the rear of the crowd, standing alone
in the shade. Later in the afternoon, while Apelu was seated with

the other chiefs enjoying their first leisurely beers, Nu'upo caught Apelu's eye from down by the beach. He was gesturing for Apelu to meet him at the edge of the village. Apelu excused himself, saying that he wanted to bathe and change. For the ceremony he had been decked out in a lava lava made from a fine mat, and the skin of his upper body had been generously rubbed with glistening coconut oil. The fact is he would have vanished from there as soon as he could slip away even if he hadn't seen Nu'upo. Apelu had endured about all he could of speeches and sermons and ceremonies— performance *Fa'a Samoa*. He hadn't been around that many people at once in a long time. His nerves were still those of a hermit, and it was even worse being the focus of so much attention. He had planned on hiking back to his shack alone, changing, and then going for a swim. He might as well see what Nu'upo was up to. Being around Nu'upo wasn't the same as being around people.

"Well, it's a proud day for the Soifua clan." Nu'upo was seated in the shade of a stone wall at the very end of the village. He didn't sound sarcastic.

Apelu stopped, looked down the empty road toward the village, then uncinched and took off the cumbersome mat lava lava. Underneath he had on a pair of athletic shorts. He folded up the fine mat and handed it to Nu'upo, who took it. Apelu pulled a pack of Marlboro Lights 100s out of his shorts pocket and lit one. "A man's got to do what a man's got to do," he said.

"Feed the village. The village likes to be fed." Nu'upo stood up, tucking the fine mat under a scrawny arm. "A well-fed village is a happy village. Congratulations. Should I elevate my terms of addressing you to their proper chiefly status?"

"That would be funny."

"Then let's save it for when we really need to be funny."

"I had to get out of there." Apelu started walking up the road toward Va'oto.

"I thought you held up quite well, so I thought I would re-ward us." Nu'upo picked up a plaited palm frond basket that clinked. He found a place for the fine mat on top of the basket and followed Apelu. A ways up the road Apelu reached over and took one of the basket handles, and they walked the rest of the way like that in silence, the basket of bottles and discarded finery swaying between them.

———————— o ————————

They were into the second bottle of vodka now. The beers were finished. Nu'upo had lost his cup. And Apelu wanted to talk about his Auntie Sia for some reason. He had forgotten the point he wanted to make, how it connected to or answered something Nu'upo had said, but he wanted to go there anyway. Maybe the connection would appear. Nu'upo was now drinking his vodka out of an empty mackerel can he had found in the garbage. He toasted Apelu with a high chief's salutation, and they both laughed.

"No, listen up. My Auntie Sia could fill half of the back of a pickup truck but she had a lot of class. She lived in LA. She was high maintenance. One of the things she was famous for was her plastic vegetables. She had this thing, this obsession, about how when she served a meal the arrangement of food and colors on the plate had to be balanced just so. She had eaten in too many fancy restaurants. So she found somewhere these realistic replicas of vegetable servings—a nice pile of green peas, or tiny carrots in a glaze sauce, sliced zucchini, even beets—and when a dinner plate needed some extra color, she would plop a piece of plastic food in there. Looked good enough to eat. She would just wash and reuse them."

"I don't like your Auntie Sia."

"That's all right. She liked herself enough to cover that."

"Was that story going somewhere?"

"Well, think about it. You're there in her fancy house up some Hollywood canyon, sitting at her fancy dining room table, and she puts a plate of food in front of you. That's how she did it, just like in some restaurant. No family-style serve yourself. And it's a really good looking plate of food, smells great. But which food on your plate is not real? How do you tell? Touch it? Sniff it? Stick it with a fork?"

"Oh, I get it. You're talking about reality and illusion."

"And if it's your first time at one of her dinner parties, you don't even expect that you are going to be lied to. And it's not a joke. You're not supposed to draw attention to the fact that your peas refuse to get on your fork."

"Now I like your Auntie Sia more, but if you're looking for a metaphor, what's the other part?"

"I guess I was thinking about the ceremony today. How parts of it—the preachy parts, the Jesus lip service stuff—were like chunks of reusable molded plastic rhetoric tossed onto a platter of otherwise nutritious traditions."

"God's good ministers, huh? Let's not go there. Look at it this way—at your lovely Auntie Sia's dinners at least the lies would taste like lies. You could tell right away what wasn't meant to be swallowed." Nu'upo had stopped drinking. Maybe it was the mackerel can, but Apelu had gotten drunk with Nu'upo several times before, and always there had been a point when Nu'upo would stop drinking, as if the alcohol had been just a means to an end, a path up to a plateau of visored clarity. He could get scary then if you didn't join him there.

Apelu went on: "But what people say and seem to believe isn't the same as a plate of food. I'm not talking about burned-out skeptics like you and me. I'm talking about everyone else in the village who was there, including my son, who listened to all that stuff. You and I have already tasted that plastic and spat it out. For them it's like watching Auntie Sia's meal being served from outside her dining room window. There is no way they can test it to see what's real and what's bogus. What about them?"

"Touching—the skeptic's lament for the innocents."

Apelu poured the last of the vodka into his cup. Now they would both be done with drinking. "You were the one who talked about feeding the village. I'm just fretting about what they're being fed."

"Words, just words. Those premolded pieces you're so worried about just pass right through them undigested. There are levels of skepticism after all, you know."

Apelu got up from the table and walked to the screen door. "I'm talking about dogma here, and all religions are about dogma. You are presented with this prepared plate of moral food, some of which is real and valuable and some of which is bogus, just there to please some hierarchy's sense of order. And when you look at it through that window it might as well all be fake."

"Or it might as well all be good chow. Obviously, if you are looking in a window at people sitting down to dinner, you're hungry and you don't belong there."

"But if so much of what is on their dogmatic plate is so blatantly bullshit, how can you trust the rest?"

"I've never eaten bullshit. How is it fixed?"

"Just a slice of a pile of brown plastic pies. I prefer the artificial cow patties, actually." Apelu opened the screen door and tossed what was left of his vodka out into the darkness of the yard.

"It's good to be a picky eater," Nu'upo said. "It keeps you thin."

A pair of headlights turned into the bottom of the lane and began their crawl and bounce up to the *fale*.

"*Tofa,*" Nu'upo said. He slipped past Apelu at the screen door before the lights reached them and vanished into the darkness. Apelu cleared the table of empties.

It was Bobbie bringing Sanele home, only Sanele wasn't ready to be home yet. He was still on a party high and had borrowed a couple of videos from a kid in the village and wanted to watch at least one of them down at Bobbie's. Could he? Bobbie said that she didn't mind, that one of the movies looked interesting and she might watch it. She gave Apelu a curious look. "You all right?" she asked.

Apelu waved them off. "Go, go, enjoy. I'll see you in the morning, son."

The next day Apelu took Sanele out to Toʻaga, and they removed all the plastic survey markers and stakes from what Apelu believed to be the approach to their land. For the hell of it, they pulled up a bunch of other ones too. Then Sanele had the bright idea of moving the stakes around, so they put them back at different locations. They had fun.

Only about a tenth of the Territory's land had yet been surveyed in a hundred years of surveyors being around. Something about straight lines drawn on a map pretending to be a depiction of—no, a dictation of—terrestrial reality just couldn't find a foothold in the Samoan mindset. The dictionary definition for the Samoan word to jostle—*feuʻuaʻi*—was to move backward and forward, as a boundary. That's what edges were meant to do— keep moving, be alive. Having land surveyed was breaking an old taboo, a sin of pride against the community, an assumption that somehow you could stop time and space and screw up everyone else's freedom and natural flow. Apelu took one of the stakes with its plastic ribbon and stuck it into a crack in the reef a dozen yards off shore.

A couple of days later, in Pago, Apelu found out what the surveying was all about. He had come over on a day trip to register his new title at the Territorial Registrar's Office and officially accept responsibility for the family lands associated with the title.

"Well, if any of your family's land is near the new hotel, I guess its value will increase," the registrar said as she filled in the paper work.

"Which hotel is that?" Apelu asked.

"The one they want to put in there along the National Park beach."

"Who is this they?"

"The money guys are all from off-island, Hawaii, Asia. Part of a chain of resorts called Paradise Escapes."

"I hadn't heard."

"Oh, they haven't officially announced it yet, but everybody knows about it. The money guys were on island a couple of weeks ago and met with the governor; got their local incorporation papers signed. I got them here. Then two days ago they came in here to file their land survey plots."

"The off-island money guys came back?"

"No, they're long gone. One of the Po'o boys filed them, or tried to. There were still several chiefs' signatures missing. The land of three different families is involved. All the chiefs have got to sign off on it."

"So, you turned him down?"

"Sent him back to get the rest of the signatures. That's my job, to be a bitch. For instance, here," and she handed Apelu several pieces of loose paper. "Now you have to take these over to the Office of Samoan Affairs for them to sign off on it, then you come back here and pay your registration fee."

"So simple."

"Seldom is. These things usually hit a hook that they get hung up on for a while. Congratulations on your title, by the way. Be a good chief."

"Feed the village," he said and left.

It was only a half mile hike down the main road in town from the Registrar's Office to the Office of Samoan Affairs, through the center of what once had been the old US Naval

Station. Many of the old Naval Station buildings had been knocked down in the fifty years since the Navy had left, so that fact—that name on the land—was harder to remember even for those who were old enough to remember when all the buildings had been there and the Naval Station was basically off-limits to Samoans without business there. The place had changed. It had lost even its *palangi* name, which in its time had erased the original place names. Now it was just sort of "downtown."

The old Naval Customhouse on the dock was gone, for instance. Every school kid of Apelu's generation knew that the last hanging of a native by the Navy had taken place there. For many years Apelu had associated the English word "custom" with hanging. When asked, anyone's uncle would tell you the story—the crazy man running across the Naval Station Parade Ground on a Sunday morning after church, waving a bush knife over his head, chasing another Samoan man. For some of the spectators, dressed all in white and on their way home from church and a London Missionary Society style hell-and-brimstone sermon, it must have seemed like some staged morality play. The man with the knife caught up with the man he was chasing and with two slicing strokes almost decapitated him. Somewhere else the subject of their fatal dispute might have been a woman, but here in Samoa the bad blood was as usual over land, a boundary dispute. The murderer surrendered himself peacefully, was tried in the naval court, and was duly hanged. Samoans weren't too happy about the last part—it seemed cold-blooded so long after the fact—so the Navy never again imposed the death sentence. But now that building, along with that piece of local lore, was gone. Apelu was sure that Sanele and his mates didn't know the story.

As he walked Apelu considered the registrar's news about To'aga. It fit in with Nu'upo's theory about why the surveyors had wanted to take out their boulder. "They got plans for that land," Nu'upo had said. "A chunk of history sitting on it would throw a monkey wrench into them. The *palangis* got mainland laws about messing with stuff like that. I figure they were just going to turn the motherfucker over and pretend it wasn't there, avoid the hassles with permits, archaeologists, and all that shit." But neither of them could figure out what sort of plans anyone would have for a place where no one would go. Apelu wondered how Japanese and Australian vacationers would deal with a headless bellhop at their hotel room door.

There was a hassle, a hook, at Samoan Affairs. One of the chiefs who had to sign off on Apelu's papers—the District Governor—was not available. In fact, he was in Hawaii for medical treatment. Apelu had to leave his papers there. The woman he left them with was a cousin of his. She promised him she would personally look after them and contact him as soon as everyone that had to had signed off. He gave her the number at the lodge to call.

At headquarters, Apelu photocopied his plane ticket and filled in a request-for-reimbursement form; then he went to see his captain to report in and get his signature on the reimbursement form. Apelu hadn't missed any of this paperwork world. The captain wasn't in. Apelu spent the rest of the afternoon before leaving for the airport writing up an incident report about the surveyors and the dozer. It was a multi-pager, but Apelu didn't make any recommendations for further action or arrests. What was the point? And he wasn't sure what, if any, criminal codes had actually been broken. He did note that they had not obtained a land use permit and that a government vehicle had been used on a non-government job, but that really wasn't any of his business.

Apelu found out that Edgar had had his preliminary hearing and that his *palangi* lawyer had gotten the charges reduced to two—possessing an unlicensed firearm and unlawful use of it. Edgar had pled not guilty to both charges and was out on bail. No trial date had been set. The AG's Office liked to plea bargain away such cases. It would probably never get to a point where

Apelu might actually have to testify to anything. Of course, Edgar was prohibited from leaving the Territory until the case was resolved, and the word was that Edgar was not happy about that. He had probably thought he could just skip out on the whole thing, forfeiting bail and the gun.

Apelu wanted to get back on the afternoon plane because his son-sitter Bobbie was back on Tutuila now, so he got to the airport early to make sure he got a seat. And lo and behold there was Edgar, along with two of his mates, heading back with him. Edgar made a point of glaring at Apelu and then ignoring him. One of the other *palangis*, the one who had interceded about the gun, nodded to him.

"Returning to Ofu?" Apelu asked.

"Yes," he said. "It seems someone has undone much of our work."

"Weird things happen out there in To'aga," Apelu said.

Back on Ofu, word about the purpose of the surveyors' work had preceded them. The family that ran the lodge refused to put them up. The lodge was the only place to stay, and no one in the village wanted anything to do with them. The Paradise Escapes news was not welcome. This was not a community where economic development trumped all other considerations. The *pulenu'u* was forced into putting them up for the night in his open guest *fale*, but now—faced with the village's silent disapproval—even he was trying to distance himself from them. All he could offer was a "just doing my job" defense. All the surveyors returned to Pago the next day. Apelu and Sanele moved several more of the stakes with yellow plastic ribbons out onto the reef in a semi-straight line parallel to the beach. They looked better out there, festive, incongruous.

The surveyors returned on the next boat. They drove a big white fully loaded rental van off the ferry's ramp onto the dock. They were self-contained now. They drove the van out to To'aga and pitched two big army surplus tents, fired up a generator, and established their base camp in the bush. The place they chose to take their stand was one of the few large tree-cleared spots in To'aga, the land behind the old Navy dispensary.

——————— o ———————

There are certain things you just don't do in a Samoan village after dark if you want to stay beneath the other world's radar—like sweep the floor or look in a mirror—but one of the basic rules is that you don't make loud noises. The second night that the *tā'aga*, as the villagers now called the *palangi* surveyors—the word meant gang, as in a gang of thieves—were encamped at To'aga, Apelu could hear the *thump thump* bass of a country and western song come and go with the breeze from that direction. The next night it was even clearer. Hours later he was awakened by a single distant gunshot, waited for more, then went back to sleep. Would he have to go out there and be a cop again?

For some reason the surveyors had not removed the stakes and ribbons from the reef. Probably they had never seen them, not being the types to go to the beach. But someone from the village had seen them and, hoping to make some mischief, had reported to the National Park that there was a line of survey flags along their precious coral reef inside the park. Bobbie and her boss were on the next morning's plane.

Bobbie's boss in this case was not Chief Biologist Martin Berm but her big boss, the park superintendent, Ilmars Dolbrecz. Apelu knew Superintendent Dolbrecz from a case a few years before. Apelu had needed the superintendent's permission to search a steeply ravined section of the National Park on Tutuila for a body that they had every reason to believe had been dumped off a cliff face there. Ilmars had resisted him to the max, as if letting him intrude local police business inside the park was like a surrender of national sovereignty. He was a large and bitter man, bitter in the way only bureaucrats can get, when even cooperation is thrown down as a challenge. He was known by his first name rather than his last for a couple of reasons. All previous park superintendents had preferred the first name title—as in Ranger Rick—and Samoans had trouble learning to say his second name with all those consonants clumped together like that.

Ilmars resembled his name, large-boned and hard-featured, with a hawk-nosed face that belonged above a uniform. He was paler and more slouch-shouldered than Apelu remembered him. Perhaps he had some other disease besides being an asshole.

Apelu drove with them in the Park Service truck out to the beach at To`aga where the stakes and ribbons still adorned the reef. Ilmars did not enjoy his stroll on the beach. He pulled out a digital camera identical to the one Drew the archaeologist had used and took some shots; then he handed the camera to Bobbie, who waded out onto the reef—it was high tide—and took more shots from different angles.

"Inspect for ancillary damage. Write it up," was all Ilmars said before turning and trudging back to the truck. He spent the rest of the day resting at the NPS cabin, then left on the afternoon flight. His total conversational exchange with Apelu had been his initial flat "Hello."

Sanele, of course, was glad to see Bobbie back. They were becoming like siblings. They shared little secrets and had snits with one another. Though Bobbie ruled, in some ways Sanele seemed older, and she would defer to that then have to put him down. It was like having a family again for Apelu. He enjoyed it and ignored it equally. That night they cooked dinner for him at the NPS cabin, then argued over which video to watch. Apelu fell asleep in the midst of the movie, and Sanele had to wake him for the hike back up to their *fale*. At the top of the climb they could just hear the music coming from To`aga.

"It's them, isn't it?" Sanele asked.

"Yes, it's them, confusing being loud with being brave."

In the middle of the night Apelu was awakened by another distant gunshot, then another and another, then silence. Apelu rolled over and went back to sleep. You had to trust To`aga to take care of itself.

———————————— o ————————————

In the morning Apelu and Sanele were surprised to see the park ranger's pickup crawling up their lane a little after dawn.

"Hey, you guys, you want some breakfast?" Bobbie called cheerfully as she pulled up beside the *fale*.

"Bobbie?" Apelu asked. This was not normal behavior.

"Well, I woke up to the leftover casserole from last night and realized it would never again be as good as it would be for breakfast today, and there's a lot of it."

"Meals on wheels," Apelu said.

"Some leftover dinner rolls, too. They'd just get stale."

"Cool," Sanele said. Bobbie passed the casserole dish and a bowl of rolls from the seat beside her out to Sanele, who took them into the *fale*. Now it was Apelu's turn to give Bobbie a curious look and ask, "Are you all right?"

"Of course. Just feeling neighborly. A nice morning and all." Bobbie got out of the truck.

Sanele came back out of the *fale*. He had put on a T-shirt above his lava lava.

"I made coffee, too. Sanele, get the thermos, would you? It's in the niche beside the tool box."

"Where?" Sanele said. "I can't see it."

Bobbie went and looked in the bed of the truck. "Darn, it's not here. I must have left it on the counter. Sanele, be a sweetheart would you and run down and get it? The cabin is open."

"Can I take the truck?"

"No," Bobbie and Apelu answered simultaneously.

Sanele shrugged and headed off down the lane. Bobbie turned and watched him until his back had disappeared. "Apelu, I have got to talk to you," she said with her back still turned to him. "It's daylight now, but I still have to talk about it."

"Something about Sanele?"

"No, not at all, but, well, yes, I guess, partly."

"Come inside."

They sat at the table.

"Last night," Bobbie started then stopped.

"Yes?"

"Last night after you guys left it took me a while to straighten up the cabin and get to sleep. Oh man, this is so strange." She stopped. Apelu waited.

"Well, I couldn't get to sleep and I was sitting out in the dark on the porch. You didn't hear anything?"

Apelu said nothing.

"It was pretty still, just the sound of the surf, and I was sitting there, feeling pretty good, tired but not sleepy, and I heard this noise, far away at first, of people coming up the road from the village, not voices, just the sound of footfalls and the sound of bodies moving. Do you know how much I like you two guys?"

Apelu nodded. "Go on."

"Well, it kept getting closer, and I moved all the way back into the darkness by the door. Then I saw them moving in front of the light coming off the ocean, coming single file in a slow trot up the road. They were all dressed like chiefs, with fine mat lava lavas around their waists and just glistening skin above. The first man was huge and carried a war club with lots of teeth on it." Bobbie was staring at the table top, seeing something else. "I wasn't dreaming. I wasn't stoned or drunk. The big guy in front cut off the road, angled toward the bush beyond my place, and the rest of the line followed. They were running in unison, like a dance, and I began to feel their pulse in the earth through my feet. Except for the voice of their bodies they were silent. Then the moon broke out of the clouds and I could see each of them clearly because now the line passed less than twenty yards in front of my porch, and each man was different, himself, many shapes and ages. I don't know how many men there were passed by me. Thirty? Fifty? I felt totally vulnerable and then totally safe because none of them seemed to notice I was there. There were several men with only one arm. Oh, Apelu, it all sounds so crazy, but I was all alone, and for some reason I was sure they were headed here, to your and Sanele's home, from the angle they took off from the road, and they all looked so . . . so . . . fixated, I guess. And I didn't know what to do." Bobbie put her slim golden arm down on the table, and Apelu covered it with his, his palm around her elbow. "Then the last man in line, the youngest and trimmest, the rear guard, stopped and looked right at me there in the double darkness of the doorway and he saw me, registered me, then trotted on. And he looked like Sanele. It was like a punch in my stomach. I almost threw up. They all trotted up a path into the bush where there is no path. I checked this morning—not a footprint, not a broken twig. I am so glad you two are all right. I just had to come up first thing to make sure. You are all right, aren't you?"

"We're fine." Apelu patted Bobbie's arm then took his arm away. "They weren't after us. Did you hear gunshots last night?"

"No. Where?"

"To`aga. It would have been later."

"I didn't hear anything. Who were those men?"

"Warriors on a mission, it sounds like."

"What mission?"

"Taking care of To`aga."

"Were they real?"

"Real enough to let themselves be seen by you."

"But Sanele was here all night with you, wasn't he?"

"Sound asleep."

Sanele came striding back up the lane, swinging a big thermos by its handle.

"Don't tell him," Bobbie said.

"Not a word."

Sanele bounced up the steps and through the screen door. "Here's the coffee. Let's eat."

Bobbie got up and gave him a big hug.

"What's this for?" he asked with a small smile as Bobbie held him.

"For being such a sweetheart and getting the coffee," Bobbie said and stepped back, taking the thermos. "Thanks for shaking it up."

"I prefer my coffee shaken not stirred," Apelu said.

CHAPTER 7

———— o ————

Finding Edgar's body was the easy part. Finding his head was something else. In fact, his body had been discovered before the *pulenu`u* came to report the murder to Apelu. The other surveyors had found it after searching for several hours. They were searching for Edgar because he hadn't come back to camp the night before after going out on patrol.

Going out on patrol, the other surveyors told Apelu, had been purely Edgar's idea. He had become convinced that they were being watched at night, that there were people out there in the bush spying on them. He did have a second weapon—a rifle with a night scope on it—and had started slipping out of camp after lights out. No one could sleep with the sound of the generator running, so they would turn it off when everyone else had gotten tired of Edgar's music and wanted to go to bed, and Edgar would put on his jungle fatigues and paint his face like a Navy SEAL—Edgar claimed to have been a Navy SEAL—and would slip into the bush on his "night surveillance" mission. He was usually half drunk by then. The others would go to sleep.

But that morning Edgar was not back in his cot when they got up, so they had to go look for him. They had been awakened by the shots in the night but figured it was just Edgar letting off boozy steam, firing at infrared shadows. Why own a gun if you can't shoot it?

Edgar's body was finally found not far from their camp at the old dispensary. The reason they hadn't found him earlier was that everyone was looking on the ground for Edgar. They found his rifle, but no signs of Edgar. The sun was up over the ridgetop by then and it was getting hot. They were taking a break in the shade when one of the men felt something dripping on his head, sticky stuff like bird shit, only dark. He looked up and found Edgar—a beefy headless corpse dressed in jungle camouflage that failed to fully hide him in the jungle canopy, draped at the waist over a stout tree limb twenty-five feet off the jungle floor. A bright blue-and-white kingfisher was perched on the blood-black collar of the uniform, pecking at the insects on the flesh and fibers and tubes and bones that had once been a neck.

By the time Apelu got there to hear the story the crime scene had been greatly disturbed. They had gotten the body down from the limb by making a ladder up the tree trunk with pounded-in survey stakes and lowering it with a rope.

You wanted to make sure it was really Edgar? Or were you going to give mouth-to-trachea resuscitation? Apelu wondered but didn't ask.

They had all handled the weapon, but no one could remember exactly where they had found it.

Apelu climbed up the makeshift stake ladder to look at where the body had supposedly been found. There wasn't much to see. It was a long ways down to the ground, so he didn't look down as he hung onto the limb. He looked up to catch his breath before heading back down, and there, stuck by its many teeth in a greener limb six feet further up the tree, was the probable murder weapon—a large hardwood war club, its razor sharp edges dark with dried blood, flies buzzing around it. By sheer will

Apelu forced himself up onto the limb. Then, holding onto the trunk with one trembling arm, he grabbed the handle of the club and gently worked its teeth free from the limb. When it came loose, its weight was such that it almost pulled him from his grip on the trunk, and he let go of the club, which fell to the ground and bounced. "Don't touch it," he yelled down. Slowly, very slowly, he made his way off the limb and back to earth.

The most interesting thing about the club, even more interesting than its heft and craftsmanship and gore, was the bullet hole through the head of it. There were splinters of wood around the hole and on one side powder burns, but the wood had not shattered at all. There was blood inside the bore. Apelu sent one of the surveyors back to their camp to get a large plastic garbage bag he could put the club into. It was the most fascinating piece of evidence that Apelu had ever run across. Henceforward he would always think of that club as his, as if it had been left there as a present just for him. The club would turn up in many future dreams, but first he would send it off for fingerprinting.

Apelu conducted a cursory examination of the corpse, which seemed to bear no other wounds. In the left pants leg pocket of the uniform were two unused clips of ammo. In the right pants leg pocket was an almost empty plastic flask whose contents smelled like whisky of some sort. Apelu put everything back where he had found it, then, with the help of the surveyors, managed to get the corpse into two more garbage bags—one from the top, one from the bottom. Without his head, Edgar was even shorter.

"No head?" Apelu asked when they were done.

"No, we haven't found it," the same spokesguy said. "What kind of person would . . . ?"

The rest of the operation—taking statements, getting the body to the airstrip, commandeering the afternoon flight, notifying headquarters—took most of the rest of the day. The other surveyors took down their camp, sticking everything into the van, which they parked by the airstrip, then flew back with the body. As the plane lifted off then turned back toward the slanting western light and Pago, Apelu called it a day.

Apelu had refused to take Sanele or Bobbie with him when the *pulenu`u* had come with the news that morning. Sanele definitely wanted to go along. In his mind Edgar was the guy who had taken a shot at them and in a way, by doing so, had ended Sanele's childhood with that sharp echoing report. When Apelu got back to their *fale* after taking a swim and washing off, Sanele was full of questions, which ended with, "Why take his head?"

"What better trophy? Take the head, you know they're dead. American Indians used to mutilate the bodies of their defeated enemies so that they would be unfit to fight in the afterlife, but I doubt Samoans took heads for any such sophisticated reason. Your grandfather once told me about how when he was a boy he and some of his mates found a skeleton with two heads up in the high jungle behind Leone and thought they had found the bones of some sort of prehistoric freak until one of their dads pointed out that it was nothing more than a wounded warrior headed home with his trophy who didn't make it home. Taking someone's head pretty much depersonalizes him, makes him a nobody. And it's not easy to do either. Have they taught you in school about the guillotine?"

"That machine for chopping people's heads off? No, but I've seen it on TV shows."

"Well, a French doctor invented that machine to make beheading people easier, because even with sharp-edged metal axes the executioner had to hack away."

"That's sort of sick, Dad."

"Nah, it's history, I learned about it in a course at the Police Academy. There was even some doctor—I can't remember if it was Doctor Guillotine or some other dude—who studied the heads after they were chopped off by the machine and discovered that they were still conscious—I mean their eyes could still blink and focus and respond—for minutes afterward. I've always wondered what they would be thinking about."

"Maybe like, *Duh, I'm dead, how come I can still see things*?"

"What if that moment is the same as eternity?"

"Pretty scary, Dad. Dude leaning over you, breathing in your face."

"If you're a Frenchman, maybe you're waiting to see angels."

"If you're a criminal, maybe you're waiting to see devils."

"Last thought, angels or devils, heaven or hell. It's all in your now detached head."

"That's not what they say at church, I don't think."

Apelu looked at his son. They were seated in a patch of banana trees up the ridge right above their *fale* where they could see the southern ocean as the sun set. Apelu was holding one of the beers he had brought up from the lodge. Sanele was absent-mindedly plaiting together long pieces of grass into a slim green cord. Apelu noticed how big his son's hands had become, a man's hands. His eyes were on the sea.

"Did we really used to eat people, Dad?"

"So I've heard, but I don't know anything about that. I've heard people don't taste that good."

"Then there must have been some other reason."

"Like what?"

"Like then that person couldn't come back either because now they were part of you."

Apelu finished his beer. The last light was dying in the sea sky, blood-red fingers blunted in clouds, a yellow that fell short of being gold, the promise of rain. Sanele stood up, then offered his hand to Apelu to help him up. He took it.

"What's for dinner?" Sanele asked. "I'm starving."

———— o ————

Next morning there were only the three of them—Apelu, Sanele, and Bobbie. Apelu knew it would be pointless to ask in the village for volunteers. "Look," he told Sanele and Bobbie, "how often in your life will you get to go head hunting?"

Apelu really didn't think they would find Edgar's head, but he'd been a cop long enough to know that he had to waste a bunch of person hours hunting for it. Negative evidence was a concept that Apelu had grown more comfortable with as he grew older—that absence not only made the heart grow fonder but also proved something. Zero could be a prime number. Zero he could understand.

Sanele was already familiar with how Bobbie did her reef transects. "It's the same only it's on land," Apelu explained. They set up about two yards apart and started walking To'aga, starting at the tree where the body had been found, circling it in lengthening arcs, looking for Edgar's head.

"What if it's up in a tree, too?" Bobbie asked.

"Then we'll never find it."

"Besides, who would put a trophy up a tree?" Sanele said, whacking the underbrush around him away with a stick. "In fact, who would drop a trophy in the bush?"

"Nobody," Apelu said, doing the same thing with his own stick, "but we've got to look."

"So that your dad can tell his bosses that the head isn't here," Bobbie said, whacking away at her end of the line. "It's like those pieces of the reef where there is no live coral, we record those too, remember?"

"That's different. It was underwater for one thing, and you were paying me, or said you were paying me. When will I get paid for that?"

"I'll pay you both the same rate Bobbie paid," Apelu said, "by the hour."

"X times zero is still zero," Sanele said.

"That's one time when zero is a problem," Apelu agreed.

After that, conversation pretty much muttered out. After two hours of increasingly lackadaisical circling, Apelu called it off. He had Sanele measure the distance they'd come from the tree and then work out a number for area searched that he would put in his report. Apelu was no good at such formulas, but Sanele was in his second semester of geometry. They stopped for water and some snacks that Bobbie had brought. The western edge of their search circle had brought them up against the vague edge of Nandiaka. As Bobbie and Apelu rested in the shade Sanele wandered off.

"You didn't tell him anything about . . . about what I told you, did you?" Bobbie took a drink of water.

"Nope."

"That club you found?"

"Like the one you described, only with a bullet hole through it."

"Apelu, could either you guys move down to my place or could I move up to your place until I go back? It would only be for a night or two."

"No problem. Whichever works best."

"Well, I sort of prefer my place because it's got a bathroom."

They could hear Sanele returning through the bush. "Hey, you guys, come look at this," he said as he came out into the open. They got up and followed him. Sanele led them into Nandiaka, over the crushed *fale* foundation, and back to the new boulder. Sitting on top of the boulder was a head.

The head had been carved out of a coconut and crudely painted with white ulu sap to look like a *palangi*. Its eyes—two chunks of charcoal—stared blankly ahead. The head sat in a dried pool of what looked like real blood.

"Edgar, what have they done to you?" Apelu said after a long silent mutual pause for staring back.

"Strange sense of humor," Bobbie said.

"I could do better," Sanele added and stepped forward to pick up the head.

"No, leave it, son. The message isn't just for us."

"Could I make a suggestion?" Bobbie asked. "Could we get out of here? Please."

———— o ————

They walked back to the NPS truck and then returned to Bobbie's cabin. Waiting for them there, seated cross-legged on the porch, was a young man dressed in a lava lava and a T-shirt. He was waiting for Apelu. The young man rose and was very polite, used elevated chiefly terms addressing Apelu. Bobbie and Sanele went inside.

"Chief, my uncle wishes to meet with you to show his respect."

"Why does he not come himself?"

"He wishes to show his respect in the proper way, at his *fale*."

"I appreciate your uncle's kind invitation. Is there something I can do for him in return?"

"My uncle only wishes to make things right again. He wishes to make amends to both you and the ghost who guards To'aga."

"Your uncle's name?"

The name the young man gave him was the name of the bull-dozer driver at Nandiaka.

"If your uncle wishes to offer an *ifoga* to myself and the ghost then he should come to my *fale* tomorrow midday. We will meet with him there."

The young man thanked Apelu sincerely. He had done his difficult duty, gotten his answer, and was off the hook. "I will take your chiefly wishes to my uncle," he said, ducking his head down respectfully. "Thank you for your answer and for your love for my family." He bowed once more and was gone. Apelu watched him head down the road toward the village.

"He's gone already?" Bobbie came out of the cabin with two glasses of iced tea. "What was that all about?"

"*Ifoga* at my place tomorrow."

"What's an *ifoga*?" Bobbie handed him one of the glasses.

"An apology ceremony."

"An apology for what?"

"Don't know for sure. We'll find out tomorrow."

———————— o ————————

The *ifoga* was an essential part of the Samoan system of social control. When a member of one family brought harm to a member of another family—murder was the usual offense—the highest available chief from the offender's family would present himself in front of the *fale* of the victim's family chief. As a way of humbling himself in apology, the visiting chief would sit on the ground outside and pull a fine mat over his head. In theory he was offering himself as payment for the shame the offender had brought upon his family, but in practice his life was not taken. Instead, he was left to sit there in the sun or the rain for as long as the victim's family chose. How long he was allowed to humble himself and what gifts of reparation—in fine mats, tapa cloth, food, cash—were deemed appropriate were determined by one of those wonderfully complex and slippery formulas that hold traditional societies together. Considerations factored in included the severity of the offense, the status of the victim, the status and age of the chief sitting out there, family histories and relative wealth, the peace of the village at large, and the future relationship of the families involved. The practice bought time for tempers to cool and for the chiefs of other families to gather and give temporizing advice. Apelu had seen his share of *ifogas* in his police work. Sometimes an *ifoga* had already commenced by the time the police arrived at a crime scene. The courts even took into consideration the speed and appropriateness of *ifogas* when they got around to sentencing offenders months later—a good *ifoga* might mean less jail time.

That afternoon Apelu hiked up to Nu'upo's camp. He had only been there a few times before. It was a long hike up. Nu'upo wasn't there. Apelu left a note: "Nu'upo Aitu, Guardian of To'aga, *ifoga* at my place tomorrow, high noon. Come as you were."

Apelu and Sanele spent the night down at Bobbie's. No visitors, no troops marching by. Apelu had trouble getting to sleep and then had troubled dreams. It all had to do with sharing the sleeping cabin with a woman—the smell, the sense of her in the house. He dreamed about being lost in an unknown jungle that sometimes was a city, trapped in a maze of first trees then streets, trying to get somewhere important.

―――――――― o ――――――――

The next morning Apelu and Sanele strung two twenty-foot lengths of clothesline from their *fale*'s eave to the corners of the cook shed roof, threading the rope through the grommets of a new tarp that Apelu had bought for just this purpose—to make a sort of people port out of part of the yard. The tarp was blue. They strung it so that rainwater would spill off the low end away from the house, though there was no rain that day, just a hot sun after the morning cliff mists burned off. Apelu took the old *laufala* mat from the floor of his room and placed it on the earth beneath the tarp. The blue light of the sun through the tarp made the space feel underwater, jewel-like there against the dense green jungle and the shadow of the house.

When Nu'upo showed up around midday, he was wearing a formal black lava lava and a fresh white long-sleeved shirt. He looked scrubbed and respectable and old in a village way. It was a good disguise.

"Is it that machine driver?" Nu'upo asked.

"Yep, he wants to make peace."

Nu'upo produced a pair of sunglasses and put them on. "Motherfucker," he said. "You can handle this, chief. I'll stay, but pretend I'm not here."

Bobbie and Sanele were there. They had been to the bush store and were preparing food in the *fale*. Apelu had made Bobbie return her park pickup to her cabin. He told them to stay inside the *fale*. Bobbie had not met Nu'upo before, and to avoid her Nu'upo pretended not to speak English, ignored both her and Sanele, and sat cross-legged in a back corner of the tarp's blue shadow.

This was not a normal *ifoga*—no one in Apelu's family had come to harm—but he would observe the basic protocols, let the man approach and sit outside to state his case, make his plea. The sun was at its height when the small troop came walking up the lane to the *fale*. They approached without greetings. In front was the young man sent earlier as messenger, bare chested now, wearing a fresh lava lava and carrying a pandanus mat under one arm. Behind him came his uncle, the bulldozer driver, holding onto the forearm of a woman Apelu took to be his wife. The man wore a blindfold or a bandage around his eyes. Behind them were four or five other older people Apelu recognized from the village. The young man spread the mat on the ground in a flat spot about ten yards in front of where Apelu sat in the blue shade of the tarp. The woman led the driver to the mat and they sat. Another woman from the group behind came forward to give the driver's wife a black umbrella, which she opened, creating a round circle of shadow around them. The rest of the group, including the young man, sat in a tight half circle another ten yards behind them.

To Apelu's surprise, the first voice came from behind him— Nu'upo sounding like an orator chief—"*O le malie ta'u malie,*" Every shark must be paid for. Apelu knew it was one of those high speech proverbs, but he wasn't sure what it implied. Something about retribution.

The man with the blindfold, sitting on the mat within the black umbrella shadow, answered with another proverb—"*Ou te nofo atu nei, a ua le la le mumu ifafo,*" I sit here before you like the sun that shines—an opening apology. He followed this with the proverbial plea that Apelu's mind might be like cool water while he spoke.

Nu`upo had no more to say.

"What business brings you here today?" Apelu asked.

"I come to humbly seek your forgiveness and your assistance." The man ducked his head down so that Apelu could see just the top of it; then slowly he sat back up. "I have been told that your title has claims on the land where I was told to go. I did not know this before. Please accept my apology for not knowing what I should have known."

"Your apology is accepted," Apelu said. Behind him Nu`upo snorted softly.

"And I have come to ask for your help, to intercede for me if you can with that guardian of To`aga, so that this curse may stop with me." As he said this he lifted a hand to his bandaged eyes. "Let the blindness stop with me. Let not my children also go blind."

"Please," the woman said. "Some of my children are already beginning to lose their sight. They are innocents. They are without blame. They will never set foot in To`aga, I promise you that."

"Nor will I ever return there," the man said. "We are poor. We have little to offer except our promises and our undying respect."

"I have no powers with the guardians of To`aga," Apelu said.

"But they are your cohorts. We all know that now. You fight on the same side. They will listen to you. There must be something you can do." The woman was now pleading the case. "For my children's sake."

Nu`upo leaned forward to whisper to Apelu, telling him what to say.

"Your children will do well if you do as I tell you," Apelu then told them. "Every day for the next ten days have them bathe in the sea as the sun is setting. Pulp the stems of an even number of the *ogo mūmū* plant, mix it with fresh water, and use it as drops in their eyes and ears."

Nu'upo leaned forward and whispered more.

"This treatment should take place when the cicadas sing in the evening. It should not be done during daylight. In fact, keep your children inside during the day, away from the sunlight. Do not send them to school or to church for those ten days."

The woman nodded. Her expression brightened. Here was something she could do.

"As for your condition," Apelu addressed the man, "there is no medicine that can help you here. Perhaps in the hospital on Tutuila they can help you, but there are no possible cures for your eyes here on Ofu. The spirits will not let the medicine work. It is part of the curse."

"Thank you," the man said, "for lifting this curse from the rest of my family. We will do as you say and abide by our vows to respect To'aga. Please let the guardians know that. We have brought you humble gifts to show our love for you."

The woman gestured with her head, and the young man brought forward three baskets woven from coconut fronds and lined with banana leaves and set them on the ground in front of Apelu, who thanked them. It was over. The woman rose, then helped her husband to his feet. The others also rose, prepared to leave, when Sanele and Bobbie came out of the *fale*, carrying plates of sandwiches, plastic cups, and a pitcher of iced tea. In polite Samoan Sanele invited them to stay and share some food. The group stopped, confused. This was not traditional. They looked to Apelu, who smiled and said, "Please, sit and eat."

The young man spread the mat again, in the shade of the mango tree at the top of the lane, away from the *fale*. Bobbie placed the plates of tuna fish sandwiches on the mat, and Sanele passed out and filled the cups. There were polite murmurings, then the woman lowered her head to say a prayer. She had not gotten three words into it before Nuʻupo cried out in a voice both old and imperative, "No praying here. You will undo everything." She stopped. Hesitantly, confused, they began to eat in silence. Their spirits brightened though when Sanele came back from the *fale* with a big bag of potato crisps and passed them around.

Apelu turned to face Nuʻupo. "So?"

Nuʻupo leaned close to speak just to Apelu. "The driver's eyes got infected from that spray of rock dust he sent up when he rammed the boulder. Who knows? Maybe the doctors can save his eyesight, but I doubt it. It's been too long. The kids' stuff is just hysterical empathy. The *ogo mūmū* drops won't hurt them unless the woman makes it too strong. They'll be all right."

"The no school and no church bit?"

"Poor kids deserve a vacation after what they've been through. They'll be better off for missing ten days of that shit. What's in the baskets?"

Apelu gestured for Sanele to come and bring the baskets into the shade beside Nuʻupo. One held *umu*-baked taro and breadfruit. Another was filled with fresh reef fish. The third held just a very large octopus wrapped tightly in leaves. Its skin still held some of the phosphorescence of life.

"Oh, yummy," Nuʻupo said in English and started selecting taro and breadfruit to put in the basket with the octopus.

The *pulenuʻu*'s big F-150 came bouncing up the lane, scattering the group beneath the mango tree. The *pulenuʻu* and both of the Poʻo brothers were in the front seat. The *pulenuʻu* came out of the driver's side door with surprising speed for such a big man. "I thought he might be here," he said. "Sergeant, I want that man arrested," and he pointed a beefy finger at Nuʻupo.

"Arrested for what?" Apelu asked.

"For the murder of Edgar Houston."

"That was a pretty athletic crime for such an old man."

"Then he had accomplices. He was opposed to the surveying. He was probably the one who messed around with their surveying markers. He's the only Samoan crazy enough to be out there at night. I want him arrested and questioned and fingerprinted, the whole nine yards."

"I think I would need more than your suspicions to arrest him," Apelu said.

"Then I'll make a citizen's arrest, I'm the law here. Boys," he said, turning to the truck and waving for the Po'o brothers to join him.

Apelu was still seated on the mat. He turned back toward Nu'upo, but Nu'upo was no longer there. There was just a pile of clothes—the black lava lava and white shirt—with the sunglasses sitting on top of them. The basket of octopus, taro, and breadfruit was gone too.

CHAPTER 8

———————— o ————————

I T WAS HEADLINE NEWS. OF COURSE IT WOULD BE. APELU HAD
never thought about it, but even the wire services had picked
it up. Sanele brought the news when he came back from seeing
Bobbie off on the afternoon flight. The story filled half the front
page of the *Samoa News*. Although they got a bunch of stuff wrong,
they got the missing head right. Pages two and three were filled
with the wire service stories with headlines like TERRORISTS
OR SAVAGES? DECAPITATED CORPSE FOUND. None of the
articles mentioned Apelu by name. He was glad for that. The wire
service stories were fixated on the missing head and the geo-
graphic location—"On a remote South Pacific island once inhab-
ited by tribes of headhunters . . ."

What was it about *palangis* and their revulsive fascination
with beheadings? It wasn't so many centuries since it was their
nicest traditional method of executing one another, but now it
was only savages or Arabs who stooped to such barbarism. Was
it because it was so personal, not to mention messy? Much better
to vaporize scores of unknowns somewhere over the horizon by
pushing the right buttons or induce death by lethal injection.
Americans were very fond of capital punishment. But for sure if

you wanted to get widespread *palangi* attention these days just chop somebody's head off. It didn't matter who or where or for what reasons or by whom—*palangis* loved hating it. It struck an unconscious chord in their own unexamined past. The severed head—the ultimate Solomon solution to the mind/body quandary. All that was missing were photographs.

Sanele also brought a manila envelope from Apelu's captain at headquarters, which he didn't immediately open. Two men had followed Sanele home from the airstrip. Apelu recognized one of them, a tall skinny Samoan who was a reporter for the *Samoa News*. The other guy, a big blond *palangi*, Apelu had never seen before. He had a camera on a strap around his neck. Apelu met them in front of the *fale*. They wanted to talk. Apelu had nothing to say besides, "No comment, under investigation." The blond guy took a couple of photographs. No, he would not take them to the crime scene. The crime scene was on private land and off limits. No, there were no suspects at this time. The Samoan reporter of course knew about Ofu's reputation for being haunted and asked if there might be . . . well, something supernatural about the crime.

"I wouldn't know about the supernatural," Apelu said, "but it certainly was an unnatural crime."

The *palangi* scoffed at the idea that ghosts or "hobgoblins" had anything to do with the murder. He called it a "convenient excuse" for not having any actual suspects. "Was it a racial crime?" he asked. "I mean, the murder victim was white, and the murderer or murderers would have been Samoan, I presume."

"Like I said, we don't have any suspects at this time, either Samoan or Caucasian, and there were three white men out there in the bush with Edgar Houston that night."

"Surely you're not suggesting that a white man or men could commit such an act?" The blond guy sounded truly offended.

"And are you suggesting that only a Samoan could do such a thing?"

"Mr. Houston was here conducting a survey for some sort of development project, wasn't he? I suppose there might be people on the island with strong feelings about such a project."

"All those matters of motive and opportunity are being looked into."

"There are reports that the suspected murder weapon was a Samoan war club, and that the beheading was done in a traditional Samoan way."

"No comment on the forensics. That's not for me to say. In fact, that's it, gentlemen. Good day."

"One last question." It was the *Samoa News* reporter. "Is the head still missing?"

"Yes," Apelu said, turning to go.

"Did you look for it?" the *palangi* wanted to know.

"A search of the area was conducted."

"By who? By you?" the *palangi* asked. He sounded incredulous.

Apelu walked up the steps to his *fale's* screen door. Before he went in he turned back and looked the *palangi* in the eye and said, "Don't go there."

The contents of the manila envelope from the captain were predictable—several blank incident report and arrest affidavit forms and copies of memos from the governor to the commissioner and from the commissioner to the captain, the gist of which was to close the case ASAP. The international coverage was not just embarrassing but detrimental to the image of the islands as a tourist destination that the governor was trying to establish. The implications for the Paradise Escapes venture on Ofu were especially troublesome. The governor was worried about the off-island money guys pulling out before they had spent any money. The governor mentioned that the National Park brass were also not happy and were concerned about the safety of their personnel and park visitors. As if there were any visitors, Apelu thought. To insure that the message was clear, the captain had slapped a Post-it note on top of the commissioner's memo—"Arrest someone." Apelu slipped all the papers back into the manila envelope.

———— o ————

When Sanele had headed down to see Bobbie off on the afternoon flight, Apelu had sent the basket of reef fish from the *ifoga* down with him for the lodge. He had no refrigeration at their *fale*, and it was much too much fish for them to cook and eat. As a result they had been invited down to the lodge for dinner to eat their fish. Sanele welcomed the invitation as it meant he could call his girlfriend Filemu and chat. After all, there he was at the scene of the biggest breaking story of the hour. So they put on clean clothes and went down around dusk. It was a particularly benign and beautiful sunset, with the last rays slanting through the jungle and the bush birds all calling out their evening news in competition with one another. The air was soft, like an extension of their skin, connecting them to the sea and the sky and the greenness around them, that time of day—that light—when human skin is at its most beautiful. The high clouds held the day's brightness long after the sea had swallowed the sun. There was no need to talk.

The only other guest at the lodge for dinner was the Samoan reporter from the *News*. The blond *palangi* was not there.

"Where's your sidekick?" Apelu asked as they sat down to eat.

"He's not my sidekick," the reporter said, reaching for the platter of pan-fried reef fish. "He's a freelancer, works for the tabloids."

"What's a tabloid?" Sanele asked.

"A newspaper with a lot of photos and no community to call home," the reporter said, and that was the end of dinner table conversation.

As they were finishing dinner, the blond *palangi* came into the lodge. He gave them a cheerful "Hey, guys," then went to the cooler for a beer. A place had been set for him at the table, and he sat down there. The girl from the kitchen, who had started clearing the table, replaced the food dishes in front of him. As he served himself, he talked as if they had been waiting there for his report.

"Well, Detective, I found your secret crime scene, and it is a pretty spectacular spot. Could I have that soy sauce, please."

"Yes, spectacular," Apelu said. "How did you find it?"

"Oh, I got a little help. I love these people here. They're so friendly."

The Samoan reporter was staring blankly at the blond *palangi*.

"I found myself a guide, who took me right there. While there was still enough daylight to get some shots, too. Spectacular spot. She told me part of the story about the place—about how no one ever goes there and no one looks after the place but how it is always perfectly clean and taken care of. Great copy."

Sanele gave Apelu a twisted-face look—like what place is this guy talking about? Apelu raised his eyebrows back at him—patience.

"Pretty amazing construction, considering . . . you know . . . for Stone Age primitives."

"But then, it is made of stone," Apelu said.

"Yeah, that's right. Is there any more salad?" the blond *palangi* asked the girl. "No? Well, would you mind getting me another beer, then?"

"I'll get it," Apelu said. "How deep would you estimate it to be?" he asked as he got beers from the cooler for himself and the blond *palangi*.

"Oh, I'd say fifteen feet deep at least, but in such a perfect bowl shape and so smooth. Not much water in it though, for a well."

"No, there seldom is." Apelu sat down across the table from the blond *palangi*. "Tell us about your guide."

"Come on, Detective, you're not going to get her in trouble for showing me where it happened, are you? She was just being helpful. She even posed for a couple of photographs at the edge of the well, so I could show its human scale. I had to use the flash, but I think they'll come out all right. Pretty girl, friendly, spoke English. I met her on the road walking out there. She took me right to it when I asked."

"And she told you that was the scene of the crime?" Apelu asked.

"You coppers always want to keep everything a secret, but people know what's going on, especially in a small place like this. She even knew my name."

Apelu didn't even know the guy's name. "And did you learn hers?"

"Sure. I had her spell it out for me. Here," and he pulled a reporter's steno pad out of a side pocket of his walking shorts, flipped to the end of the used pages. "Sinalelagi. She told me that g is always pronounced ng. Is that right?"

"Yes, Sina-lay-langi," Apelu said. "That's right."

"You know her?"

"No, but did she wear her hair down?"

"She let her hair down when she posed for the photos—great hair, straight and black and all the way down to her ass."

"A nice smile?"

"Great contrast in all those shadows."

"It was a nice sundown."

"Neat light. Nice place you got here."

"Thanks. We like it, nice and quiet and . . . friendly."

The Samoan reporter's mouth had fallen slightly open as he stared at the blond *palangi*. Sanele looked back and forth between his father and the blond *palangi*.

"Yeah, friendly. She said she'd try to stop by my cabin later, if she could get away, so that I could interview her more about the place, the history, the legends—background stuff. She seemed to know a lot."

"I'm sure she did," Apelu said. "Another beer?"

"Yeah, why not? In fact, give me two and I'll take them back to the room with me. Maybe she'd like a beer." He turned to the Samoan reporter. "You know, I think I'll stay another day or two, not go back on tomorrow morning's flight. I mean, like her hair totally covered her back and her ass."

Apelu handed him two unopened cans of Budweiser.

"Hey, thanks. See you guys tomorrow," and he left, the screen door slamming shut behind him.

A very long silence followed. Sanele was looking to his dad for an explanation. The Samoan reporter was staring at the screen door. Apelu took a sip of beer, his eyes wrinkled between a smile and concern.

"The Tuiofu's well," Apelu finally said.

"The King of Ofu's ancient sacred well?" the Samoan reporter asked.

"The same. The one spot in To`aga forbidden to everybody, especially strangers. It's way short of where the body was found."

"But why would someone—" Sanele began.

"I wouldn't question her motives here tonight, if I were you, son. There's nothing we can do about it. The thing about To`aga is that you have to let it all play out. You really never can have control over what goes on there. It will happen with you or without you. It will just happen the way it wants to happen. That's what's so scary about the place—it's beyond all human control. It's its own reality."

"And Sinalelagi?" Sanele asked.

"The tabloid man may have met his match," the Samoan reporter said, then stood up and followed the blond *palangi* out the door, letting the screen door slam behind him.

——————— o ———————

The tabloid man did not make it onto the next morning's flight. In fact, it took another forty-eight hours for him to be medevaced out. The doctors could find nothing wrong with him, except for the fact that he couldn't move, would neither eat nor drink, and failed to respond to any human communication. He left the Territory without having said another word. The Samoan reporter stole the film from his camera and had it developed. The last half of the roll had been exposed but there were no images on it, just white light.

——————— o ———————

The recent events at To'aga—starting with the first Samoan surveyors being spooked off, then the gunshots and Edgar's arrest, then the scene at the boulder with the bulldozer, Edgar's beheading, the dozer driver's curse and subsequent ifoga, and now the *palangi* reporter's possession—had not been lost on the Ofu villagers. It was both an affirmation—like people living on the San Andreas fault being reminded by a five-point Richter temblor that they lived in an earthquake zone—and the cause of some serious questioning. Several generations of Christian *faifeaus* had assured the villagers that their faith in a living Jesus had put an end to all such pagan happenings. There was no room for two systems of belief, or at least that's what the village *faifeau* said.

Before the blond *palangi* had been declared incurable, a number of the village women healers had been called in by the family that ran the lodge to see if they could revive the stranger. They spelled each other around the clock massaging him with coconut oil and herbs. Nothing worked. Maybe *palangis* required a different cure or maybe his dose of possession was just too dense to crack. How long had the succubus been with him that night? Also, Nu'upo was not around to supply the *taulasea* with all the herbs and root squeezing they needed in their non-stop massages of the victim. 'Auro they called him, the golden one. They managed to keep him alive until he was taken away. That was considered a victory.

The second day of the taulaseas keeping the golden one from death happened to be a Sunday, and the faifeau in his sermon remarked upon the fact that several of his deacons' wives were absent from the service. He prayed that their absence did not mean that they had fallen back into heathen practices. Of course he knew where they were. After the service he fined the deacons whose wives were missing. This was war, God's war. To'aga must be made history, its powers cancelled forever.

The faifeau knew about the ifoga and the bush medicine prescription for the bulldozer driver's children, and that Apelu had told the mother to keep her kids away from school and church. What was worse was that the treatment was working. The relieved mother had spread the word that already their sight was returning to normal, except for one daughter who seemed to enjoy going blind. Apelu discovered all this Sunday afternoon, when the faifeau paid him a visit, accompanied by a handful of largely reluctant church deacons. The faifeau was very frank. Apelu appreciated that. He was also impertinently imperious, which Apelu did not appreciate. He wanted to know why Apelu and Sanele did not come to church. What church did they belong to if they didn't belong to his, the only church on the island? Why had Apelu not honored him with an envelope of money after he, the faifeau, had delivered God's invocation at Apelu's saofai? Instead he had used his money to get the chiefs drunk on beer. Where was Apelu's respect for God? Why did he align himself with irrational heathen beliefs? And what did that awful, immoral man Nu'upo have to do with this? These actions must cease.

They were all seated in the blue pool of light beneath the tarp. Sanele had brought out more laufala mats from the fale for the visitors to sit on. Apelu listened to the preacher's pumped-up, self-righteous rant. He knew that the performance was more for the deacons' benefit than for his. Apelu found it ironic that this man of God was attacking irrational beliefs.

"Do you not believe that the Son of God is your savior who died for you?"

"I'd hope if there was a God he would treat his only son better than that."

"Do you not believe even in God himself?" The *faifeau*'s voice was in full pulpit mode by now so this was meant to be a rhetorical question, but Apelu had had enough and interrupted him.

"I have my self-delusions, Reverend, but among them is not that after I'm dead I'll be alive or that some supreme being is made in my image. You are not my *faifeau*, not my chief, so I'm not at all sure what you think you're doing here uninvited, but I don't have to listen to this and you've got other things to do, I'm sure. So, *tofa*, goodbye, have a nice day," and Apelu stood up.

The *faifeau* struggled to his feet. He had to—to maintain his dignity he could not be spoken down to. "I will have you removed from here, Soifua. The commissioner is a Christian, a leader of our Territorial church. He will hear our pleas to have this godless policeman removed from us."

The deacons were now also standing.

"And why have you not taken that devil Nu'upo into custody? Who else could have killed that *palangi*? Unless, of course, if you are in league with him to stop progress that would enrich the village, would enhance the spreading of the word of God, and would kill once and for all these pagan superstitions about To'aga."

"You can go now, Reverend. Chiefs, thank you for stopping by. Come again any time, but without him." Apelu turned and went up the steps and into his *fale*.

Inside the *fale* Sanele was seated at the table. He did not look happy.

"I didn't think that was cool, Dad."

"What's that?"

"How you treated the *faifeau*. You're supposed to treat them with respect."

"Son, let's say he wasn't a *faifeau*, just some guy who came up here and spoke to me that way. Then could I talk to him like that?"

"I don't know. Maybe. But he is a *faifeau*. Everybody knows that and treats him like one."

"Well, he's not my master. So I can treat him the same way I'd treat any other man."

"So, you don't believe in God, Dad?"

"I believe in what exists, what can be experienced."

"Is that a god?"

"You can call the sum total anything you want. It doesn't matter, because you can never experience it all. So whatever name you give it won't begin to contain it."

"What about Sarah?"

"Sarah was great. Sarah's gone."

"She's not waiting for us?"

"Only in our past, in what we experienced and remember."

"We won't see her again?"

"I see her every day in other things I see."

"Me, too. Does she ever speak to you?"

"No, son, she never speaks to me."

"She speaks to me sometimes, at funny times. She's always happy, making jokes—you know, the way she always did—making fun of me or making me laugh."

"That's not a bad afterlife."

"I guess not, but you know Mom thinks Sarah is waiting for us in heaven, that we'll get to meet her again."

"That's too bad."

"Why?"

"Because we won't, and your Mom's fake future only means she's living in the past."

"In the past? Like in the Bible? Mom says everything is explained in the Bible."

"Excuse me, son, maybe everything can be explained by your mother's faith, but the Bible doesn't explain shit."

"Dad!"

"Sorry, son, but the Bible is not about explaining things. Show me in the Bible where it attempts to explain things like why the jungle is green and the ocean is blue, why Venus is sometimes the evening star and sometimes the morning star, why all the beings we know need sex to reproduce, why fire burns or people have to die. It doesn't explain anything really. It's not about reality. Ninety percent of it most Christians ignore because it doesn't make any sense to them. Did any of your mother's Catholic preachers or teachers ever even mention the Old Testament books of Tobias or Nehum, Baruch, or Sophonias? Besides, religion is all about mysteries, not about understanding. It's a fantasy game, like some disk you could stick into your Xbox and play, advancing from level to level ever farther away from the real day outside. It's a waste of time, an easy addiction. And when the pushers get together and organize to keep the addicts addicted it becomes more than just a bad idea. It becomes a scam, a social parasite. The promise of an afterlife is a great excuse for not living this life fully."

Apelu felt very calm as he delivered this confession of sorts to his son, this admission of his not thinking like everybody else. He leaned against the kitchen counter, looking out the screen at the jungle rustling to a fresh sea breeze. Maybe he could get this clear with his son, an understanding, and they would never have to speak about it again—like the talk about where babies come from.

"What if you're wrong?" Sanele asked.

"Then your mother is right. Come on. It's a beautiful afternoon. Let's go for a walk." And they went for a walk on the beach, skipping stones off of wave tops, seldom speaking and then only about what was around them. Sanele found a rusted-shut sea-man's jack pike stuck between two coral heads.

"A piece of the past," he said. "It's not good for anything, but I'm going to keep it anyway."

———————— o ————————

That night Apelu finally sat down and wrote out a full incident report about Edgar Houston's death. He took his time, first drafting and editing it in longhand, then carefully block-printing it onto the forms the captain had sent him. He filled in an affidavit for arrest form too—for the three *palangi* sur-veyors who had been at the camp in To'aga that night, the only people with the opportunity and capability of taking Edgar's life as they had described it. For motivation he sug-gested, "Revenge on a total asshole." The governor and the commissioner and the captain wanted a suspect, now they had three. Apelu was sure the other surveyors had all left the Territory by now. So nothing would come of his arrest affidavit, but he made the best case he could. Maybe that would quiet things down.

———————— o ————————

Apelu didn't know what else to call them but a posse. There was the *pulenu'u*, the *faifeau*, Danny and Ace Po'o, and three silent but serious men from the village. They presented themselves as "volunteers" to bring in Nu'upo. Apelu ran into them at the air-strip when he met the morning plane to send his paperwork off to headquarters.

"We were just going to go up to your place," the *pulenu'u* told him from the driver's seat of his F-150. "We figured you might need some help finding Nu'upo out there."

"Thanks, but if I wanted to find him, I'm pretty sure I could do that by myself."

"So that means you don't want to find him?"

"I have no reason to go searching for Nu'upo and bring him in. He's not wanted for anything, not even questioning. He's not a material witness or anything."

"You don't think he's involved in all this . . . these outrageous events, disturbing the peace of the village, not to mention supplying unlicensed drugs to these bush doctors?" This was from the *faifeau*, who was sitting in the front seat of the truck with the *pulenu'u*.

Apelu couldn't imagine either of them trekking through the bush, calling out, "Yoo-hoo, Nu'upo, come out come out wherever you are." He had to laugh.

"I don't see how this is a laughing matter, Soifua," the *faifeau* said. "The village has had enough of Nu'upo and his antisocial behavior."

"Just being antisocial isn't a crime, Reverend, even here."

"If you refuse to pursue this as a police matter," the *pulenu'u* said, "then we will proceed with it as a village matter."

"Whereas forcible abduction is a crime. It's called kidnapping."

"Nu'upo is hardly a kid," the *faifeau* again, "and he is no longer welcome here."

"Well, I can't stop you, I guess, but I doubt you'll find him driving around in your truck. But if you do find him, I'm here to protect his rights. I wish I had my traffic citation pad with me, because I'd write tickets for both of you not wearing your seat belts. Have a nice day in the bush."

The *pulenu'u* jerked the truck into gear and jolted away, surprising the five men in the back of the truck, who were jostled together. Apelu waved after them. Vigilantes, he thought. I've never had to deal with vigilantes before.

<hr>

○

When Apelu got home he found Nu'upo sitting on the ground beneath the blue tarp. Sanele was seated cross-legged with him on the mat, and they were so engrossed with something on the mat between them that they never looked up until Apelu was standing above them.

"Bring anything to eat?" Nu'upo asked without looking up. Between their crossed legs on the mat was a jumble of sticks and braided coconut fiber cordage.

"Uncle Nu'upo is teaching me how to make a wild fowl trap," Sanele said. He was holding two hooked pieces of wood about a foot and a half apart in front of him. Nu'upo was trying to fit other pieces into them.

"This motherfucker here is the hard part, this is the trigger," Nu'upo said. "Hold your hands steady, boy." Then to Apelu, "What are we supposed to eat for breakfast? Sunshine?"

"They're looking for you, you know."

"So I heard they would be. So?"

"So maybe they were going to give you breakfast."

"Breakfast of chumps," Nu'upo said in English. "Then this piece back here holds the noose in place. See?"

"I think we've got to set it up someplace for me to see it."

"Okay, okay, doubting fucking Thomas," Nu'upo said, wrapping all the pieces up together in a dirty piece of cloth.

For breakfast Apelu fixed them tea and peanut butter sandwiches. Sanele found some ripe bananas.

"So, Dad, what do you mean they are looking for Uncle Nu'upo?"

"They want to hunt him down like the wild pig that he is," Apelu said, blowing on his hot, kerosene-burner boiled tea.

"What? Dad!"

"No, you are what you eat, boy. Your father is just a domesticated pig and you are just a hot dog or maybe a piece of pizza." Nu'upo was devouring breakfast. "I am a wild pig. Thank you for the compliment, Apelu."

"Uncle Nu'upo, was that you on top of the rock?"

"What rock? If it was edible, maybe." Then to Apelu, "That's it?"

"No, I think they want to exile you. They're tired of you."

"Who is tired of me?"

"Mainly the powers that be, the *pulenu'u* and the *faifeau*."

"Well then they can just ignore me. I ignore them and it is very comforting."

Sanele laughed.

"Apelu, this boy has got a lot to learn. We'll start today with this motherfucking bird trap. You can spare him, right?"

Apelu looked at Sanele, whose face had opened and lit up. Apelu tried to remember what it was like to be sixteen when boredom—its own purple patented emotion—was the biggest enemy. "Yeah, sure. Take some sandwiches with you. Sanele, clean up first." It was true there was a posse out looking for Nu'upo, but Apelu was pretty sure they would never find him.

They were soon gone, and Apelu had the place to himself. The rest of the day was pleasantly quiet. There was always work to be done in the scattered plantation plots above the *fale*. Apelu sharpened his bush knife and wandered off to see what task that needed to get done would grab his attention first. As always he moved and worked slowly. It wasn't just the heat of the day, but also that things done quickly were usually done badly as well. Working by himself he could find that pace that freed his mind to go wherever it wanted to go as his body took care of the familiar physical stuff. He stopped and sat often, all of him in a perfect private idle, about as present as a jungle breeze. He felt hidden by the bush, just another shadow in the shade. The jungle birds ignored him.

He brought taro and breadfruit, coconuts and firewood back to the *fale*, then went down to the beach for a long float, letting the current of the outgoing tide pull him west with the setting sun, then slowly side-stroking back to where he had started. He watched the afternoon Twin Otter flight from Pago land and then take off.

Apelu was on the sand track going past the lodge, headed home, when he heard someone calling out. It was Drew the archaeologist, walking toward him from the Park Service cabin. He must have come in on that flight. He was still in uniform.

"Coming back from a swim? This must be an agreeable posting if you enjoy such things."

It had been such a nice day all by himself. Apelu decided not to answer. Drew didn't seem to notice.

"I was wondering if we could get together, say like this evening, and discuss your . . . ah . . . current events over here."

"Officially?"

"Well, I was hoping we could be a bit more informal than that. You know, the Park Service has its concerns, which, I believe, are parallel to yours."

There was probably no way of escaping this, Apelu thought, might as well get it over with. "Let me change. I'll be back down in half an hour."

At the *fale* there was no sign of Sanele or Nu'upo. Apelu washed off with fresh water and changed into a clean pair of shorts and a T-shirt. He took the shortcut down to the lodge and picked up three cold beers before going to the NPS cabin—might as well make this as painless as possible.

Drew was sitting on one of the plastic chairs in the tent in front of the cabin, leaning forward, elbows on his knees, a pair of Benjamin Franklin spectacles halfway down his nose, intent on the keyboard and screen of his laptop situated on another plastic chair in front of him. He didn't want a beer, thanks. Apelu went into the cabin to stick two of the beers into the small freezer compartment of the fridge. There was a large yellow box in the front room that hadn't been there before. It was just like one of the surveyors' cases, only it had a green and white Property of National Park Service sticker on its side.

Drew was closing up his laptop as Apelu came back out of the cabin. "So."

"So, Doctor."

"No, call me Drew."

"Well, I thought that seeing as you were addressing me by my title, I'd address you by yours."

"Shall I call you Apelu?"

"That would be fine, Drew."

The conversation didn't get much warmer than that. The gist of Drew's news was that he had been sent over by his boss, Park Superintendent Ilmars, to put together a report that could be sent back to their Pacific Basin Regional Office in Oakland, hopefully explaining to their bureaucratic satisfaction what was suddenly going on in and around their most removed and obscure slice of National Park. It would seem that the Smokey Bear guys read the tabloids.

"How is Superintendent Ilmars doing?" Apelu asked as he went to get another beer.

"Why do you ask?" Drew called after him.

Apelu came back with a new opened beer. "Well, he didn't look so good when he came over here. Just wondering if he was feeling all right."

"He is concerned about the publicity To'aga is getting."

"Is he concerned about the new resort rumors?"

"Yes, of course, that too, but those are just rumors about something we have no control over. He does wonder if these recent . . . events . . . might have something to do with those rumors."

"How would that be?"

"Oh, if there wasn't an element here that was against the development, maybe for selfish reasons, or wanted to have the development in some other location, say over on Olosega?"

"No, I don't think so."

"But there is some local opposition, isn't there? In the village, I mean. Isn't that why the surveyors had to camp out there instead of staying somewhere civilized? And that crazy man who stopped the bulldozer?"

"Actually, I stopped the bulldozer, and the crazy man is easy to explain—it's old Foisia, the guardian out there. Before the bridge was built he guarded the channel to Olosega against intruders. I guess now he guards To'aga instead."

"Foisia? Do you know where he lives? The superintendent is concerned about the safety of our people out there. Maybe I could talk with this Foisia, sort of get him on our side, point out that the Park Service's mission is to guard the place as well. Maybe you could set up a meeting with him for me."

"That would be tough. He lived about ten generations ago. We could leave a little peace offering for him, though. He seems to have developed a liking for Marlboros and vodka. I know the place where we could leave it."

"What do you mean he's been dead for ten generations? Oh, you mean the original Foisia. The name and the position have been passed on, just like with other Samoan titles. That is one persistent cultural trait whose survival surprises me, considering how much else has vanished."

"No, there's no current Foisia, just the original."

"He was alive hundreds of years ago, and people saw him last week threatening the bulldozer driver?"

"He lived hundreds of years ago, and people thought they saw him last week."

"Apelu, I don't feel that you are being straight with me. Don't try to bullshit me. My doctorate is in cultural anthropology. Being an archaeologist is just my trade. I have studied the history of this society. I can draw a line between what is actual and what is obfuscatingly disingenuous."

"Is what?"

"Is invented to blur the boundaries of the real."

"Don't get excited, Doc. It's just a legend playing itself out."

"I think you're drunk, or stoned or something. You are not making sense. Perhaps we can continue this conversation tomorrow, earlier in the day, when you are less . . . less preoccupied. Good evening."

——————— o ———————

It was a good evening, with one of those orange and purple sunsets. Apelu had taken the last beer from the freezer before he left. He drank it with his meager meal of leftovers before he went to sleep. Sanele was still not back. Apelu convinced himself not to worry about it. Soon the boy would be wholly on his own. This practice was necessary. He was a sensible boy. But the *fale* felt empty as he went to sleep.

CHAPTER 9

——————— o ———————

APELU WOKE EARLY AND RESTLESS. IN THE FIRST BLUE-GRAY light he opened a can of tuna fish and made himself a sandwich and ate it standing at the kitchen screen, blankly staring out, listening to the birds waking up. They actually had to practice a bit before they found their proper voice. He slowly filled four large plastic water bottles from the hose and put them in his string sack, with a loaf of bread and a couple more cans of tuna fish on top of them. He took his bush knife when he left.

The easiest way up to Nu`upo's camp was to take the road through the village then head up a four-wheel-drive track to the ridgeline. The track was maintained by the Communications Department to service a receiver/transmitter station at the highest point on Le`olo Ridge. Several village families had plantations at level spots on the way up. Nu`upo's camp was near the top, a ways off the road down a canyon toward the north shore. It was a four-mile hike altogether, with one mile of it seriously uphill. Not a single vehicle passed Apelu in either direction the whole way. The village dogs didn't seem to notice him. It was an overcast morning and no one was out. It was as if there had been an emergency evacuation overnight and he had the island entirely to himself. It was good walking weather. He took his time, maybe two hours.

Apelu was looking down at the road, judging the ruts on a sharp curve, and he almost walked into the back of the *pulenu'u*'s F-150 parked in the middle of the track. It sat low on the road. All four of its tires were flat, slashed. It was locked and deserted. Apelu stopped and drank some water, then circled the truck in a widening circle—nothing. He walked on. The trail off to Nu'upo's camp was only a hundred yards or so further up the track.

He smelled it first. It wasn't fresh. It was wet with the dew of the night, but it was the gray smell of a dead fire. The smell grew stronger as Apelu walked down the trail to Nu'upo's camp. All the birds—the honeyeaters who always announced your passage through the bush—were silent. He saw the scorched trees before he got there. Nu'upo's simple Samoan *fale* and its surroundings had been torched.

Apelu kicked through the still smoldering piles of ashes, burning a toe, uncovering a few cooking pots and the metal tube frame of a chair, but nothing else, no bodies. Again he circled the scene, looking for more but again finding nothing

He made the hike back down in half the time it had taken him to get there. The newest and fanciest two-story house in the village was the *faifeau*'s place beside the new church. Apelu stopped there first, but the *faifeau* wasn't there. The *faifeau*'s wife was very cold to Apelu. She acted like a *palangi*, standing in the doorway of the house, not inviting him in, treating him like a dangerous stranger. Her husband had left on yesterday afternoon's flight for Pago. Village business. Apelu's next stop was the next most ostentatious house in the village, the *pulenu'u*'s, who also was not home. The *pulenu'u*'s son answered the door. He didn't know where his dad was. The boy was a couple of years older than Sanele. Rap music was playing inside. The boy seemed distracted, disjointed in his speech. It was only about ten-thirty in the morning, but the kid was stoned and home alone.

"I haven't seen my dad since yesterday, man. I guess he's busy. Hey, how did Sanele dig those videos I loaned him? Dug your saofai, man, cool party."

The longer Apelu stood there at the door the more nervous the kid got, so Apelu stretched out the silence.

"Anybody else home?"

"No, man, just me. Look, I'll tell my dad when he gets home that you stopped by, okay?"

Apelu turned to go, then turned back. "Are you stoned, son?"

"Hey, no, man, no way, just chillin', just chillin'. I'm cool. I'll turn down the music, dude, no problem. Tell my dad you were here and all." He was trying to smile, nodding his head.

"Just chillin'," Apelu said, then left.

───────── o ─────────

Back at the *fale*, Sanele was sound asleep on his bed when Apelu got home. He let him sleep. Sprawled on his stomach like that he looked so huge. Some permanent image in Apelu's brain had his son the size where he could just stoop down, scoop him up, and lay him, still sleeping, over one shoulder. There was a disconnect. Call it time.

When Sanele woke up in the middle of the afternoon Apelu fixed him some food, and as he ate, Sanele told him about his adventures with Uncle Nu'upo. They had hiked up to Nu'upo's camp and then down that canyon, where they set up two of the wildfowl traps. After that they continued on down the canyon to another smaller camp at a falls above a small cove on the north shore. Uncle Nu'upo showed him how to throw a net to catch the small silver fish inside the reef. Sanele didn't catch any, but Uncle Nu'upo did, and they ate them raw there on the beach. They were good. By then it was getting late and Sanele wanted to head home, but Uncle Nu'upo said it was too late to go so far and that it would be good for his father to spend a night without him. So they spent the night there. Sanele apologized if he had made his dad worry.

Apelu told him, no problem, he was a big guy now who could take care of himself and Apelu knew he was safe with his Uncle Nu'upo. "By the way, was your Uncle Nu'upo with you all the time?"

"Pretty much. He did go off at one point in the afternoon to check on our bird traps while I was trying to learn how to throw that stupid net. We didn't catch anything. And he went out night fishing, but I was too tired and went back to sleep. He doesn't sleep much, you know. He's kind of wired for an old guy. You know, he seems to be always nibbling on something—leaves, berries, nuts, I don't know what. He just picks things and eats them. Weird. Those little silver fish were good, though. I could eat more of those."

But in the morning, Sanele said, Uncle Nu'upo seemed to have lost all interest in him. He asked Sanele if he had any money, then walked him to a trail along the north shore that was a much easier, if longer, trek out to the road by the bridge at the opposite end of To'aga from home. Nu'upo just pointed him east on the trail and left him there without saying a word. Sanele had had to walk the whole way back. There had been no traffic on the road.

"I remembered the names of a bunch of the places, even going backward," Sanele said. "Oh, and Bobbie's Park Service truck was parked near the new road into Nandiaka. Is Bobbie back?"

"No, just that Drew dude."

"Dweeb."

Apelu watched his son eat. His skin was as sleek and brown as a piece of the finest teak, except for the wispy jet black whiskers on his lip and jaw and chin. How much of innocence is a mask and how much is a blessing, Apelu wondered.

"Your Uncle Nu'upo isn't anybody's standard model," Apelu said, still watching.

"That's okay. He's different, but he's cool too. He told me about his wife who died and that he had a boy about my age."

"Once."

"Once what?"

"I mean the boy was your age once and still is in Nu'upo's mind."

"Yeah, I figured it was something like that. Dad, can I make another phone call from the lodge?"

"Your girlfriend?"

"Yeah, and Mom in Apia, if that's all right. I wonder how Issy and Toby are doing. If that's all right?"

"That's all right," Apelu said, swallowing hard, wishing he still had more of that innocence. "That's fine. Say hello for me. Let me know how they're doing."

Apelu dreamed about Sarah that night. Sarah in To'aga. Sarah in Nu'upo's north shore fishing camp. Sarah wandering the rocky shoreline, just a toddler with no one watching her. Sarah laughing at the waves. Then Bobbie, thin blonde Bobbie, coming out of nowhere to scoop Sarah up out of the wave foam, both of them laughing in the retreating surf. Then bigger waves, waves that rose without breaking, a thousand-year memory wave as blue and half as tall as the sky. The wave that woke him up.

———o———

Apelu really didn't want to see Drew again. He had avoided him entirely the day before. But in the morning on his way to the village to seek out the pulenu'u again he stopped at the Park Service cabin to see if the archaeologist was still on island. He was, and he was seated at his laptop as before in the tent in front of the cabin.

"How's your report going, Drew?"

"That really isn't any of your business."

"Okay, but it is my business that you were out on my family's land in To'aga surveying yesterday." Apelu decided to make himself comfortable, pulled up a lawn chair, and sat down.

"I wasn't surveying your land. I was only ascertaining the precise location of the petroglyphic boulder. For my report."

"Which is none of my business. You can do that?"

"Yes, I can conduct a survey alone. It takes longer, but at least I know that it's been done accurately."

"No, I mean you can just wander off park land and survey on private property without asking anyone?" Apelu lit a cigarette.

"I wish you wouldn't do that."

"What? Question the legality of your actions?"

"No, smoke. I am allergic to tobacco smoke."

"I'm Samoan. I'm allergic to trespassers."

"Look, I was asked to investigate your find and report on it."

"Not by me you weren't."

"I was asked by your government, by the Territorial Historic Preservation Office, which is part of the Office of the Governor, who is your boss, I believe."

"They know better than to go onto family land without asking permission first. They'd get their asses kicked."

"Are you threatening me?"

"Nowhere near as much as you threaten me, Drew." Apelu took a drag on his cigarette and looked at Drew. Sanele was right. He was a dweeb, basically harmless, too full of himself to be much of a threat to anyone else.

"You're not going to put that out, are you?"

"Open air, nice breeze, free country, legal age. I could see why Smokey Bear might have a thing about smoke, but you don't fight forest fires, do you, Drew? You just write secret reports."

"The repercussions of my report will not be a secret to you, I hope. I believe my superintendent will share it with your commissioner, and your incompetence and lack of action will be duly rewarded." Drew stood up and went into the cabin. Apelu waited. Drew came back out of the cabin, sucking on a bronchial inhaler. Apelu finished his cigarette and flicked it toward the bush.

"I had the opportunity," Drew said, taking the inhaler out of his mouth, "to meet with your mayor here for his input. He was very clear on the fact that you have done next to nothing to solve the Houston murder case and bring some sort of peace back to this village. In fact quite the opposite, according to the mayor." Drew stayed standing by the cabin door. "For instance, you have refused to take into custody for questioning a prime suspect, a Mr. Nu'upo, whom the mayor believes—and he was an eyewitness—was the person pretending to be your mythical guardian Foisia on top of the boulder and who was also in all probability a conspirator, at the very least, in Mr. Houston's gruesome murder." He took another hit on the inhaler. "Instead, you—" Drew stopped to catch his breath, then started again. "I also spoke with my superintendent yesterday, who had heard from your commissioner that you had filed an arrest affidavit for the three other surveyors, charging them with Mr. Houston's murder, which is totally unbelievable, ridiculous."

"Did the mayor tell you about his torching Mr. Nu'upo's house?"

"I don't know what you are talking about. According to the mayor this Nu'upo character doesn't have a house here, or family, or land. He is just a vagrant, and a dangerous vagrant at that, a drug dealer. The mayor seemed intent on bringing him in himself, seeing as you have refused to lift a finger."

"I guess your bottom line, Drew, is that none of this happened on National Park land, so you and Superintendent Ilmars have no jurisdiction, no say whatsoever over any of it." Apelu got up to leave. "And, Drew, stay off my family land or I will kick your fucking ass."

Half of the island's half dozen operational vehicles were parked in front of the *pulenu'u*'s house as Apelu walked up. Young men and boys were seated on the ground in the shadow of the house's western shade. They nodded to Apelu as he came toward them. Inside the house a *fono* was in process. The *pulenu`u*'s American furniture had been pushed back against the walls, and eight of the village chiefs were seated in an irregular circle in the middle of the floor. When Apelu entered they greeted him almost silently and made a space for him in their oval. Apelu left his flip flops at the door and joined them. Chief Tiafatu sat at the head of the circle, empty spaces to his left and right. He welcomed Apelu by the title Apelu still thought of as his father's, then he reminded Apelu that he was seated among them not as a policeman but as a voice in their *fono* deliberations, representing only his family.

The matter before the *fono* was of an emergency nature—the whereabouts of the *pulenu`u*. Two nights had now passed since he had last been seen in the village. His family was worried. He had not left the island as far as anyone knew. He had gone into the bush to find Nu`upo and had not returned. Everyone knew about the *pulenu`u*'s tires being slashed and that replacements would not arrive until the next boat from Pago at the earliest. Everyone knew how incensed the *pulenu`u* had been about the attack on his truck. Everyone knew that the *pulenu`u* had gone back out two nights ago with the Po`o brothers to find Nu`upo. Everyone knew that the Po`o brothers had returned the next day, worn out with the search on foot and a night in the bush, but that the *pulenu`u* had refused to come back without Nu`upo. But when Apelu asked, no one admitted to knowing about Nu`upo's camp being torched.

It was decided that the `aumaga*, the young men of the village, would be sent out to look for the *pulenu`u*. The Po`o brothers had guessed that he would have spent the night back at his truck, where he had stored some food and water. The *pulenu`u* had been worried that more damage would happen to his precious F-150 up there in the bush. The `aumaga*, under the direction of two of the younger chiefs, would start their search for the *pulenu`u* there. They would also be looking for Nu`upo. The *fono* would like to speak with him, if he could be found. Where were the Po`o brothers? Apelu asked. He was told they had left on the morning plane for Pago. Apelu was beginning to think that Ofu would be a more peaceful and less confusing place if there were no flights to and from Pago Pago.

The meeting broke up. The young men went out. One of them, Apelu noticed, was the *pulenu`u*'s son. One of the chiefs with a working pickup gave Apelu a ride back to Va`oto. He had to walk past the Park Service cabin, but the truck and Drew were gone.

At home Sanele was constructing his own wildfowl trap. "See, I used hibiscus for the trigger arm. It's springier. What do you think?"

"The proof is in the catching," Apelu said. "Maybe a piece of old inner tube would be even snappier."

"Yeah, got any?"

"No."

"So?"

Apelu watched Sanele secure a joint of the trap with strands of braided coconut fiber. "It might work if it rains. The hibiscus will just break if it dries out."

"We'll see." Sanele didn't look up from his work. "You know, Uncle Nu`upo told me an interesting story as he was getting ready to go night fishing and trying to get me to go along. He was shredding dried coconut fronds and tying them into small bundles for torches. He said that once when he was night fishing at To`aga this strange thing happened. He knew he was out there all alone when he saw a torch burning yellow and red moving quickly across the reef in front of him. He could see the light and a silhouette, but it had no bottom, no feet. It seemed to float across the reef."

"*A ue o lama a le aitu*," Apelu said.

"Yes, it was the ghost torch," Sanele said. "That's exactly what Uncle Nu`upo said. How did you know?"

"And what did Uncle Nu`upo say he did then?"

"He said he stopped fishing because . . ."

"Because the ghost had taken everything."

"Yeah, right. That there would be nothing, no fish or crabs or clams or sea cucumbers left on the reef, because the *aitu* would have taken them all."

"Smart choice."

"You knew that story?" Sanele looked up from what his hands were doing.

"Version of it."

"What are *aitu*, Dad?"

"No knowing for sure until we are one."

"Are they real?"

"Is Uncle Nu`upo real?"

"Yeah, but."

"He sees them."

———————— o ————————

The `aumaga` expedition returned empty-handed, and the next morning there was another meeting of the village *fono* at the *pulenu`u*'s house. Apelu suggested that they switch their search area to the reef at To`aga. They sent half the `aumaga` there and they found the *pulenu`u* there, seated on a high brain coral head at low tide—naked, wet, alive, and babbling, a burned-out coconut frond torch in his hand.

They took the *pulenu`u* home and hid him there, but no one could get him to respond to a sensible question with a sensible answer. The *taulasea* were called in with their herbal massages, but nothing worked. After a while all the *pulenu`u* would say were Samoan children's nursery rhymes, and those he voiced as questions. When he was awake he played constantly with his genitals and he seemed to know only one English word, *mother-fucker.* The family tried to keep it all a secret.

———— o ————

It didn't come as much of a surprise. After a couple of quiet days Apelu received a memo from his captain, calling him back to headquarters for a meeting. This time Apelu took Sanele with him. There was no high school on Ofu or Olosega, and if he was going to keep Sanele there, he would have to set up some sort of home schooling routine. Sanele didn't mind going. He would get to see his girlfriend, Filemu, and pick up some different CDs. He had tired of the music he had brought with him. They left on the morning flight with Drew, who ignored them.

The flight to Pago was very rough. The pilot warned them to keep their seat belts tightened. They hit several walls of squalls that the plane could not climb over. There was lightning and sheer winds, and the little Twin Otter, with only ten passengers aboard, bounced all over the sky. At one point the pilot took them down to a couple of thousand feet and headed south away from a particularly nasty piece of blackness.

Apelu had given Sanele the window seat and sat beside him. Sanele saw the whale first, off their left wing, heading south with them. Or maybe the pilot had seen it first and was following it, because that's what they seemed to be doing. Sanele nudged his dad and pointed, so that Apelu could lean over and watch. The whale was making time. From above, though huge, the whale looked sleek, like an elephantine trout. It was swimming hard, flexing through the waves. Soon all the passengers were on the left side of the plane, watching the whale, and the plane tilted down on that wing until the pilot compensated and yelled back through the open cockpit curtain for everyone to go back to their seats and buckle up.

Drew hadn't moved from his seat under the right wing. "Quit following the whale and get us back to Pago Pago," he yelled back at the pilot.

Sanele and Apelu watched the whale. Suddenly it raised its flukes into the air and slapped the ocean twice with its broad airplane-shaped tail as if to tell them to fuck off. The pilot did, slipping west again around the squall line.

"Cool," Sanele said.

"Never seen that before," Apelu said.

"What's with Drew Dweeb?" Sanele asked.

Drew had moved to a first row seat behind the co-pilot and was now leaning forward, questioning the pilot, who had dropped his earphones down around his shirt collar so that he could hear Drew. Drew was taking notes.

"Drew is finding fault," Apelu said. "That's what Drew does, he finds fault with things."

"Why?"

"It makes him feel better about himself, I guess. He's one of those people consumed with feeling good about themselves."

"Why?"

"Because, I guess, that doesn't come naturally to him, and he's smart enough to know that other people just normally feel good about themselves and he doesn't know why he is missing out."

"So he takes notes?"

"I think it is called an obsession."

"Like being a perfectionist? That's the right word, isn't it?"

"Something like that, only it's not about being right but about being perceived as seeming right by making other people look wrong. It's an expression of insecurity, really."

"There are people who actually work that way?"

"Wait till you get married, son. You'll see what I mean," Apelu said.

147

The plane was gaining altitude again, slipping around the towering thunderheads. The pilot had put his big padded earphones back on, silencing Drew.

———— o ————

The captain sent Apelu straight up to the commissioner's office. Apelu didn't know this new commissioner well. The Department of Public Safety changed CEOs more often than the Territory changed governors. The position was a revolving political door. The only constant was that the new governor-appointed boss was never someone from the Department. No one ever rose up through the ranks to be the chief. It was always someone from outside—a campaign manager, an unre-elected legislator, a paramount chief who could use a government director's salary. Like most bureaucratic departments, Public Safety survived and continued on the strengths—or at least the immutability—of its second-tier career officials. The head was changed so often that the body had learned to survive by ignoring it.

This commissioner was also a businessman, with multiple financial fingers in pies all over the island. He didn't need the paycheck. So, of course, everybody wondered why he had adopted the job. He was young for the job, too, only a few years Apelu's senior. Apelu didn't know what to expect when he knocked on the commissioner's door.

"Detective Soifua, have a seat." The commissioner was standing at a window that looked out onto the parade ground in front of headquarters building. He was packing a pipe with tobacco. This was such an unreal, movie-like thing to see a Samoan do that Apelu was taken aback. He hadn't seen a Samoan with a pipe since his Auntie Palepa died twenty years before, and who knew what she smoked in it. Still standing at the window, the commissioner lit the pipe. As he was doing so, between puffs, he looked at Apelu and asked, "You don't mind do you?"

"No, of course not." Apelu took a chair in front of the commissioner's desk.

The commissioner was tall, with a once athletic build now gone slightly pear-shaped and a thick head of prematurely silver hair. "You didn't know that I am from Olosega, did you, Detective?"

"I knew your family name had a branch there, but not that you were of that branch."

"Your family is from Ofu, isn't it?"

"One branch of it, yes."

"And you just took a title there?"

"Yes, my father's title."

"That's excellent, excellent."

Apelu had been watching the commissioner with his pipe and had decided it was not just some affectation. Once he had gotten it lit and had taken a few firm puffs he seemed to forget it was in his hand. He had to relight it now.

"Excellent?" Apelu asked.

"What better keeper of the peace to have there than a chief who is from there?" The commissioner sat down behind his desk. "Especially when strange things begin to happen." There was a pause that Apelu didn't fill. "I believe you have been made aware, Detective, that both the governor and the national park superintendent were concerned about the bad publicity following that *palangi*'s beheading."

"Yes, sir. I was."

"And you responded with a full report—which I read—and an arrest affidavit for the three other *palangis*, which I have also read."

Another pause as the commissioner relit his pipe again. Apelu said nothing. He liked the smell of the pipe tobacco in the room. Its smoke was pale blue in the slanted sunlight.

"Is that right, Detective?"

"I wouldn't know if you had read them or not, sir, but I did send them over."

"I think Dr. Wentworth had something to do with Danny's enhanced sensibility," Martin said. He was acting a bit like Sanele, sort of peevish.

"Look, Martin," Danny said, "the resort is a bad idea. I see that now. I'm not stupid."

"But you are one of the people who brought this on us."

"I was only along for the ride. I hadn't been here since I was a kid. I saw the whole thing differently after I got here, after I went back to Ofu. Before it was just an easy way to make some big bucks. Land that no one was using, that deserted beach. Even the National Park being there was a selling point. The money was all lined up. It would be good for the island—jobs, money coming in, better air service, put in a bigger runway."

"Where? On top of the reef?" Martin was being Martin.

"So now I see the idea sucks, all right?"

The waitress came back into the room carrying steaming bowls of entrees. Apelu ordered another round of drinks. The waitress left.

"Martin has a plan on how to stop it," Bobbie said, helping herself to the dishes on the lazy susan.

"It's a brilliant idea," Danny said. "I think it will work."

"We get the whole reef there at To`aga designated as a federally protected special marine preserve. No reef, no beach, no resort. Simple." Martin had not yet taken a bite of food. The rest of them were digging in.

"And how do we do that?" Apelu asked.

"We make it special," Bobbie said.

"Indispensable," Danny added.

The stage was now Martin's, and as he took it he also served himself some food and took a few bites. His previous peevishness fell away. He started in the middle, then stopped himself. "No, let me start at the beginning," he said. The beginning was a memorandum of agreement Martin and the park had entered into a number of years before with a university in Texas to conduct a joint bioactive species research project in To'aga. Martin would select and collect different species from the reef and send them back to Texas for testing for bioactive properties. It was a kind of prospecting, only it wasn't precious metals they were searching for but creatures that secreted enzymes that might be of pharmaceutical value. "Pretty standard research stuff," Martin called it. About nine months before, Martin had discovered a small sponge species on the reef. "They were rare. I'd find them tucked in the folds of the deeper coral, and in a small circle around them no other feeder species would be present." He collected a few and sent them off. It turned out to be a previously unknown species of sponge. In fact, they named it after him—something *bermia*.

Recently Martin had heard from the university that they needed as many samples of that specific sponge as Martin could supply. The sponge's bioactive qualities were proving very promising. Research wanted to move into development, but they had been unable to synthesize the sponge's active properties and To'aga was its only known home.

"But I stalled them," Martin said, "because I knew nothing about the sponge's reproductive cycle, and I was afraid I might over-harvest them."

"What's it good for?" Apelu asked.

"HIV, they hope. Something in the sponge's makeup seems to weaken the reproductive powers of the virus so that stronger drugs can get to it and contain it. That's what they hope."

"And we hope?" Apelu asked.

"That if Dr. Wentworth and I can finish up our research there and draw up our final report with the university researchers, we can get the reef its special protection status." Martin took a triumphant mouthful of lemon chicken.

"Martin explains it really well in a guest editorial he wrote for the *Samoa News* about why the resort should be stopped. They should run it sometime this week," Bobbie said.

"He did?" Danny asked.

"Yes, we have to raise a public outcry against this travesty," Martin said between forkfuls.

"We do?" Apelu asked. "I thought your marine preserve would be enough to make them pull out."

"The people should know about this," Martin said.

"Yeah, sure, but how about after the fact?" Apelu said.

"Is the timing really that important, Apelu?" Bobbie asked.

"Maybe not. It's just against my nature to show my hand before I play it. But Martin may be right, lay the groundwork."

"I'd like to work it out so that a part of the profits from any drug they do develop comes back to Samoa," Martin said. "What do you think?"

"I'll wait till your egg foo yung hatches. When are you going back to Ofu?"

"In two days, on Thursday afternoon's flight," Bobbie said, "before the superintendent returns from his off-island leave."

"Until then I'm acting superintendent and I can approve the travel," Martin added, turning the lazy susan to get some sweet and sour pork.

"Sanele and I are going back then too. We'll see you there."

Apelu ordered the shrimp fried rice to go and had the waitress fill another Styrofoam plate with table leftovers. As they were leaving, Danny asked him where he stayed while on Tutuila.

"Oh, my main house is here, being neglected. We stay there, chop the weeds away."

"Do you have a phone there?" Danny asked.

"The number's in the book," Apelu said. The fact was he couldn't remember the number.

———— o ————

Danny called before Sanele had finished eating the takeout.

"I didn't want to talk about this in front of Bobbie and Martin. Got a couple of minutes?"

"Sure. Shoot." Apelu got a cold Steinlager from the fridge and opened it. The only phone in their house was on the kitchen wall, with a twelve-foot cord. Apelu sat at the kitchen table and watched Sanele eat as he listened.

"I was wondering if anyone had approached you for your signature."

"No, and I don't hand out autographed photos of myself either."

"I meant your signature on the To'aga survey report. Your signature was one of the three other chiefs' signatures they needed in order to be able to file it with the Registrar's Office."

"It was?"

"No one told you? That's why Chief Tiafatu wanted you to take the title so quickly, so that they could get your signature too. It's the only one they're missing now."

"Oh."

"They tried to file it with just the *pulenu'u*'s signature and their skewed survey boundaries, but the registrar wouldn't take it. She said the chiefs whose lands bordered on the survey had to agree to it too. That's you, Tiafatu, and another guy over here on Tutuila, in addition to the *pulenu'u*. I thought that Tiafatu would have asked you to sign by now."

"I don't think my title's official yet. The district governor still has to sign off on that. Maybe that's it." Sanele put the now empty Styrofoam containers in the trash, took his glass of iced tea, and left the kitchen. "Besides, by now I think he should know that I wouldn't sign anything giving up my family's land."

"They were going to cut you in."

"Buy me off?"

"Every chief has got his price, they said."

"Tiafatu?"

"His price was high, but he's in."

"Danny, why are you telling me this?"

"I'm just wondering how serious they are about all this now after everything that has happened and the *pulenu'u* . . . the *pulenu'u* on the disabled list and all."

"So you're not still in touch with them?"

"No. That night up in the bush with my brother and the *pulenu'u* going a little . . . a little crazy, I told them I thought the whole thing was wrong and that I was bailing out. The next day my brother brought me back here to put me on the plane to Honolulu, but I wouldn't go, so he told me that if I screwed up the resort deal he would break both my arms. I haven't heard from any of them since."

"What does Bobbie know about any of this?"

"Only that I'm still here and on her side now."

"What's the other chief's name, the other signatory?"

"You know, I don't know his title name, just that everybody calls him Roketi. He lives in Pago Pago, up the hill."

"Danny, are you coming back with us to Ofu Wednesday?"

"I plan to, yes."

"Good. We can talk more about this there, and, Danny."

"Yes?"

"Danny, don't do anything to hurt Bobbie. Do you hear me?"

"I wouldn't do anything to hurt Bobbie, ever."

The next two days went quickly. There was a lot of reclamation work to get done around the house and yard. Wednesday afternoon Sanele took off to see Filemu when she got out of school and didn't return until late, in a much lighter mood.

Thursday afternoon they were all there in line at the Manulele Airlines check-in counter, everyone except Danny. Bobbie kept looking over her shoulder.

"He should be here," she said. She pulled out a cellular phone and hit a number on her speed dial and listened to it ring. Danny never showed up.

Martin's guest editorial was in Thursday morning's *Samoa News*. Apelu read it as they were waiting to board the plane. It was very strident. Apelu doubted that most Samoans reading it would grasp the emotion behind that stridency or share the author's outrage.

Aside from a young mother carrying an infant, the four of them were the only passengers. They were all seated toward the front of the plane. The seats in the rear had been folded down, and boxes of cargo had been strapped over them. The Twin Otter was fully loaded and took more of the runway than usual to get airborne, but the flight was smooth under clear skies. The patches of cloud below them were almost too white to look at in the afternoon sun and cast pockets of deeper blue shadows on the French blue sea. Sanele dozed beside Apelu, and across the aisle Bobbie stared out the window. Apelu watched the dials on the instrument panel in front of the co-pilot that he could see through the open cockpit curtain, judging their progress by the air speed and altimeter gauges and the pilot's throttle adjustments. They slowly lost air speed and altitude as they approached Ofu, whose ragged green cone on a plate of bright blue slowly emerged out the cockpit window. The usual approach from the west, the plane bouncing gently in the headwind, the normal trades. Under the left wing Apelu could see Ofu village and the dense jungle thigh of Le'olo Ridge rising up, caught in patterns of acetylene sun and deep shadow. In front of them, beyond the far end of the narrow runway, ran the long curving beach of To'aga. Sanele woke up. It was good to be home.

The co-pilot reached overhead to push the flaps all the way down for landing. The pilot's right hand pushed the throttles forward. They were in their final approach, just off the end of the runway, when everything changed. Instead of the usual powered touch-down they were suddenly floating. The headwind blowing over To'aga had died as if a switch had been thrown and had turned into a capricious tailwind, as if To'aga was sucking them in. In the cockpit, Apelu could see the pilot's panic. He killed the throttles to stall, and the klaxon stall alarms went off, but they were still hanging on the tailwind. The short runway was vanishing beneath them and they were still yards above touching down. They yawed so that all Apelu could see out the cockpit window were the tops of coconut trees along the right side of the runway. The pilot pushed the nose down and jerked the throttles back toward full speed. The Twin Otter's wheels smashed into the runway. They bounced. The pilot pulled the plane left, then slammed it into the macadam again and thrust the throttles into reverse.

Sanele grabbed his father's arm. The look in his eyes was one of complete incomprehension. The plane was not stopping.

"No hydraulics!" Apelu heard the pilot yell.

The plane veered to the left. The young mother behind them screamed. They ran off the end of the smooth runway and started to bounce. Out Sanele's window Apelu could see the lodge and its cabins whisking by behind the trunks of coconut trees. Then there were two big jolts that threw all of them forward against their seat belts and loosened the cargo behind them, and the plane came to a stop. Apelu watched Bobbie throw up.

———————— o ————————

The general opinion was that the crash was miraculous. It took some time—because the pilot had been knocked unconscious by a falling overhead instrument panel when the plane had stopped and everyone had to crawl out through the cockpit to exit because the cargo had shifted so much they couldn't get to the cabin door—but everyone aboard escaped alive and basically unscathed. There was no fire. Somehow the pilot had missed all the trees lining the lawn that ran the length of the space in front of the lodge's cabins off to the left of the end of the runway. Not even he knew how he had done that. Without hydraulics he could neither break nor steer, and he had lost his hydraulics, snapped the tubes where they ran above the wheel shocks, the first time he'd hit the runway.

The pilot was very shaken, more so than anyone else. Bobbie was mostly embarrassed about throwing up. Sanele's summation was that it would be something neat to tell his kids about someday. Martin concluded that the pilot was an incompetent.

The Twin Otter got the worst of it. Manulele Airlines' only plane now sat, broken in several different ways, on the lawn in front of the last, the NPS, cabin, its nose almost in the bush where Bobbie's phantom warriors had once vanished. It would take a week at least to get the parts and mechanics here to fix it. They would have to come by boat, the only way to reach Ofu now. And they would have to cut down several trees to get the plane back on the runway.

CHAPTER 11

———— o ————

I T WAS SUNDOWN A COUPLE OF DAYS LATER AND APELU WAS floating on his back, alone, about as far out as he could get within the fringing reef at high tide. The sky was calm and clear. From where he floated off To'aga he could see the precipitous south side of Ofu and west side of Olosega cast in dramatic silhouettes, their peaks still aflame in the setting sun as if in homage to their volcanic ancestry. He was there for a reason. He was watching. And as he watched he was rewarded—there on a ridgeline high on Olosega a pencil thin finger of smoke appeared, indistinguishable from the forest mist except for its pure verticality in the still air. He fixed the position as best he could in the map of his mind, then darkness cascaded as it does in the tropics, and he turned onto his side and started his slow side stroke back toward the beach. The old man would wait until darkness to start his fire. Apelu wondered if fires started any better on Olosega than on Ofu for him.

Martin and Bobbie had already resumed their reef research and had again recruited Sanele to help them. The three of them spent every day in the waters off To'aga, so the next morning Apelu hitched a ride with them in the NPS truck and asked them

164

to take him to Olosega. He had some police work to do over there, he told them. Sanele asked his dad why he was carrying Sanele's school backpack.

"I might not be back by tonight," Apelu told him. "I brought extra stuff. Can you stay down with Martin and Bobbie at the cabin if I don't make it back?"

Apelu had Martin drive him almost all the way through Olosega, past the church at the far end of the village.

"I think the house is around here. You can let me off. Thanks."

Martin was eager to get to work and miffed that Apelu had taken him a half hour out of his way. Nobody asked any more questions. Martin quickly turned the truck around and headed back toward the bridge to Ofu and To'aga.

This would be another four-mile hike, but this time through country with which Apelu was wholly unfamiliar. Olosega was unknown to him. He could see from the map that the only way up Olosega's central Matagia Ridge was from its southern end at Lemaga Point. The ridge rose to over two thousand feet. Nu'upo's fire had been near the top. It had to have been Nu'upo's fire. Who else would be crazy enough to spend a night up there? Apelu had brought what he hoped to be enough supplies for a two-night stay.

Nobody appeared to notice him slipping out of the southern end of the village. He took his time on the two-mile hike down the coastline. This was virgin territory for him. He saw no one. Now and then the trail took a turn into the bush over coral slab walkways and through jungle tunnels thousands of years in the making. He could tell from the birds that this trail was now seldom taken. He stopped near the south point to eat and drink and watch the ocean breaking. Behind him the ridgeline rose to a collapsed caldera knife-edge back the way he had just come. The next two miles would be uphill.

The trail was clear at first, but then it became quizzical. Apelu would lose it, then backtrack and find it again. He regretted that he hadn't brought a bush knife. For long stretches the trail followed the edge of the cliff, and he was slowed by the view, the birds beneath him, and the need to move carefully over crumbly rock. He stopped often to just sit and drink some water and watch. Less than three miles west of him was Toʻaga straight on, a view of it he had never experienced before—its entirety in one panorama, the great sweep of its bright yellow, almost golden beach and the rise of the ridge behind it like the face of an apocalyptic green wave about to break.

Apelu knew from the legends that the ancient village of Olosega had been located somewhere up here, back in the days when a village required the best possible defensive position against its neighbors. Then there must be water up here somewhere, he thought. And if he could find the water source, he would probably also find Nuʻupo nearby.

When the trail got close to the peak of the ridge, it left the cliff face and petered out in thick montane jungle. Apelu backtracked again. He remembered seeing the tops of a few tall coconut trees from the trail. Coconut palms did not just volunteer themselves in the jungle. People had brought them there at some time or another. Coconut palms were like dogs—if they were wild it only meant people had abandoned them. He got his bearings on the old tall coconut trees, and then he retraced his steps to the end of the trail and cut in that direction. It was fairly easy going. The thick canopy kept the jungle floor passable, and even though the sun was now near its zenith there was a coolness in the shadows of the high bush, a cool quietness with just the sound of the breeze in the trees above him. He came to an overgrown stone platform that he had to step up onto, then another—level, human-made platforms with straight hand-laid stone retaining walls. There were a couple of breadfruit trees and off to one side a patch of red ti plants grown wild, the plant Samoans planted only around graves. High above were the frond fingers of the coconut palms he had aimed for. He sat down on the edge of one of the walls.

Well, this was once home for someone, Apelu thought. Kids took that trail to and from the beach without really thinking about it much. Penthouse living without an elevator. He lit a cigarette.

"Nu'upo, I have come. I have brought cigarettes," he said in a normal voice. Then he just sat and smoked for a while. "Old man," he called out louder in Samoan, "I can smell your anus from here and it smells sweet just like a volcano." He smoked some more. "All the old wives in the village miss your after-midnight visits."

Apelu stubbed out his cigarette and waited. There was no response. The effort of the climb came over him. He found a patch of ferns back on the platform, flattened them, wrapped a lava lava around himself, and went quickly to sleep.

———— o ————

Apelu woke up when Nu'upo dropped the big tree limb on him and sat down on it. "What do you mean *old* wives?"

"Get off me, you old fart."

"So, are you here to arrest me or what?"

"Arrest you for what? What have you done?"

"Where are those cigarettes? You know, you should have more respect for your elders."

"Excuse me, do you know there are red ants all over this fucking log? Get up."

"My volcanic anus protects me. You'll learn over time that in the dark all cats are gray and that good pussy is ageless."

Apelu had twisted around so that he could get both of his hands on the ground and now he heaved himself up, pushing the tree limb and Nu'upo off of him.

"Okay, you win. Give me a cigarette," Nu'upo said, brushing red ants off his legs.

Apelu pulled out his pack of Marlboro Lights 100s and handed one to Nu'upo along with his lighter. "Saw your burnt-out camp. My condolences."

"Non-attachment is where it's at. Bring me any other goodies?"

"A couple of cans of tuna, a bottle of vodka."

"Let's go then. This spot is too public, too many *aitu* watching us."

"They won't follow us?" Apelu said, picking up his backpack.

"They're a lazy bunch, these Olosega spooks. They don't want to stray far from the house, still waiting for Junior to come home with an extra head or two. Come on."

— o —

The name Olosega meant the fort of the *sega*. *Sega* was a bird, the blue-crowned lory. The lory was an elusive if gregarious forest bird. They were extremely rare on Tutuila, but much more common here on Ofu and Olosega. Apelu was sure there was a story behind the island's name, but he didn't know it. As he followed Nu'upo through the bush Apelu inadvertently stepped on a dry fallen limb that cracked like a pistol shot, and a flock of *sega* exploded from a tree above them. Their flight was ballistic, as if a cannon had fired a cluster of emerald and lemon, purple and blue projectiles. Apelu had never seen so many *sega* in a single flight. In a second they were gone.

"Watch out for our cannibal warriors," Nu'upo said without looking up. Apelu knew that story—the *sega* making its nest in the dead man's skull.

Suddenly they were out of the bush and back at the cliff's edge. Apelu stopped to catch the view and Nu'upo vanished over the edge. Apelu went to look where he had last seen him. Nu'upo's voice from below said, "Grab that root and swing down. There's a step you can't see."

"There is?"

"Only a fool could miss it," Nu`upo said, "or a dead man."

Apelu did as he was told. He grabbed onto a big root that stuck out of the ledge like a handle and stepped off into the void. His feet found a ledge on the face of the cliff. He looked down. About a yard beneath his feet was a wider ledge, where Nu`upo stood. Apelu turned carefully around and then jumped down to join him. Below that ledge was a sheer drop of a thousand feet.

"Remind me to lose that bottle of vodka," Apelu said, looking over the edge.

"There's another way out for drunks," Nu`upo said as he turned and walked along the ledge, which gradually widened as it turned into a crevice in the face of the ridge. The crevice wasn't deep, maybe twenty yards, and at the end of it Apelu could see the mouth of a cave. A small stream trickled out of the cave, across the ledge and over the edge.

"You've got to watch your step there along the edge," Nu`upo said. "Where it's green it's slick. That could be a nasty fall. Welcome to Plato's place."

Off to one side on the ledge in front of the cave's entry were the blackened rocks of a cooking fire and a pile of firewood. The cave's mouth was maybe eight feet high and half again as wide. Nu`upo disappeared into its darkness. Apelu followed him. When his eyes got used to the gloom there was nothing much to see—a pile of vegetation for a bed, another pile of coconuts, a bush knife sticking out of one of them. Nu`upo's once-yellow fanny pack hung from a rock outcrop. The stream ran down a well-defined channel about two feet wide through the center of the cave. The back of the cave disappeared into darkness, but there was, deep in the shadows, a small splash of green sunlight at the end of the tunnel.

Nu'upo picked out two husked drinking nuts and picked up the bush knife. "Happy hour," he said. Back out on the ledge he deftly cracked the tops of the drinking nuts and removed their caps. They each took a long drink from their fresh *niu*, then Apelu took the bottle of vodka from his pack and opened it. He topped off each of their *niu* with vodka, and they stirred them with an index finger. They toasted each other and drank. The nuts were topped off again with vodka, and they both found positions to relax on the ledge. The afternoon sun came all the way into the crevice. An on-shore breeze came up the ridge face.

"So, how did the Dow Jones do today?" Nu'upo asked.

"About the same as yesterday, I'm sure." Apelu took a sip of *niu*.

"Mergers?"

"Too few, I'm sure."

"You know, dark rum is totally better than vodka in these things."

"I know, Myers's. None available."

A pair of very white, large—three-foot wing span—birds floated up on the sea breeze thermal just yards off the edge of the ledge in front of them. Each bird sported long white tail streamer feathers almost as long as their wing span. A black bar accented their eyes. Apelu had never been so close to a White-Tailed Tropicbird before.

"*Talofa*, Tava'e," Nu'upo greeted them. "They're my neighbors here. Their nest is the next floor up. They're busy these days with a new family. They leave me alone. I leave them alone. They taste too fishy for my liking anyway. *Manuia le afiafi*." Have a nice sunset, he called to them. The birds turned their heads to look at them as they went up on their air elevator, a proper couple not so sure they were pleased with their new neighbors but too polite to protest.

"We will never understand them, you know," Nu'upo said as they watched the pair wind-brake and settle into an out-of-sight cliff cranny above them.

"Why is that?"

"What *tava`e* sees is not what we see. She sees things we will never see—colors, details, the closing distance of things. Her world is like a series of revolving spheres with her at its center. Our world is like a plain on which we are wandering, lost. Our world is made up of corners and shadows and things we can't see. Her world is a clarity of the space surrounding things, where nothing is hidden, nothing is ever out of focus. Even her sense of time is different, more precise. Her world is air. Our world is dirt. To her, our vision would be like being blind."

"It has to do with flight."

"Flight is only an expression of it, as little of it as we can try to understand. Just trying to imagine that exhausts us. But flight is just a fraction of the differences between us, a simple symbol of the distance. At least they don't shit on us, piles of guano that we are to them. More vodka."

Apelu passed the bottle, but Nu`upo refused it. He held out his *niu* to be refilled. Apelu did. "And the *pulenu`u*?"

"He learned to see even less than the rest of us piles of ambulatory excrement. He had his head in the clouds up his ass. He was so blind he could see only himself and he thought that—that and his big motherfucking truck—was the world."

"Then you heard what happened to him?"

"It was written long ago in the sky he never looked up into. He is probably wiser now."

"And the *palangi* reporter?"

"Best piece of pussy that cocksman ever had. I'm sure he saw visions spared most of us before she fucked him brainless. Don't you see how appropriate every ending is? Even the fat surveyor without his head to feed himself. Ha! I love it. We are given these glimpses of the higher order, and they are always some sort of obvious corny punch line we should have expected but didn't."

The light of the setting sun now filled their west-facing crevice. Nu`upo held out his *niu*, and Apelu poured the last of the vodka into it. Nu'upo took the bottle from Apelu. "It is empty now," he said. "This is what happens to emptied vessels," and he threw the bottle in a high looping arc into the face of the sun. But it never made it. It fell in twirling reflective spangles into the void below them. They never heard it land.

They finished their drinks as the sun sank behind the ridge above To'aga. Nu'upo made a fire before last light. They ate Apelu's cans of tuna fish along with a day-old cooked breadfruit and a *poi* Nu'upo made of mashed papaya, bananas, and some berries and greens Apelu didn't recognize. As they ate Apelu asked whether Nu'upo's change of islands was temporary or permanent.

"You think you can tell the difference?" Nu'upo asked. "You think there is a difference? No, Ofu had gotten entirely too hectic for me. I couldn't sleep at night for all the spirit clamor coming out of To'aga. *Aitu* eating everything in sight. Villagers trying to hunt me down like a wild pig—which I am, which I am. The place was getting crowded. Now I even get tourists up here. I'm running a motherfucking mobile bed and breakfast. You did bring breakfast, didn't you? No, I'm staying away from Ofu's bad juju at least for the time being, and time being what it is—like not under my control—who knows how long that will be? Who cares?"

They talked about Sanele for a while. Twice Nu'upo called him Etuane by mistake, not hearing it. Apelu remembered that Nu'upo's minister father had always been referred to in the village as the Reverend Etuane. Nu'upo divided his vegetative mattress into two separate adjacent beds. The darkness brought a chill into the cave. Apelu wrapped himself in both the lava lavas he had brought with him, made a pillow of the backpack, and went quickly to sleep. The one time he awoke, slapping some insect off of his face, he sensed that he was alone and that Nu'upo was gone, and he reached out in the blackness to where he should have been. But he was gone.

<hr>

○

In the morning there was no trace of Nu'upo. His bush knife and fanny pack were gone. Nu'upo had left the leftover *poi* from the night before in half a coconut shell. Apelu ate it. It was tastier a day old. Apelu packed up his few things then walked up the lava tube cave toward the morning splash of sunlight at its end. The cave narrowed as he followed it inward until he had to stoop and if he reached out he could touch both walls. The floor was slippery along the stream, so he took off his flip flops and walked barefoot in the stream. The water was cold. The rocks were smooth. The jungle-filtered sunlight came through a hole about three feet in diameter in the roof of the lava tube. Worn smooth steps in the rock led up to it. Roughly beneath the hole a pool had been cut into the rock floor. Water seeped through cracks in the wall at the end of the cave and was caught in the pool before spilling out a channel into the stream—ancient Olosega's secret source of water. The back of Plato's cave was a life-giving spring.

He dipped his cupped hands into the pool and drank. The water was cold and clear. He drank again, deeply, then filled his plastic water bottles. Then, on an impulse, he stripped off his clothes and slipped into the pool. Its chill was a shock that shrank his scrotum and his cock and tensed his long muscles. It was a work of will to totally submerge himself, only to burst quickly back up for a gasp of air. He could endure it only for a minute or two, rubbing his hands over his limbs and trunk, hair and face— a bath like a bird would take, flapping its wings. He dried himself with a lava lava, enjoying the shivering and the tingling of blood rushing back to his skin.

Apelu climbed up the stone steps into the sunlight. He emerged into a field of boulders and tumbled rock. A half dozen strides away from the opening down to the spring he couldn't see where the entry was, it was so well hidden in the confusion of rocks and shadows and brush. He found his way pretty easily back to the trail out and down.

Apelu didn't see a soul until he got to the church in Olosega, and there most of the souls were inside the church, dressed all in white. Once again Apelu had lost track of the days of the week. It was Sunday morning. A choir was singing. In the shade of the church's porch five young girls in white dresses held infants too fussy to be inside with their mothers. They never looked at him as he walked by on the sand road, a whitewashed stone wall between them. It was as if he were invisible, though one of the infants started screaming. The rest of the village was deserted, as were the road and the bridge and the road into To'aga.

For some reason Apelu felt young this morning. He was untired by the miles he had covered, had not even raised a sweat. He mentally checked for the old familiar pains—from that scar on the sole of his foot, the pinch in his hip, the stiffness in his thumbs—but all were absent. The colors of everything seemed especially bright. He welcomed the sun on his skin. The road felt soft beneath his feet, almost springy. And he was horny, horny in that almost anonymous, universal way that he once had been as a teenager. He spent a few seconds wondering what those greens and berries were that Nu'upo had mashed into the *poi*, then dismissed the thought with a doesn't matter, no way of knowing, so what. As he walked down the road in To'aga every wave breaking on the beach had its own sound, and the trees along the road were alive with birds.

The old brown pickup truck was only semi-wrapped around the coconut tree. It was so rusted out that it had structurally collapsed before it could fully wrap itself around the tree. Even though Apelu knew that it hadn't been there the day before, the truck already looked like it had been there for years. The windshield had collapsed inward, the front bumper was in the weeds, and a front fender had fallen off. A tiny red-headed honeyeater hovered in front of an askew rearview mirror, challenging its reflection to a duel. Apelu knew the truck and its owner Loki. As he approached it he could see the skid marks in the road sand—the driver had braked and tried to miss something in the road and had hit the tree instead. There was nobody in or near the truck. No blood either. He could smell gasoline.

At Va'oto, Apelu stopped first at the NPS cabin before going up to his *fale*. Martin had set up a sort of mini lab under the tent in front of the cabin. There were plastic buckets filled with seawater and reef creatures, stacked plastic containers, specimen bottles, laboratory scales, calipers, notebooks, rulers, maps, charts, a camera, and a laptop. The ammonia smell of the reef was mixed with a hint of other chemicals. Martin was busy at work, too busy for Apelu. "Sanele's not here," he said, barely looking up. "Went to church with Dr. Wentworth."

Martin called Bobbie Dr. Wentworth only when he was pissed at her. "What's Bobbie done now?" Apelu asked, looking into the buckets.

"It's what she's not doing. We have a lot of data to record and order."

"It's Sunday, Martin, the traditional day of rest."

"It's bad enough she refuses to collect data on Sunday and that she won't let me collect data, but the least she could do is help me here with this recordation instead of running off to some over-long church service."

"You're not a Christian, Martin?"

"Actually my parents were Jewish, but that has nothing to do with it. We have a deadline to meet."

"What was it, Martin, park mission number four? To maintain a good relationship with the natives. Well, Bobbie's right, you would not be maintaining a good relationship with the natives by being out on the reef on Sundays." Apelu picked an interesting piece of elkhorn coral out of a bucket.

"Put that back. Don't touch anything. Besides, how would the villagers know if we were on the reef today? They're all either in church or eating and sleeping."

"Oh, they'd know."

Martin was bending over, taking a digital photo of something that looked like a deformed sea slug laid out beside a centimeter ruler. "And where have you been? Your son stayed here last night and kept her up half the night watching some inane video starring that Samoan wrestler."

"How was it?"

"I told you—inane, a pointless plot fragmented by repetitive violence, with a stupid predictable ending."

"Watched the whole thing, did you?"

"Look, Apelu, can't you see I'm busy?"

"Okay, I'm out of your way. Tell Sanele I'm home, would you? Oh, by the way, what happened to Loki's truck? Do you know?"

"That wreck in To'aga? Why don't you check with the police? Oh, that's right, you are the police. Right on top of that one, aren't you?"

"Martin, I think you're working too hard. You are aching to make enemies."

Martin straightened up, put down the camera, took off his glasses, and massaged his eyes with his fingertips. "Yes, perhaps I am. Sorry. Perhaps I will take a little break," and he sat down in a plastic lounge chair.

Apelu went into the cabin and plunked ice cubes from a freezer tray into two tall glasses. Back out under the tent he filled the glasses with water from one of his plastic bottles and handed one of the glasses to Martin, who was still sitting there staring straight ahead, blinking.

"Thank you," Martin said. "Sorry about the . . . the negativity. I . . . "

"Forget it," Apelu said, swirling the water around the ice cubes in his glass. "Spring water," he said.

Martin took a sip. "That is good," he said. "The accident happened late yesterday afternoon, around sunset. We were back up on the beach, packing up, when we heard the crash and ran to the road. It happened not too far up the road from where our truck was parked. There was the driver, an older man, and a woman I took to be his wife and four kids who had been riding in the back of the truck. Everyone was very excited. The woman was still stuck in the passenger side seat, and a couple of the older kids were trying to yank the door open to get her out. The husband was lying in the road, yelling something in Samoan. Bobbie and I helped free the wife while Sanele tried to talk to the husband, calm him down. No one was seriously hurt. They must not have been going very fast." Martin had finished his water. Apelu poured him another glass over what was left of his ice cubes.

"Of course, Bobbie and I didn't understand anything that was being said. It was all in Samoan. We got them all into our truck and drove them to the dispensary, but of course no one was there at that hour. So we took them on to their place in the village and left them in the care of their family. Sanele pieced together the story for us as best he could. He said the truck had been attacked by a giant wild boar, which had charged at them, picked up the truck in its tusks and thrown it into the tree. Everyone said the same thing and that the boar was so big and old and gray that it looked almost white coming at them. Of course, they were embroidering the part about the pig attacking them, but I did see some large hoof prints in the road that could have been made by a pig. I don't know anything about land animals. There was also an empty bottle of vodka in the road. Maybe the driver was drunk." Martin paused. "Lucky no one was hurt."

"I wonder how big and white the boar has gotten in the telling by now," Apelu said.

"Yes, of course hyperbole would have set in by now, like a fungus on the facts. I still can't understand that, the need people feel to exaggerate when the facts are fascinating enough in themselves."

"No, you wouldn't understand it, Martin. Just as well. I don't think of it as a fungus. I think of it as fermentation. Not something being covered up, but something evolving into its next state—the past becoming a memorable event."

"You are too philosophical to be a Samoan, Apelu."

"But I am a Samoan."

"Then you are too philosophical to be a cop."

"I'll buy that."

"This is nice water."

They sat in silence for a while, listening to the wind ripple and flap the tent fabric. Martin seemed calmer.

"Apelu, you know that big black rock at the water's edge roughly in the middle of To'aga's beach? It is the only basaltic erratic around there, maybe eight feet high above the ground."

"Yes, I know the rock you mean. It even has a name, Matato'aga, the eye of To'aga."

"I've noticed that absolutely nothing grows on or around that rock. Now, why would that be? I've looked at similar boulders at both ends of the beach where the cliff face is closer and more big rocks have made it to the water, and they are covered with the creatures you'd expect. But not that one."

"You will never see a Samoan fishing or reef gleaning around there either, either at night time or day time."

"And why is that?"

"It's just a place to avoid. It's *tapu*."

"The *pulenu'u* was found near there, wasn't he?"

"Yes, on a coral head in front of the rock."

"Do you think he ate something poisonous he caught there?"

"Something poisonous happened to him there."

"It's a large kill zone. I wonder what its cause is? I was thinking maybe something in the fresh water runoff through the berm there, something toxic inland seeping down."

"I don't think you are going to be able to bottle whatever it is and sell it to the drug companies or the Department of Defense, Martin."

"Maybe it's some of your fermenting facts polluting the ground water."

"There's got to be a chemical reason for everything, doesn't there, Martin?"

"I'm afraid so, Apelu. We are all just biological beings, an envelope of complex chemical reactions."

"I find that reassuring."

"Do you?"

"Yes, simple answers are always reassuring. Then you don't have to think about all the other things that the simple answer doesn't cover but just dismisses. I like simple answers as long as they're answering simple questions."

"So, a researcher's goal should be to ask simple questions?"

"I wouldn't know. I'm not a researcher." Apelu left Martin one of his bottles of Olosega water. He put it in the fridge to chill. When he left, Martin was still sitting in his chair, looking at the display screen on the back of his digital camera, flicking through the images of specimens he had taken.

"They're all dead, Martin," Apelu said, picking up his backpack.

"I know. That makes both the question and the answer simpler, doesn't it?"

CHAPTER 12

———— o ————

MONDAY MORNING APELU HEADED INTO THE VILLAGE TO GET Loki's version of the story about the accident. He was in luck. The PTA fathers had gotten the school bus running again and were taking it out for a test run. They picked him up. There were no kids on the bus, just four of the men from the village offering various opinions on what was still wrong with the engine. They had turned around at the airstrip because they had no intention of driving into To'aga. The sole elementary school for the two islands was on the other side of To'aga and the bridge, in Olosega, which is why the village needed a school bus. When the school bus was out of commission, the parents would load all the Ofu kids into the backs of the village's pickup trucks and drive them to and from school, but Loki's accident—following on all the other To'aga events of the past few weeks—had brought a complete halt to all traffic between the two villages. No one would take a truckload of school kids through there now. Which is why they had resurrected the school bus, but now nobody wanted to drive the school bus through there either. While all the fathers on the bus agreed that their kids should go to school, they all tacitly agreed not just now, maybe later after things in there resolved themselves a little better, things quieted down, and current events could become recent history.

Loki's story differed from Martin's in only a few details. The giant boar was indeed old, but just old gray not white, and, no, the empty vodka bottle hadn't been his. He hadn't been drinking. He wasn't drunk. In fact, the vodka bottle had come out of the sky and smashed in the windshield just moments before the boar appeared and charged the truck.

Apelu wrote out the accident report just as Loki told it to him, then he had Loki sign it and date it. Loki's wife wasn't there. After the accident she had trouble walking and by Sunday was unable to walk at all. They had to carry her to church Sunday morning, and after the service the *faifeau* had insisted they leave her there, in the church, where he and his wife and the wives of the deacons could take care of her and pray for her under the watchful eyes of Jesus. Loki seemed relieved to have her out of the house and pleased with his new notoriety in the village. He wondered out loud if the government had funds set aside to help victims like him and his family. His truck was gone. It was a public road, after all, and the accident was not his fault. Maybe the government and the park people could share the cost. Apelu had to tell him that he didn't think so, that he had never heard of such a fund. Of course Loki had no insurance. The idea of insurance was so foreign to the villagers as to make absolutely no sense at all.

As long as he was in the village Apelu thought he might as well walk over and see Chief Tiafatu. He first stopped by the small bakery the chief ran because it was close to Loki's place, and found Tiafatu there, seated behind the wheel of his pickup truck as two of his bakery boys loaded racks of fresh bread in the back. The chief was glad to see him.

"I was about to head up to your place to find you," he said.

"And drop off a couple of loaves of bread for me?"

"After I made my deliveries, and have a little talk. Busy? Get in."

Apelu walked around the front of the truck and got in the passenger's side. The boys were finishing up loading the truck, tying a tarp over the top. Then they hopped onto the tailgate, and Tiafatu pulled away.

"Been over to get Loki's story?" Tiafatu asked.

"Wild Pig Survives Truck Attack."

"Any money in it for him? New truck?"

"Not a chance."

"Figures. I had to ask. Loki is one of my family's men. You know, Apelu, people are beginning to talk about how before we had a policeman here there was no need for one, but now that you are here officially it just seems to be one thing after another." Tiafatu stopped at the first bush store in the village, and the boys delivered an order of bread.

"A cop-caused crime wave?"

"No, not that anyone blames you, just that it seems like more than a coincidence, especially seeing as much of what has happened has taken place out near your land in To'aga."

"Is it my land now?"

"As far as I and the rest of the *fono* are concerned, yes, Nandiaka is now yours to shepherd."

"A flock of stones and trees."

They made their delivery to the second bush store, and the boys stayed there, closing the tailgate. "There is a lot of tension in To'aga," Tiafatu said. "It has to be relieved."

"How would that be done?"

"As in all things, by finding the consensus, reaching an agreement. Quell tension and anger with compromise, the Samoan way."

The third bush store in the village didn't buy Tiafatu's bread—a longstanding quarrel between the two families. Tiafatu headed south out of the village toward the airstrip and Va`oto. Apelu figured the chief was giving him a ride home, but when they got to Va`oto he kept driving toward the cliff-edge turn into To`aga.

"What sort of agreement?" Apelu asked.

"A boundary agreement."

So, here comes the pitch Danny had been wondering about.

"Your new title provides certain . . . certain benefits for you and your family, a chance to make decisions that will benefit both you and them and the whole village." They were bouncing gently down To`aga's sand road now. "As chiefs we must always be aware of how our stewardship will affect future generations of our family. We must contain the past, the present, and the future."

They passed Loki's wrecked truck, and Apelu was getting impatient. "So, you want me, as my family's chief, to sign off on the bogus *palangi* survey that gives away part of my family's ancestral land?"

Tiafatu slowed the truck to almost a crawl. "Nandiaka is near here, isn't it? You have no idea where its traditional boundaries actually are, do you? For decades your father and the title holder before him, your great uncle, ignored Nandiaka. A child had died a violent death there. The land was *tapu*. Nothing would grow there. Your family's land shrank at the same rate that your family's interest and investment in the land shrank. Nandiaka is nothing today but a name out of history, but you want to make that name, that ignored memory, a cause of trouble in the island. Maybe the villagers are right, maybe you are the source of all the bad happenings."

"Stop, pull over. I'll show you Nandiaka."

"No, I won't stop here. I am the only one now who will drive through here, just to make my deliveries in Olosega, but I won't stop here. I am not a fool." He drove on, speeding up a little.

After a bouncy silence Tiafatu addressed Apelu by his chiefly title and changed his form of speech to polite chiefly Samoan. "Sir,

I assure you that your cooperation in the matter will only benefit you, your family, and the village. We must all pull in the net together. We will have the survey redone, showing the proper boundaries, with your title's land duly acknowledged. It was the *pulenu`u*'s idea to take Nandiaka in the surveying. I never agreed to it. All that you are placing on the mat is a corner of an accursed piece of worthless land, but when the mat is turned what will come back to you—and your son, your family—are rewards that will outlast your days, the means of bettering your family's lot financially. And it will secure the peace at To`aga, make it safe again."

"Agreeing to give my family's land to build a *palangi* resort hotel in To`aga will secure the peace?"

"Oh, that place will never get built. To`aga would never allow that to happen. It would make everything impossible for the *palangis*. You know that. But meanwhile they will have signed a lucrative long-term lease with the landowners, and you and the poor *pulenu`u*'s family and others in the village would benefit from the lease payments, and the village economy would benefit. Sir, this consensus will not be whole without your acceptance. All the rest are in agreement."

"You are among the others who would benefit, aren't you, Tiafatu?"

"Yes, some of my family's land is within the new boundary, and I am happy that I can help my family by my decision, and I have promised that a generous portion of our blessing will be shared with the church, so that my catch of fish will be shared with all. It is what a chief does—bring in the harvest then share it fairly among his people."

"And my family's cut would be?"

"To be determined, but as you are the last to speak your voice will be heard."

"And do the villagers desire this?"

"The people desire what their chiefs are wise enough to decide. The flight of the bird follows its head."

"Has the village *fono* decided?"

"It is not their decision. These are family lands, not village communal lands."

They were safely out of To`aga by now, on the long causeway down to the bridge to Olosega.

"As the newest member of the *fono* I am seeking their counsel on this matter. I would like to call a *fono* meeting before I decide to sign or not."

"That is your right, but you will only be piling fuel on a fire. Sir, if this is not done in a proper, quiet, chiefly manner and resolved, I cannot insure that peace in To`aga can be restored. There are forces at work beyond our control."

They were on the bridge to Olosega now. "Tiafatu, that sounded vaguely like a threat."

"There are easy ways to do things, and there are hard ways to do the same thing. You can climb up the coconut tree feet first if you choose, but you will look like a fool to all who see you."

They bounced off the cement edge of the bridge onto Olosega's sand road. The few racks of fresh bread in the back of the pickup jumped up and down. They drove on in silence.

———— o ————

The textbook had the title *World Civilizations*. Apelu thought that was a pretty big project to take on, but it was a big book, about three inches thick. Sanele remembered that his last day in that class the homework had been the chapter on the Aztecs. Apelu quizzed him on the previous chapter, about the Egyptians, and his son seemed familiar with that—the pyramids, papyrus, hieroglyphics and all—so he set him to reading about the Aztecs.

"You know, in school we skip chapters," Sanele said.

"What? And miss one important culture or another? Wait, give me that book." Apelu was curious. He turned to the table of contents, then flipped to the index—nothing about Samoa, Polynesia, Oceania, the Pacific, not even Japan aside from World War II. The only culture between India and America mentioned was China. A third of the globe totally ignored.

He handed the textbook back to Sanele. "Let's see, today is Tuesday, isn't it?"

"Let's call it Tuesday," Sanele said.

"Friday afternoon I want you to teach me all about the Aztecs. I forgot. Okay?"

"You going to take my tests for me after I teach you everything?"

"Won't have to."

They had done pretty much the same thing for geometry, biology, health, and all his other subjects, including something called "Language Arts."

Apelu left Sanele sitting under the blue tarp with his books and went down to the lodge. He wanted to call his cousin at the Office of Samoan Affairs and find out if the district governor had signed off on his title papers. No one was around the lodge. As he picked up the phone he saw a note on the pad beside it, "Apelu, call Engine Ueba," and a Tutuila number. He dialed the number, and a male voice answered. "US Coast Guard. How can I help you?"

"Is Ensign Weber in, please?" Apelu guessed at the name.

"One moment, sir."

What the Coast Guard was concerned about, the young officer explained, was that in the week since the Manulele Airlines plane had crashed, privately owned boats, mainly fishing boats, had begun leaving Pago Pago harbor with Ofu as their destination. None of these boats were licensed to carry cargo or passengers, and the ensign had some safety concerns.

The Coast Guard's presence in Pago Pago was limited to a boatless junior officer and two non-coms. Would Apelu mind, as the only law enforcement officer on the island, checking on the boats that arrived in Ofu and reporting back to the Coast Guard office any suspected commercial transportation of goods or people? At the very least could he call in now and then with the names of vessels that stopped there? The ensign was apologetic to the point of being sheepish.

Next, Apelu called his captain at headquarters to ask whether he was permitted to conduct investigations for a federal agency. The captain told him that it was okay to inform them about what boats came and went, if he wanted to and it didn't interfere with his other duties, but that federal regs about shipping were none of their business and he should ignore it.

"In any event, the harbor is miles away from my house, and I have no vehicle to get there," Apelu told him.

"Then screw it."

"What about my promised vehicle?"

"I don't know anything about that, Soifua, and stop whining."

I wasn't whining, Apelu thought as he hung up, just asking. He saw the school bus drive up the road to the end of the airstrip and start a slow three-point turn. He ran out the front door of the lodge and waved them down before they had started back toward the village. They waited for him.

The school bus was running smoother, but the men onboard told him it still wasn't right, something to do with valve lifters. Apelu had them give him a ride to the harbor at the far western end of the village.

It was a small harbor behind a high seawall. Usually there were no boats there, discounting those rotting up on the hard and the irregular visits of the small inter-island ferry. This morning four boats were moored there—two twenty-foot, double-hulled, open-cockpit, single-outboard local fishing *alia* needing paint jobs, and two larger, American-style, twin-engine sportsfishing cabin cruisers. The *alia* had no names or numbers on their hulls. The cabin cruisers were *Dream World* and *Inca Queen*. Apelu copied down their names and numbers.

Did the Incas come before or after the Aztecs? Apelu couldn't remember. He would have to ask Sanele on Friday. As he sat in the shade of a huge mango tree beside the road above the harbor, he noticed a figure moving in the deck shadows of *Dream World*, so he waited there. He had nowhere else to go, really. The sun was heading into its zenith. The shaded figure—a male—disappeared back into the cabin. Apelu watched a village fisherman retrieve his woven-vine fish trap from the shallow waters off the beach. He watched sooty terns return to their nests in the cliff face of Nu'utele Island across the harbor channel. Language Arts, he was thinking. What the hell is Language Arts? Then the big man appeared on the sunlit deck of *Dream World*. It was Danny's brother, Ace. He looked misdressed in swim trunks and a black T-shirt. Dogs return to their vomit, Apelu thought.

Apelu's deal with Sanele was that he could work for Martin and Bobbie in the afternoons, if he spent the mornings with his school books. By the time Apelu got back to the *fale*, Sanele had gone to work. On his way back, Apelu had stopped at the lodge again to call his cousin at Samoan Affairs. The district governor had still not returned and signed his title papers. He also called Ensign Weber back and reported the four boats in Ofu harbor. He asked the ensign to check on who the registered owner of *Dream World* was. It took a couple of minutes, but the answer came back one Roketi Fitimanu of Pago Pago village. Roketi of Pago Pago, the other chief to sign off on the To'aga land lease boundaries.

When Sanele got home at dusk, Apelu walked down to the NPS cabin to talk to Bobbie. He was wondering if she had heard from Danny Po'o. He found her rinsing off their gear with fresh water.

"No, I haven't heard a thing from him."

"That's strange. No explanation for missing the plane or anything?"

"No, and when I tried to reach him he didn't answer his cell phone. Screw him."

"You're not worried?"

"Well, a couple of nights after we got here I got a call from his brother Ace, who said Danny had asked him to call me. Danny had to go back to California on some urgent family business. He'd be in touch. Well, he hasn't been in touch. He didn't even have the balls to call me himself."

Bobbie stood up from where she was crouching with the hose and their diving gear, kicking aside a pair of fins. "It's happened before, okay. A couple of dates, then just as we start getting intimate, the guy disappears. Why am I telling you this? He couldn't stay and play anymore. He had to go home. End of story. I had the feeling that he may have already been married anyway. Like you. So don't ask me any more about Danny Po'o." She turned off the hose.

Apelu thought about telling Bobbie what Danny had told him about Ace's brotherly threat to break Danny's arms if he fucked up the resort deal. He decided not to mention it. Now she could just write Danny off and get on with it, but if he told her then she would worry, too, get caught there between those two opposites.

"Then his brother Ace started asking me all these really dumb questions about the park and what Martin and I were doing. What a zero." Bobbie took a towel from the back of a chair and dried off her hands and arms and walked into the cabin. Now Apelu was wondering, not worrying, what was with Danny.

Martin was busy in his makeshift lab. He was humming to himself as he worked. "Thank you for leaving that extra bottle of spring water, Apelu. I really enjoyed it ice cold. Wherever did you find it? If you get more, please think of me. I know that it's only water, but a glass of it really perks me up. I'd like to have a chemical analysis of it done, see what minerals are in there."

"You would. How's the research going?"

"Well, well. That boy of yours is a big help. We should be done with the mapping and sampling by the end of the week. Then I just have to work it all up. I'm sure I can make the case for special preservation status when I get back to Pago."

Back at the *fale*, Sanele was seated at the table, reading his *World Civilizations* textbook in the light of the kerosene lantern.

"Dad, did you know that the Aztecs believed in human sacrifice? They had special sacred places where they would cut people's hearts out and offer them up to their gods."

"That's pretty extreme even for a religion, isn't it?"

"The preferred sacrificial offerings were young girls and boys."

Later, after dinner and after Sanele had gone to sleep, Apelu pulled the zip-lock freezer bag out from beneath the floor boards and sat for a while where Sanele had sat by the lantern, looking at pictures of Sarah.

○

As usual, the jungle birds awoke him. Apelu felt like taking a dawn swim. He had had a sweaty, bad-dream night. Maybe the sea could wash the residue of Sarah memories off of him. It helped.

On his way back to the *fale* from the beach, Apelu noticed activity in front of the NPS cabin. Martin was up early and busy. Apelu didn't want to stop and talk, but there was something about Martin's behavior that struck him as strange. Usually Martin was very slow and methodical as he worked, but now he was striding back and forth among his tables doing seemingly random things. Then he kicked a box beneath one of the tables and something glass shattered. This was not Martin. Apelu tied his towel around his waist over his wet shorts and walked slowly toward the cabin.

"What's up, Martin?"

Martin swirled around. "Oh, it's you. Nothing. Nothing is up. Everything is down, shut down, kaput." He kicked another box.

Bobbie came to the screen door. "Stop breaking things, Martin. I am not cleaning up what you break. Hello, Apelu."

"Oh, bloody hell," Martin spat out, as he picked up his fins and snorkel mask from a table and stomped off around the tail of the derelict Twin Otter toward the beach and To`aga.

"Bad hair day?" Apelu asked.

"Worse than that. Come in and get a cup of coffee. Been for a swim?"

They brought their coffees back out beneath the tent where it was cooler. Already you could tell it was going to be a scorcher. Not a coconut frond was moving, and the sky showed only the skimpiest lingerie of clouds. Bobbie slipped her slim legs up under her in her chair and took a two-handed sip from her coffee mug.

"Call from the superintendent early this morning. He just got back from the mainland and discovered what Martin was doing out here."

"Playing at the beach instead of watching the shop?"

"Worse. Guess again."

"Playing at the beach instead of watching the shop while stranded on a paradise isle with you?"

"That's not bad, but you're getting colder."

"Give me a clue."

"Progress."

"Progress? Martin is taking too long with this research? He's supposed to be doing something else more essential? He's not getting anywhere with you?"

"Quit it, Apelu. This is serious."

"Then be serious."

"Our asshole boss has pulled Martin and me off this job, cancelled it, and called us back to Tutuila immediately."

Apelu looked at the abandoned Twin Otter, grass already growing long around its wheels. "The immediately part is going to be problematic, but what's that got to do with progress?"

"That editorial Martin wrote for the *News* has come back to bite him in the ass. Ilmars thought it sent out exactly the wrong message—that the park was opposed to private enterprise and local development. Progress. That it made us come across as anti-progress, anti-development, just what the hardcore locals always thought—that we were here to freeze them in time, turn them into some sort of Stone Age theme park. I don't know. I don't pay attention to any of that stuff. It's just politics. Old farts listening to themselves spout off. It is so dysfunctional." Bobbie stopped to scratch her foot.

"So, Park Superintendent Ilmars is pro-resort?"

"I don't know if he's pro-resort. I don't know if he's pro-anything. He just wants Martin to halt this special marine preserve research and get back to the office. Me? I kind of like it here. There won't be a boat for another four or five days. It would be nice to just kick back for a while and relax."

"Martin didn't seem very relaxed."

"Oh, Martin is plenty pissed. Want more coffee? No? Okay." Bobbie shifted in her chair, reversing her legs tucked beneath her so that now Apelu was looking at the soles of her feet, not her knees. "After the phone call Martin threw a snit about how Ilmars has always hated this place, this assignment, and about Ilmars's disdain for the rent-a-park deal and the local chiefs' greed, about the insult of managing a park that no one comes to visit. Oh, Martin was quite specific about what a disaster Superintendent Ilmars has been. It looks like he'll kill any attempt Martin will make to get the reef special status, probably kill the Texas university research deal as well. Martin has invested a lot of time and energy on those projects. Oh well."

"And you?"

"As far as I can tell I was never mentioned in the conversation. Martin was acting superintendent. I was just following orders, I guess. It was a guy thing." The last two words were pronounced with quotes. Bobbie got up from her chair. "Well, I ought to go find him, I guess, before he starts kicking the coral and hurts himself. I've never seen Martin act this way." She took Apelu's empty cup from his hand as she headed for the screen door. "Catch you later."

———— o ————

Back at the *fale* Sanele had started his schoolwork.

"Dad, you said I had to do every other problem at the end of each geometry chapter. What about World Civ, every other question too?"

"You got to write them out?"

"Yeah."

"Then answer every one. The writing practice will do you good. And make it legible, so that I can read your answers. You done with that Aztec chapter already?"

"It was sort of interesting."

"What's the first question?"

"'Every known civilization has practiced some type of organized religion and believed in one or more deities. In your own words describe and discuss the religious practices of the Aztecs.' What are deities?"

"Gods. I don't know if that's true or not, the part about every civilization having organized religion. There was never any type of organized religion here in Samoa before Christianity got imported."

"But they had a deity, right? Tagaloa."

"Creation myth, not like anybody worshipped him."

"You don't believe in religion or God, do you, Dad?"

Apelu was tying fishing lures. The *atule* were beginning to run. It was what Sanele had caught the day before. Soon there would be a lot of them. Last night when Sanele was cleaning the fish, Apelu had checked the color of their stomachs. They all were yellow, so Apelu was fashioning *atule* lures with yellow feathers. If the first *atule's* stomachs had been white or black, as they were some years, he would be using white feathers or black feathers. It was a tradition as old as catching *atule*. He concentrated on his work and tried to ignore the question.

"Dad? You heard me."

"Why don't you just answer the questions in the book?"

"At Sarah's funeral Mom called you an atheist because you refused to pray for her soul. That means you don't believe in God, while everybody else does. Why?"

"It's the worship thing, I guess. I'm not into worship." Apelu held up his finished lure and admired his work, then started another.

"What's wrong with worship?"

"Just answer your questions." After a while, without looking up from what he was doing, Apelu spoke. "Let's call what we're talking about 'It,' just to be neutral, because there is no need to name It, personify It. No need to worship It, because It has no self-consciousness, no self at all, really." He glanced up. Sanele was watching him. "It has no need for our adoration, our prayers. It is powerless to do anything for us beyond maintaining the balance that sustains the conditions that make life and consciousness possible. It is a greater entity than us, sure, the way a charge in a power line is greater than the charge of a single electron passing through that line, but we are each an electron that adds to, is part of that power. It's not separate from us because we are all part of It. So worshipping It is like worshipping ourselves and our own invention, a pretty ridiculous proposition, just a way of feeling self-important. That would be like me worshipping this lure I created. There is no point in calling it God or any other name, for that matter. It's not a conscious being. It's everything together, most of which we will never know. That's my understanding anyway, and that's not a belief, because believing means making a leap of faith, and I am not making that leap. I don't see the need to." Apelu looked up again, and Sanele was looking past him, out the window, a curious look on his face. They talked no more about it.

Apelu put his lures away and got ready to go into the village, while Sanele continued his schoolwork.

"By the way, son, I don't think Martin and Bobbie will need your help on their job anymore. Looks like it's been called off."

"But we only have a couple of days' work left to do."

"Well, check with Bobbie then. Martin is not in a good mood."

In the village Apelu spoke with several of the other chiefs from the *fono*. They agreed that it would be good to have a meeting to discuss To'aga. Everyone was talking about it, and as usual when something became the primary topic of gossip there was more misinformation than real information—speculation offered as fact, rumors hardening into positions. The other chiefs would confer on the time and place and let Apelu know.

The *fono* was held at Chief Tiafatu's guest *fale* the following afternoon. It was raining, but by the time of its scheduled start at two p.m. all the *fono* members were there except for two older chiefs who had been stuck on Tutuila since the airplane crash. Apelu

195

didn't know every face there. Every pillar was taken. At the very last minute the *faifeau* ducked under the eaves out of the rain at the far end of the *fale* and sat down outside the circle of chiefs as he was not a member of the *fono*.

As host, Tiafatu welcomed them, then in a move that surprised everyone he deferred to the *faifeau* for an opening prayer. As the minister began intoning his invocation, Apelu did not lower his head and he noticed that several of the other chiefs likewise refused to offer the usual respect. As a non-chief and an outsider—he was not from Ofu—the *faifeau* should not have a say in the *fono*'s deliberations, but it was quickly clear from his invocation that he was attempting to establish a platform.

"Lord, give these your chiefs the wisdom to find the best solutions and direction. Let them seek the truth and act upon it, guided by your example. For we must strike down false gods and take your message and your cleansing light even into the darkest jungle. We must replace darkness with light, destroy superstition and sin with the leveling sword of your righteousness, and bring all parts of your creation into your glorious dominion."

There were another few minutes of this, during which everyone got restless. It became clear that what the reverend was trying to do was turn their discussion of what to do about To'aga into an indictment of To'aga, putting it on trial. When he finished, Tiafatu thanked him and the speeches began.

It was a long *fono* because every chief wanted to have his say. There was the matter of the children not going to school, being in the village all day causing trouble. There was the matter of no air service—money and mail and supplies not arriving. There was no means of medical evacuation. There was the matter of the—absent—*pulenu'u*. Nobody really wanted to go there, but shouldn't they have an island mayor who wasn't ga-ga? And who was going to tell the Office of Samoan Affairs who appointed him that he was now permanently damaged goods? And what about the crimes? The *palangi*'s murder, the slashing of the *pulenu'u*'s truck tires. And all those new boats coming and going in the harbor, were they fishing in village waters?

A village that normally had on its plate just the next wedding or funeral or holiday was suddenly facing a meal of urbanesque perplexities, but no one wanted to take up the *faifeau*'s indictment of To'aga as somehow the cause of all these developments. To'aga was, after all, a part of themselves, a part they might wish to avoid and ignore and cover up, but a part of themselves nonetheless, a progenitor and member of their extended family, a reality, a force to be neither fooled with nor questioned.

As the newest and most junior chief, Apelu waited his turn to speak. Although some of the matters addressed by the others involved police business, he was never questioned nor referred to. He was there representing his family, not the Department of Public Safety. And so it was when he finally spoke that he spoke only of his family's concern—that he had been asked to enter into an agreement involving his family's land that involved a survey and the possibility that a resort hotel would be built at To'aga.

Up to now no one had mentioned Paradise Escapes and the land deal. Apelu stopped to consider how to continue, and he could feel the assembly relax, a tension leave the guest *fale* like a breeze between its open pillars, a murmur and a relaxation of bodies. Several chiefs reached for their cigarette packs on the mat beside them and lit one. Finally they would get to address the real issue.

The first question, of course, was about money. Who in the village would profit from the development if it did take place?

Tiafatu answered. "Directly, the families whose land the developers desire. That is only proper. But indirectly the whole village will profit. It will mean jobs for our children and money coming onto the island."

"But that money will be coming in the pockets of strangers," an old chief observed.

197

"But the pockets will leave and the money will stay," a younger chief said.

"There will be more planes," Tiafatu said. "We would not be cut off just because one plane is broken."

"Will the visitors be *palangi* or Chinese?" someone asked. "I don't like Chinese."

Tiafatu pointed out that the *fono* had already agreed in the past to lease the beach and the reef at To'aga to the National Park and that the whole village profited from those annual payments. "This is the same thing, the next logical step."

"But does To'aga want it?" the same old chief asked. "To'aga has not been happy since all this began."

"May I speak?" It was the *faifeau*, who had inched his way forward into the circle of chiefs. The answer was no—Apelu could see it in every chief's demeanor—but this was their *faifeau*, and no one was bold enough to say the word. "I must speak. I am your spiritual counselor, your Christian conscience. It is my duty to point out the guideposts along the way to salvation.

"What is at the evil heart of all these troubles? To'aga. The Commandments tell us clearly. Thou shalt not put false gods before me, and yet some of you seem unaware that your To'aga is a false god. You seem to fear and worship it instead of Jesus and reason. To'aga is a devil, a devil you must throw out of your lives so that the Lord may fill this island and your souls. I will prove it to you.

"I have heard that this man named Nu'upo is seen by some as Foisia, the traditional guardian of To'aga. Let it be so, because as surely as To'aga is the devil, Nu'upo is the devil's lieutenant. A witch doctor and a cursemonger, a drug pusher and an atheist, a trickster and an adulterer, an outcast and a murderer."

Sitting cross-legged like everyone else in the circle of chiefs, the *faifeau* had leaned and squirmed himself forward so that now he broke the circle, his back to the chiefs beside him as he addressed the rest. Apelu held his policeman's tongue at the word "murderer," but the *faifeau* turned on him anyway. "I have proof," he said, shaking his fist in Apelu's direction.

"As you know, this man Nu`upo was once connected with our church, through his father, Reverend Etuane. When our local police failed to follow up on investigating this man Nu`upo as a suspect in the murder of the *palangi* surveyor, I mounted my own investigation through Samoan members of our church back in California. The Lord does not lose sight of these his children, even those who have fallen by the wayside."

The *faifeau* was dressed all in white and carried a black Bible, which he now held aloft. "There is no greater love than the love of Jesus. All praise his name."

A stony silence filled the guest *fale*.

"A murderer and Satan's handyman. This man Nu`upo has killed before and will kill again at the bidding of his master, *tevolo* To`aga. They must be beaten, wiped from the face of our island in Jesus' name."

Even Tiafatu seemed taken aback by this outburst. "Murderer? Nu`upo? We all know To`aga herself dealt with the *palangi* surveyor."

The *faifeau* stood up, an inexcusable offense to all the chiefs sitting there. "A murderer four times over, and with just one stroke. And this is only one proven incident. Others will follow, I'm sure, as our inquiry deepens. Before he returned to Ofu this man Nu`upo spent five years in prison for vehicular manslaughter, having killed his wife and his twelve-year-old son Etuane and two other innocents in another car in a drunken, head-on collision from which only he escaped unscathed. Devil's spoor."

The *faifeau* suddenly realized that he was not in his pulpit, but was standing, in conspicuous disrespect, in the middle of a circle of seated chiefs.

"Sit down," the old chief said. "You will be fined."

The rain had deepened as the *faifeau* spoke. It was now almost deafening. One of the chiefs called out the wish to suspend further talking until tomorrow, "to let the mats cool," and all agreed, eager to leave that place. One by one the chiefs walked off into the pounding rain. Apelu was among the first. The rain felt good, warm and scouring. It stayed strong all the way on his long walk home.

CHAPTER 13

———— o ————

I T AWAKENED THEM IN THE MIDDLE OF THE NIGHT, BUT THEY
didn't know what it was. By the time they were fully awake it
was over. It was still raining hard, and they listened through the
rain for other sounds but there were none.

"Was it an explosion?" Sanele asked.

"What is there to explode?"

"Maybe the plane blew up."

They went to the window that faced in the direction of the
airstrip and the lodge but could see no flames.

"A huge wave?"

"I hope not, for the village's sake."

Apelu went out into the rain and walked to the top of the
lane then around the edge of their compound, sniffing the air
and squinting into the enclosing blackness. Sanele waited at the
screen door.

"Nothing," Apelu said as he came back indoors and Sanele
handed him a towel. "It will have to wait till dawn. Go back to
bed." But neither of them could get back to sleep.

At first light they hiked down the lane. It was still raining
steadily but not as insistently. Everything seemed normal at the

lodge and the airstrip. The Twin Otter was still there, looking more forlorn than ever. There was no evidence of a large wave. They walked out to the rise above the beach at the end of the runway and looked up and down the coastline as far as they could see. Nothing. As they were walking back across the runway they saw Martin walking briskly back the sand track from To'aga. They caught up with him at the NPS cabin where Bobbie was waiting out of the rain, sipping a mug of coffee.

"Yep, just as I thought," Martin said. "Get in," and he unlocked the park truck. Bobbie ducked into the passenger side seat with her mug of coffee, and Apelu and Sanele climbed into the back. Martin drove back up the road he'd just come down.

They could see it even before they got to the cliff-edge turn into To'aga—the face of the cliff had come away and cascaded over the road all the way to the ocean, a new high talus slope with garage-sized boulders in it, gleaming and raw in the rain. Martin stopped the truck well before its edge and got out. "Figures," he said. "Just two or three days' work left to do, and now we will have to walk around this monster to get there. All that rain, I guess. It was bound to happen sooner or later. I guess you'd better call this in, Apelu. It looks like something needing an emergency response, if anything like that is possible out here."

"I doubt it fell on anyone in the middle of a stormy night in a place where no one goes," Apelu said, walking up to the edge of the landslide. He remembered the old chief's words—"To'aga has not been happy."

The landslide had not only buried the road, it had taken out the power and telephone poles and lines to Olosega as well. The only power generator for the two islands was on Ofu, at the harbor. Back at the empty lodge, Apelu called there first and told the guy on duty about the landslide and the fact that the lines were down. Almost immediately the power was shut off. Apelu waited an hour until his captain would be at work to call and report the landslide. The old chain of command of credit—the captain would get to report it to the commissioner, who would get to break the news to the governor. The Department of Public Safety was on the job, first on the scene. The governor would thank the commissioner. The commissioner would thank the captain. And Apelu would not get his patrol SUV because now there was no way for him to get over to Olosega to check on the commissioner's business interests there.

As he talked on the phone in the lodge's main room, he could see people from the village walking past on the road on the way to see the landslide with their own eyes. The rain had almost stopped. Apelu wondered if he should go back to the slide and keep people away from it in case there were after-slides. He wondered if there were such things as after-slides? He decided that To'aga wasn't pissed at any of those people, her people, and she would leave them alone. He went to the NPS cabin instead, where Sanele and Bobbie and Martin were having a big breakfast. Apelu joined them.

After breakfast, as Sanele was cleaning up and Martin was busying himself out in his makeshift lab, Apelu took Bobbie aside.

"Well, the natural disaster seems to have restored Martin to his old Martin self," Apelu said.

"It was so natural that it confirmed his faith in observable phenomena," Bobbie said and laughed. "But actually the familiar Martin returned last night after he decided to screw the superintendent. We are going to complete the project and he is going to push for the reef's special preservation status with or without Ilmars's permission. Even if it means his job. I think in his mind Martin has already resigned. That's why he's so cheerful."

Martin, indeed, was actually whistling while he worked, although Apelu couldn't identify the tune.

"We're going back out there today, even if we have to swim around the end of the slide."

"Sanele too?"

"We've got a bunch to get finished before the boat comes."

"It will probably be coming even sooner now."

"Then it will be long days until then. Can you excuse Sanele from his morning lessons?"

"Sure. After you leave there will be little else for him to do but study."

"Sanele," Martin called in from the porch, "pack plenty of water. We'll be gone all day."

Sanele looked at his dad, and Apelu nodded.

———————— o ————————

By two p.m. when the *fono* reconvened at Tiafatu's guest *fale*, the skies had mainly cleared, with just the last tail feathers of cirrocumulus trailing the storm. All the chiefs were back, but the *faifeau* was absent.

At the start of the meeting Apelu announced that he had reported the landslide to the government officials in Pago Pago, then the discussion of To'aga continued. One of the chiefs whom Apelu didn't know asked permission to be the first to speak. He was one of the younger chiefs and very fit. He spoke in a flat, emotionless voice, and his speech was devoid of any fancy Samoan oratory. He reminded the *fono* that there were now many more natives of Ofu living off-island than there were on-island. Why was that? Because times had changed and the jobs that paid the money that the new reality ran on were all on Tutuila or in Hawaii or the mainland.

"We are becoming an island of ghosts, alive only in the past. The real world has passed us by," the young chief said.

Apelu leaned toward a chief beside him and in a whisper apologized for his ignorance and asked who the speaker was. He was familiar with the title name the chief whispered back into his ear, but he did not know the man. Then the chief beside him touched his arm and they leaned together again. "In Pago where he lives he is known as Roketi," he said.

Roketi, the owner of *Dream World*, went on to regret that so many sons and daughters of Ofu could not live in their home because the island had failed to keep pace with the real world. "Soon they will need a time machine to get here," he said and paused.

"Is it a race that we are in?" asked the old chief from the day before. "And are we racing against Tutuila, Hawaii, and the rest of the world? I could think of better things to do with my time."

"If your son had a job here, you could grow old surrounded by your grandchildren, not left alone," Roketi answered, "and they could learn from you the proper *Fa`a Samoa*. The point is we should concern ourselves with the future, not the past. We should open ourselves to what is possible."

Apelu could see that this speech was persuasive to many of the other *fono* members. The speeches that followed confirmed this. The chiefs had had a day to discuss this matter more fully and informally among themselves. A cautious consensus of some sort had been reached among a majority of them, but there were hold-outs, mainly among the more senior chiefs. The old chief who was acting as their spokesman reminded the *fono* that they were there because Apelu had asked for their advice—the village's will—on whether he should sign off as a chief on the papers that would make the resort development possible.

"Who else among us has already signed these papers without consulting us?" the old chief asked.

Tiafatu spoke for the first time. "These are family lands, not village land. They are being leased not sold. It is not really the *fono*'s concern."

"But those decisions will affect us all, with or without my grandchildren and a time machine." The old man's voice had taken on an edge. "Nevermind. We already know the names of the other three chiefs who have signed. In any event, our son here"—and he gestured toward Apelu—"cannot sign as chief until thirty days after his title is officially registered. That is the law. So he has time to weigh his decision, to wait on developments. There is no need to rush, to race into the future. The stones speak to those who listen. Our son has done the right thing by asking for our guidance. I hope we will meet again after we have digested this meal of words, but now we have another meal to eat."

A line of young women followed the *faifeau*'s wife into the *fale*. Each of them was carrying a freshly woven placemat of green coconut frond on which a banana leaf held a pile of food—fish, lobster, pork, taro, breadfruit. With a deep bow, the women placed an offering of food before each of the chiefs. The old chief said a short prayer that ended, "And we accept these gifts of food from the *faifeau* in the spirit in which they have been offered. May we live in mutual love and respect. *Amene.*"

So, feeding the *fono* had been the *faifeau*'s fine, Apelu thought, but the man himself was nowhere to be seen.

When one of the young women returned with a drinking nut, Apelu pushed his food away from him and gestured with his eyes and head that she should take it away. She handed him the *niu* and took the placemat of food. Other chiefs were doing the same thing. Decorum did not require them to stay and eat there. The *fono* was over. Apelu said his polite goodbyes to the chiefs on either side of him and ducked sideways under the low eaves of the *fale* to leave. The young girl who had served him met him in the yard and handed him a coconut frond basket with his food wrapped in a banana leaf inside it. She smiled. It was a simple, open smile, but it meant a lot to Apelu. He smiled back and slipped away alone. He was halfway home to Va'oto when Chief Tiafatu caught up with him in his pickup truck.

"Sir," he said, pulling up beside him, "there is no need for you to walk. Get in."

Apelu put his basket of food in the back of the truck and sat in the front beside Tiafatu, who was alone. Their conversation was brief and polite. Tiafatu wanted to assure Apelu that the survey map would be redrawn, restoring the Nandiaka portion of the land to be leased to Apelu's title. He said there would be no problem waiting for Apelu's title to become official before he signed, that, in fact, the delay would work in their favor. The developers were eager to close the deal and were already offering more money to expedite the proceedings. If they had to wait an extra month or so maybe they would go even higher. Apelu thanked him and said he would not even consider signing a lease agreement until the survey map was accurate and left it at that. They rode a ways in silence.

"I've noticed the park people have been very busy on the reef," Tiafatu said. "Would that have anything to do with that piece that was in the *Samoa News* about saving the reef for science or something?"

"They are doing some sort of study is all I know. Why?"

"It didn't come up at the *fono,* but a number of chiefs have been grumbling about it. They don't like the idea of To'aga being used like some sort of laboratory animal in an experiment. Actually, I think they just don't like having the park people around at all because they don't know what they're up to out there. Besides, I thought the park people were on our side in this, that it would bring in more visitors to their park. That's what their head guy told Roketi anyway. And that archaeologist guy said that he wouldn't make any trouble about that boulder back on your piece as long as the developers agreed to make the area around it a little park so that people could visit and see the boulder."

They had pulled up in front of the lodge. Tiafatu offered to buy Apelu a beer, but he declined. "A beer" to a Samoan meant spending the rest of the day getting drunk. Apelu thanked him for the ride and got his basket of food. He would have a beer, but alone and just one.

———————— o ————————

Apelu and Sanele went fishing for *atule* that sundown on the reef off the airstrip after the boy got back from his work in To'aga. They caught a lot, quickly. Apelu's yellow-feathered lures worked every time. Sanele was impressed. On their way back, as night was filling in the spaces between the trees and the sea was getting black with just a wavering white line of surf on the outer reef, they stopped at the NPS cabin and gave half their catch to Bobbie and Martin. Apelu had considered mentioning to them what Tiafatu had told him about Ilmars's and Drew's position on the resort development but had decided not to. He wasn't sure if it was any of his business, and it was just hearsay. Besides Martin was in excellent spirits. No reason to bum him out. He would get enough of that when he got back to the office. Martin said that one more working day on the reef ought to wrap it up. There was still no word on when the boat from Pago would come, but when it did arrive, they would be ready to go back on it.

The next morning Sanele was up and out early. Apelu spent most of the day in the plantation up the ridge behind the *fale*. He was expanding it now that there were two to feed. Apelu had forgotten how much a sixteen-year-old could eat. He used the phone at the lodge to call into headquarters once to check on the boat. They didn't know when it would be coming. Public Works had loaded a big earth mover and a dump truck on it for the road work, and now the Coast Guard was wondering if it was seaworthy.

By sunset Sanele had not returned and Apelu walked down to the NPS cabin to check, but there was no one there. He went to the lodge, which was deserted. Without the plane there were no guests. He waited at the *fale* for an hour, then he took the big flashlight and headed out. There was a light rain falling again, another front coming in from the east. It was that time of year. At first he tried walking over the landslide, but it was too slippery, muddy, and treacherous, so he climbed back down and went out to the beach. The tide was out, and he easily walked around the end of it, getting wet only up to his waist. He remembered to take his cigarettes and lighter out of his shorts' pocket.

Apelu wasn't sure what part of the To'aga reef they had been working on. He walked the length of the beach, seeing no one, no lights, no equipment. A metallic coldness started seeping into his emotional veins, that going-into-battle adrenal mixture of fear and the resolve not to panic. There would be a logical explanation. Maybe for some reason they had gone on to Olosega. Maybe someone got hurt. Maybe they had caught a boat ride back to the harbor. Maybe they had just been delayed and had been walking back along the road as he was walking the beach. Although the power was back to Olosega, the phone lines were still down, so if they had gone there they couldn't have called. But he had no phone anyway.

It took him two hours to search the beach in both directions and get back around the landslide. The rain was coming down harder now and the tide was coming in. His cigarettes were ruined. The NPS cabin was as dark as he had left it. He turned on all its lights. By now he felt like cold steel inside. He went up to his *fale*, dried off, and changed clothes, found a fresh pack of Marlboros. There was nothing much that he could do but wait for the logical explanation to arrive, and that probably wouldn't arrive until the morning now. He didn't sleep.

By first light he was in the village asking around, but no one had seen the park people or his son. A few people, when they heard that they had been working at To'aga, just closed their eyes and shook their heads. Chief Tiafatu offered to get a search party together. Apelu accepted the offer and asked for a ride to the landslide. It was raining steadily now. The morning was nickel gray. Alone, Apelu walked around the slide and headed down the beach toward Olosega, still searching. In Olosega it was the same as in Ofu—no one had seen any *palangis*. The number of

Apelu's logical explanations was dwindling. He headed back to To'aga.

There were only five young men in Tiafatu's search party. Tiafatu was not among them. Apelu sent one man up to the road, another to the strip of bush between the road and the beach. A third was told to search the edge of the bush along the beach. The other two he sent out onto the reef. Apelu took the beach. Once again he was searching. This time he was looking for a clue as to why his son had disappeared. His mind ran back and forth over the same tracks.

The call came from the edge of the bush, a long high "Uuuuu." The boy there had found their cache tucked out of sight in the vines where the beach shelved above the beach. There were two small Igloo coolers, a net bag of water bottles, and several other net bags holding clothes and towels and water-tight plastic boxes with clipboards of paper inside. Apelu found three towels, Bobbie's lava lava and a dry T-shirt, one of Martin's T-shirts, and three sets of flip flops. There was no snorkeling gear. He picked up the net bag of water bottles, and it was light—only a few bottles still full. All that was left of their lunch in one of the coolers were empty sandwich and chip bags and three apple cores. They had put in almost a full day's work. Apelu turned and looked out to sea.

"They never came back in," he said.

"You mean they just vanished?" someone asked.

"To'aga took them," someone else said.

Apelu started walking toward the ocean. There was a drumming in his ears not made by the rain. The young men stood there watching him. Only one of them followed him.

"The rest of you finish the search to the end of To'aga," Apelu said. "Search well."

The one young man who walked into the water with Apelu was the *pulenu'u*'s son, the one he had caught getting stoned.

The rain made the ocean still, beaten down, a softly undulating stippled skin the color of aluminum. All they could see beneath the glassy surface was a circle of about three-foot radius around their feet. There is no other way to walk through coral in flip flops except slowly. They walked the reef slowly in the rain, two arm's lengths apart, looking down in waist-deep water. Sometimes between coral plateaus they had to swim. The water was warmer than the air. They made it to the outer edge of the reef, maybe a hundred yards off shore, then turned to cover another section headed in. The outer reef face was steep here, a quick drop into the depths. They weren't equipped to go there.

The *pulenu'u*'s son found it—a clear plastic clipboard with black-gridded plastic pages and a grease pen attached—caught in a limb of pink coral. Nearby Apelu found a mask with snorkel still attached. He could tell from the shortness of the mask's strap that it must have been Bobbie's. Within minutes they found her. The shifting tides had wrapped her around a particularly handsome head of live coral so that she looked like she was sleeping there, her arms around it, as if she and the coral were sharing a mutual dream. They found it difficult to disengage her.

When they got Bobbie's body back to the beach, Apelu sat holding her for a while. Death made him cold, as if life had left him as well. He smoothed back her short hair and felt the contusion on the side of her head. It was large. There was another near the base of her skull, the one that would have done the worse damage. The white zinc oxide cream on the bridge of her nose and her cheekbones was now a small girl's innocent makeup for a date with death.

They laid Bobbie's body out on the beach and went back to the water. They searched in tandem in silence for another hour and found nothing. The rain had not let up. Apelu sent the *pulenu'u*'s son back to the village to fetch others to take Bobbie's body back. He stayed there with her, shivering in the rain, looking out to sea. Somehow he knew his son was not also dead. He couldn't be. When Sarah died he had felt it like an amputation, an organ failure. He knew death. It was a finality, a circuit failing, a hole in his consciousness. Sanele's channel was still open, alive. He was out there somewhere. He had not lost him too. He would find him. He had to. He held Bobbie's hand until they came for her. He was frozen, almost catatonic. He had always wanted to do that, to just sit on the beach and hold Bobbie's hand. His tears and the rain were the same.

———— o ————

Back at the lodge Apelu called headquarters and reported Bobbie's death as a homicide. The National Park people should be notified. He did not report two other people missing. No one there could do anything about it, and he wasn't yet ready to admit it to himself. He was getting angry now, heating up inside. He was angry mainly with himself because he didn't know what he could do. A further search was out of the question because no one from the village would go back into To'aga. That had been made clear when they brought Bobbie's body out. Apelu got one of the bush store owners to empty a food freezer, and they put her body in there.

Unable to rest, Apelu walked down to the harbor. There were three new boats there—two more Samoan fishing *alia* and a new cabin cruiser, the *Manusina II*. The *Inca Queen* was gone but *Dream World* was still there. He stood on the dock and yelled out to *Dream World*, but no one answered. All of the boats seemed deserted. He walked back through the village in the rain. It was a ghost town—not a person, not a dog to be seen. No roosters crowed. No birds flitted between the trees. The doors of the bush stores were closed and locked. The doors of the church were closed and locked—a padlocked chain through the handles. It was as if he was the sole living thing left on the island. Puddles filled the sand road. He walked through them. He hadn't been dry since he had left the *fale* before dawn. He walked through the village and saw no one. He was a couple of minutes past the last house on the road to Va'oto when he heard the church bell ring four times behind him, almost like an all-clear signal. He walked on.

When do you go up the road and when do you go down the road? Apelu wondered as he splashed on toward home. Most of this road along the seashore was pretty much level, so was he going up the road to home or down the road to home? English was funny sometimes. In Samoan there was no distinction like that, but in English you wouldn't say going up the road when you were feeling bad. It was emotionally wrong somehow. Up and down, good and bad. Up the mountain, down into the sea. They were left and right here where he walked on a thread of road at the edge, the very boundary of both. Life and death, heaven and hell. And why was he thinking these things? Wondering like this. He was losing his focus. Then he felt it in his limbs, the exhaustion. His brain was just going first. He'd been up and on the move, soaked, for more than thirty hours. Very soon he would be no good at all, and Sanele would need him. He had to sleep, eat and sleep, get dry and warm, so that he could find Sanele. He plodded on home. His body did what he told it to do.

○

In the dream Nu'upo was wearing a suit, a good suit, a silk tie, and *palangi* shoes. He was younger. His hair was not white, and he was not emaciated. He was walking through the lobby of the Mark Hopkins Hotel in San Francisco. He had just come in the street-side revolving door. As he walked he glanced at his wristwatch. He was in a hurry. The lobby was crowded with people in evening clothes. He walked past a cocktail lounge where a man in a tuxedo was playing at a grand piano. He walked away from the crowds down a long marble corridor then through a door into a large blue-lit, tile-walled room with a deserted Olympic-sized swimming pool. He dove into the pool and stayed under water as he kicked toward the distant darkened end. He never resurfaced. There were other dreams, but that was the one Apelu remembered when he awoke. He remembered Nu'upo diving deeper and deeper into the blue light, breathing under water, searching for something.

When Apelu woke up the rain had stopped. It was still dark. He lit the kerosene lantern and forced himself to eat. He was not doing well. His resolve to not panic was being dissolved from the inside by panic. Where was Sanele? He needed his boy. He needed to know. Was he deluding himself, protecting himself with the conviction that he was not dead? Why couldn't Sanele just come walking up the track from the road with a story to tell? If he was hurt somewhere, Apelu wanted to find him. If he was a captive somewhere, he wanted to free him. If he was dead, he wanted to hold his body one last time, hold him like when he was a sleeping, almost unwakeable baby.

A while after dawn he left the *fale*, headed for To'aga. He didn't know where else to go. He had to do something. He would walk the reef alone until he found something, anything. He stopped at the NPS cabin and found a spare pair of fins and a mask and snorkel. Halfway around the end of the landslide, almost at its point, he met Martin coming in the opposite direction. Martin was dressed in swim trunks and a T-shirt. He was carrying a bundle made from a wetsuit top, his snorkel and fins sticking out of it. When he saw Apelu he said, "I want to report an attempted murder."

Apelu ignored him, looked beyond him. "Sanele? Is Sanele with you?"

"Why, no he's not. I'm quite alone. I haven't seen him."

Apelu was speechless. He felt as if he'd been dropped from a great height, was in freefall.

Back at the NPS cabin Martin changed his clothes and fixed himself a mug of herbal tea. "Where's Doctor Wentworth?" he asked when he came back onto the porch.

"Bobbie's gone," Apelu said.

"Did the boat come?"

"No, Martin, I mean Bobbie is dead."

Martin sat down. "Tell me."

Apelu told him. Martin wept for a good five minutes. Apelu let him. There's not much a guy can do at times like that for another guy. Apelu cried too, but that wasn't helpful.

After he stopped sobbing, Martin went back indoors and blew his nose and splashed cold water on his face. When he came back out he was without his glasses. Swollen with crying, his spectacleless eyes looked even more boyish.

"Sanele?" he asked.

"Missing," was all Apelu said.

"Oh God, Apelu. It was a concerted attack. All planned, not an accident. We must find Sanele. I survived, maybe he did. What can we do?"

"Tell me what happened to you. Maybe that will help."

"Okay, but why would anyone want to hurt Bobbie and Sanele?"

"Don't know yet. Just tell me what happened, Martin."

Recounting his story seemed to calm Martin down. He studied his now cold cup of tea as he spoke, sometimes going back to correct or elaborate upon details. Considering the fact that it obviously was a case of attempted—and nearly successful—murder, he did it calmly and well. As Martin talked, Apelu lit a series of cigarettes, and Martin never even noticed.

It was their last dive of the day, their last dive of the study really. There were a number of anomalies—mistakes, actually—in their earlier data that they had to correct. Bobbie and Sanele were snorkeling on the reef, and Martin was scuba diving off the face of the reef, revisiting places they'd been to before. Martin heard the sound of a boat's engines and was perplexed by it, but there had been fishing boats along there a couple of times in the previous days and he didn't think much of it. He was busy, visiting his black sponges.

When it hit him the first time it was on his butt and pushed him downward. He didn't know what had hit him. His first thought was big shark, and he became a bit disoriented in the bubbles and the turbulence. The wave surge had him too close to the reef face, so he pushed off into deeper water. Out of the corner of his mask he saw it diving at him again and he swatted at it with his clipboard, which hit it and flew out of his hand. That was no shark. It was metal. His first thought was for his clipboard and he went after it and caught it. He was in deeper, calmer water now and he looked up to see a boat's hull forty-some feet above him. He decided to descend. He could hear the boat's engines revving up again above him. He headed back toward the reef face.

This time it hit him in the middle of his back, on his tanks, and it stuck, caught a tank strap. He reached back to free himself and found that a grappling hook attached to a steel cable had caught him. He rolled over onto his back and yanked at the cable to get some slack, the way—he realized later—a gamefish did when it got snared. That told the boat that they had him, and the engines revved again and with a jerk they started dragging him out to sea, setting the hook and sending him spinning forward.

"I don't know why they didn't end it then and there. I was afraid they would. I couldn't get loose of that hook. If they had just hit the throttles and dragged me up to the surface, the embolisms probably would have killed me. Maybe they thought someone may be watching from shore and they just wanted to wander innocently away, but they dragged me slowly out into deeper water."

The grappling hook was caught on his tanks. If he were going to jettison his tanks, he had to work his way gradually closer to the surface. This took a while, being dragged. On his way up he unsnapped the buckle of his weight belt and clipped it onto his tank vest. At twelve feet he opened the buckles on his tank vest, took one good last breath of air from his regulator, and rolled over to free himself of his vest and tanks. He kicked away from the departing boat and stayed underwater as long as he could. The boat hadn't slowed or altered its course. It disappeared quickly between the open ocean swells. He floated a while. The sun was heading for the horizon. Behind him were the peaks of Ofu and Olosega. Olosega seemed to be closer, and a slight current seemed to be pushing him that way. He went with it. He had a mask, snorkel, fins, and his short-sleeve wetsuit top. He went with it slowly, as if he were out for a stroll. It would be a long night. He went for it. He just tried to keep the few lights in Olosega village in sight from the tops of the swells and kick now and then in their direction. The next morning, almost fourteen hours later, he made it ashore on the eastern, uninhabited side of Olosega.

"I found a stream, drank some water, and went to sleep on the spot," Martin said, finally looking up. "Something saved me. I don't know how."

"You are not a praying man, are you, Martin?"

"Nope. Didn't pray. It was the currents that saved me, pulled me back toward shore beyond the point. I guess. I stayed there the whole next day. Couldn't move. Found some coconuts and bananas to eat. Buried myself in the sand against the mosquitoes, just glad to be alive, getting stronger. Headed back first thing this morning." Then Martin started crying again. "Bobbie, Bobbie, what have I done?"

"Martin, would you recognize the bottom of that boat?"

Martin stopped crying. "Yes, I think so. Why?"

"Because I think they may have taken Sanele with them. Are you up to go looking?"

"Of course. Let's go. Let's go now. I have to get out of this place."

They parked the Park Service truck before the harbor and walked down to the shoreline. Martin was carrying his mask and fins. There were now just four boats moored in the harbor—two Samoan fishing *alia* and two *palangi* boats, *Dream World* and the *Inca Queen* again.

"It could have been either of those sportfishing boats—twin-engine, white-bottomed. Let me check." Martin headed back up the shore to a spot out of sight from the boats. Apelu followed.

"Do you think you can tell which?"

"My boat had a blue keel and a bad scrape on its hull, right side aft." He was quickly into the water.

Apelu walked back and found a bushy spot where he could watch without being seen. Martin was good. His snorkel tip barely made a ripple. There was again no sign of life on any of the boats. No Ace on the deck of *Dream World*. The boats rose and fell with the gentle swell. If Sanele was on one of those boats, he would be quite alone. Apelu's mind started racing again toward panic.

It only took about five minutes and Apelu caught sight of Martin's snorkel heading back away from the moored boats. Apelu met him where he had put in.

"Nope, neither," was all Martin said. "Now what?"

"Are you sure?"

"Certain."

"Shit."

"What now?"

"The other boat that was here, the *Manusina II*. Of course, they would leave. They wouldn't stay here."

Back at the NPS cabin, Apelu called Ensign Weber at the Coast Guard office in Pago. He reported the boat arrivals and departures, then asked if the ensign would check on the registration of the *Manusina II*. Again it took a few minutes. The *palangi* ensign had trouble pronouncing the long Samoan name of the registered owner, so he spelled it out for Apelu. It was obvious the young man didn't know the name, didn't recognize it, didn't know that it was the police commissioner's name.

———————— o ————————

In a way it was an easy phone call to make. Apelu had something solid, a lead, and he went right after it. However, it was not lost on him that he was about to involve his big boss in a homicide, or at least an attempted homicide, investigation. Of course, the commissioner was not available. The secretary said the commissioner wouldn't be back until after lunch.

Apelu went back up to his *fale*. He was shaking and wanted to hide it from Martin. He was beginning to doubt his self-assurance about Sanele being still alive. Had he brought his son here so that he could be killed? Had he again been a contributing cause in the death of one of his children? He remembered a bottle of vodka he had hidden once beneath the cook shed woodpile. It was still there. He took a swig from the bottle. It was hot, burning, disgusting. He spat it out. The hose wasn't running. He scooped half a mug of water from the rain barrel, then filled the rest of the mug with vodka. He sipped it. He swallowed it. There was the slight hint of gasoline. It was a bitter cup, but it was his. He sat beneath the blue tarp and finished the mug as if it were medicine or a cup of poison he was doomed to drink to kill his mind. He had a second and a third. The alcohol focused the heat of the day into his body, a fever that his morbid sweat did not break.

By the time Apelu returned to the lodge to call the commissioner again he was half drunk, but it wasn't helping. The commissioner was there. Apelu caught him on his way out.

"What is it, Soifua? Can't your captain handle this?"

"Just a few quick questions, sir. The boat *Manusina II*, is that your boat, sir?"

"Why yes it is, Soifua. What of it?"

"Well, it's been over here in Ofu, and I—"

"Yes, it probably has been over there. I leased it out last week."

"Could I ask who you leased it to?"

"I don't see why it is any of your business, Soifua, but I leased it to the National Park. I was glad to stick that jerk the superintendent with a nice stiff daily rate. They had some people over there they wanted to get back. Though it seems now, from your report, that there will be one fewer person to bring back. What's happening with that?"

"We have her body on ice, and the investigation is proceeding. Ah, sir, does your boat have a blue keel and a bad hull scrape starboard aft?"

"Blue keel, yes, but it better not have any scrapes on its hull. What are you talking about?"

"Do you know where the boat is now, sir?"

"No, I don't, but I'll find out. It better not be banged up or I'll make that asshole pay big time." The commissioner hung up. You could tell he wasn't a cop because he never got an answer to his question, he just got pissed off.

Apelu returned to his *fale* and finished his medicine beneath the blue tarp. After sundown, now deadly drunk, he returned to the NPS cabin. Martin was asleep. Apelu got the keys from where he had seen Martin hide them and commandeered the NPS truck. He drove to the harbor and swam out to *Dream World*, which was all dark. The cabin was locked. He broke in, smashing a deck chair through the door window. He searched the boat. There was no one, nothing. He cut his foot on the broken glass. He didn't feel it until he was back in the water and the salt water found his wounds. He made it home somehow.

CHAPTER 14

———— o ————

APELU WAS AWAKENED BY A TRUCK HORN HONKING. THE SUN was already high. The truck was in his yard. When he pushed himself upright from his sleeping mat, the open cut in his foot made him wince and remember the night before. Upright, his head started pounding. He cinched a lava lava around his waist and went to the door.

It was the *faifeau*'s truck. The *faifeau* was in the driver's seat. He honked once more before Apelu opened the screen door.

"Soifua," another man said, getting out of the passenger side door. "The reverend here gave me a ride over because I didn't know where your place was." He introduced himself. It was Roketi, the chief from Pago. "I want to report a crime."

They sat beneath the blue tarp. Roketi reported that the night before some vandals—village kids probably—had broken into his boat anchored in the harbor. Apelu nodded, excused himself, and went back inside the *fale*. He came back out with one of Sanele's school pads and a pen and an empty tin mug. Before he sat back down he filled the mug from the rain barrel. He was very thirsty. He wrote down the name of the boat, *Dream World*. He emptied the mug and excused himself again. He put the mug down on the sill above the water barrel and went around the end of the *fale*, where he took a long piss. His head was clearing and his foot was throbbing. He refilled his mug and made a point of not limping as he walked back to join them.

"Missing property?" Apelu asked, picking up the pad and pen again, tucking his lacerated foot under the edge of his lava lava.

"Nothing I've noticed so far. I've got to check. Maybe some beer and tinned food. I don't keep an up-to-the-minute inventory because I don't expect to get broken into, especially over here on Ofu."

"Do you have any idea who might have done it?"

"No. Why would I? Probably some kids, like I said. There is a bunch of expensive electronic equipment and fishing gear on the boat, but it doesn't look like they messed with any of that. At least one of the little pricks cut himself. There was blood all over the deck."

"I'll come down in a bit to inspect the crime scene and fill out a report for you to sign. We'll ask around the village." Apelu stood up to signal that the meeting was over.

"Okay, okay, you do that," Roketi said, getting up. "The reverend here was pointing out that none of this stuff like this that's been happening here happened before you showed up." Roketi walked back to the truck, but the *faifeau* stayed behind, standing at the edge of the tarp's blue shadow.

"We have heard that your son is missing," he said. "We are praying for him, praying for his safe return."

"You do that, Reverend. You do that as hard and as loud and as long as you can. And then if I do find him, you can take full credit for it. It's all yours. The credit will be all yours."

"No, all credit will go to the merciful Lord." He joined Roketi in the truck and they drove away.

It took Apelu a good hour to get ready. He made a pot of coffee, bathed and shaved and bandaged his wound. He bound it tightly, then put on a pair of Sanele's Adidas. He even borrowed his son's clothes because none of his were clean. He hobbled down to the NPS cabin, where the truck was parked at a strange angle on the lawn. Martin's butt was sticking out of the driver's side door. On the ground beside him was a plastic bucket. He squeezed a rag into it. What came out of the rag was dirty pink water.

"Martin."

"I'm not even going to ask. I don't want to know," Martin said, looking over his shoulder. "My days of asking questions and doing research here are over. I don't even care what happens to this truck, but the blood was just attracting flies."

"Can I borrow the truck again? Official business."

"If you can find the keys."

"I put them somewhere, I know."

"Well, find them then."

They were in the glove compartment. Martin picked up his bucket and rags and went into the cabin without saying anything more. Apelu drove away. The smell of antiseptic in the cab was strong. The steering wheel was still damp. There were no flies.

At the harbor Roketi came to the dock from *Dream World* in a small pontoon dinghy to pick up Apelu. Two boys were on board the boat, sweeping up broken glass and swabbing the decks. That's what happened when you left a crime scene alone too long— someone would clean it up. In this case that wasn't such a bad thing. They got the paperwork over quickly. Roketi had a list of what was missing, with a price tag on each—a pair of binoculars, a digital camera, a CD player, an emergency flare gun and box of flares, and three bottles of booze. At least Roketi hadn't pushed it too far. Plus, of course, damage to the boat. They both signed the crime report, which made it okay for insurance claim purposes.

As Apelu was about to disembark the *Dream World*, he saw another white sportfishing cruiser approaching the harbor's entrance through the reef cut. Even though he couldn't see the name on her stern, he knew it was the *Manusina II*.

Roketi was already in the dinghy, holding it to the hull for Apelu to get in. When Apelu paused, Roketi followed his gaze to the mouth of the harbor. "Boat coming in," he said. "Come on. I'll take you to shore."

"No, wait," Apelu said. "Let's visit them, warn them about the vandals."

"I can do that later," Roketi said.

"Well, actually, the Coast Guard has asked me to check on any new arriving boats."

They waited at *Dream World* until the new boat had stopped, an anchor was dropped from the stern, and a Samoan deckhand dove overboard with a line to secure her bow to a mooring buoy. As they motored over, the man who had tied up the boat to the buoy swam past them, heading for shore. Apelu didn't recognize him. The boat turned on its lines, showing her stern—*Manusina II, Pago Pago*.

Superintendent Ilmars came to the railing as they pulled alongside. "What is it you want?"

"Permission to come aboard."

"For what reason, Officer?"

"Owner's request. The commissioner asked me to check out his boat when it arrived."

"That's ridiculous, but come aboard anyway and do all the checking you want."

Apelu searched the boat. There was no one else, nothing unusual. When he came back out onto the fantail, Roketi and Ilmars had been talking but stopped when he returned.

"I was just warning him about the vandals," Roketi said. "It should be all right as long as someone's on board."

"No crew?" Apelu asked

"Just the boy who went ashore. It's his family's village. He lives in Pago. He wanted to see them."

"Speaking of crew, Roketi, I forgot to ask where was your crew when your boat got broken into?"

"I don't have any crew that lives onboard."

"What about Ace Po'o? Wasn't he living onboard?"

"No. Ace wasn't living onboard. Ace has never even set foot on my boat. I wouldn't let a scumbag like him close to it. I have no idea where he might be and I don't especially care, but he was not on my boat."

"Who is this Ace person and what does he have to do with me?" Ilmars was irritable. "If you are quite through inspecting the vessel for your suspicious boss, Officer, you are invited to leave. I have just come over from Pago Pago to bring Dr. Wentworth's body back to Tutuila. Would you kindly tell me where I can find her remains?"

"Yes, of course. In the freezer of Lolo's Store in the village."

"And is there any word about Martin Berm and the young native boy?"

Apelu stared at Ilmars, replaying the man's question, testing it to make sure he was thinking straight. He was. Apelu had never reported that Sanele and Martin were missing. If Ilmars had just arrived here, how would he know? Yet he did know. Apelu shook his head and walked to the stern. He leaned over the starboard rail and looked down. He couldn't see anything unusual. He slipped off his shirt, put it on the deck, and emptied his pockets onto it. Then, without saying anything, he climbed over the rail and dove off the side. The blue keel was there. A long scrape along the starboard hull was there.

Apelu climbed up over the engines back onto the deck. He turned to Ilmars. "It would seem that you don't know that the missing 'native boy' is my son. Where is my son? What have you done with my son? Where is Sanele?"

"I . . . I haven't the slightest idea what you are talking about, Officer. I know nothing about your son or his whereabouts."

Apelu grabbed two handfuls of Ilmars's NPS polo shirt and lifted him off the deck. "If I have to kill someone to find him, I will." The shirt ripped apart in his hands and Ilmars fell to the deck. "This boat is under arrest. It does not leave this harbor," Apelu said down at Ilmars as he twisted about to grab a rail and get upright.

"Under arrest for what? I just got here!"

"This boat was here two days ago. I saw it."

"If it was here, I wasn't on it," Ilmars said. "We just left Pago Pago last night."

○

When Roketi dropped Apelu back at the dock he went looking for Ace. Now Ace had something in common with Sanele—they were both missing. Maybe there was a connection. Ace's local family said that they had not seen him in more than a week; neither had anyone else in the village it seemed.

At the lodge Apelu called the commissioner, but the commissioner wasn't in. So he called his captain to report that he had arrested the commissioner's boat. The captain was not happy to hear about it.

○

Martin was coming back from the beach when Apelu pulled up to the NPS cabin. He was carrying a load of the things that had been left on the beach at To`aga. "Look what I found." He held up a pair of fins and a mask and snorkel. "These are the ones Sanele was using."

"So he was out of the water."

"They were up in the vines beyond the gear. He must have put them there after he took them off."

Martin carried his load to the tent in front of the cabin. When he came back he said, "Give me the keys. Get in." He started the truck, left it in neutral, and turned the air-con on high. "I am so tired of being hot," he said.

Martin seemed not to care that Ilmars was on-island. "I'm not leaving," he said. "I'm not leaving until we find Sanele."

"He's come to take Bobbie's body back."

"He can have her frozen remains. They're not Bobbie. She's like a specimen now, isn't she, Apelu? Just like one of my preserved undersea specimens—a piece of evidence, a part in a puzzle, just a detail that died leaving a space, a space that won't ever again be filled. It's like your black rock at To'aga, Apelu, your Matato'aga, where when the last of a species died there were none to replace it, no offspring, no hope." Martin said this as if he were a lab technician reading off a computer printout. "Remember that water you brought me? I could use a bottle of it now." He adjusted another vent to blow directly on him. "I've always hated the heat, but I never complained about it because what's the point?"

"The boat your boss came in on is the one that dragged you." Just another fact. "And he doesn't know that you're alive." And another.

For a long time Martin just stared straight ahead out the windshield. "That asshole," was all he said. Then after another while, "You know, when Ilmars called to pull me off our job, I told him to go fuck himself, that I was going to finish the field-work and write it up no matter what his orders were."

"That go over well?"

"Like a charm. He threatened me. I wish I had it on tape. He became kind of unhinged, told me—among other things—that he would write me up for insubordination and get me transferred out of here. He actually yelled at me over the phone, told me that he knew I was taking sexual advantage of a subordinate, meaning Bobbie. It got pretty heavy then. I told him I knew he was being paid off by the developers."

"You know that?"

"No, but it was something to say. I've never gotten along well with that man. I never told Bobbie about that part of the conversation. She wasn't there to hear it. I just told her we were supposed to be off the job. Maybe if I had told her . . ."

"You had no way of knowing."

"She would have been warned anyway, been more cautious."

"Ilmars claims he wasn't here when any of that happened, that he only arrived on the boat this morning."

"That should be fairly easy to determine, shouldn't it?" Martin was sounding a bit less like an automaton.

"It should be, maybe. Who knows? I'll try."

Apelu made a few phone calls to Pago. "If they call back, take a message for me will you, Martin? I've got to go change clothes, get out of these wet shoes."

---

    o

There is that moment after a deep free dive when you break the surface and can take that first deep draught of sweet air. There is that second when you awake from a falling dream and realize that you are not going to die. There is that meandering minute of returning from being knocked unconscious when the lights are so bright and the voices so distant but welcome. All those back-from-the-dead stories of lights at the end of a tunnel and bright gates opening. There is birth. And there was seeing Sanele lying asleep on the mat beneath the blue tarp.

Apelu stopped and stared, stunned. Unable to walk, he flopped to the ground and sat in the middle of the yard. He closed his eyes, took a deep breath, and opened them again. His son was still there, his head wrapped tightly with leaves resting on his crooked left arm, his peaceful beautiful face turned toward him. Apelu crawled forward on his hands and knees. Was he breathing? Would his skin be warm? Apelu sat cross-legged on the mat beside his son. He stretched out a hand, afraid to test his sight with touch. He laid his hand lightly on his son's shoulder. It was warm. It was him. He touched his face. He was saved.

Apelu let Sanele sleep. He sat and watched him breathe. He got up and brought a lava lava to drape over him. He wept, like a tide going out. He thought about what Sanele would want to eat when he woke up and got up to boil some noodles. His son slept deeply.

Sanele woke up with a start, sitting up suddenly. Apelu was behind him at the kerosene stove. In Samoan Sanele called out, "Dad, Dad, where are you?" There was panic in his voice.

"I'm right here, son."

Sanele swirled around. "You're all right? You're okay? I was so worried. Where have you been?"

"Looking for you."

Apelu caught Sanele in his arms before he could stand up. They held onto each other. The past three days disappeared. Panic drained from them.

CHAPTER 15

———— ○ ————

S ANELE'S STORY WAS SIMPLE. HIS LAST TASK THAT LAST DAY of the dive was to get all their gear assembled so that they could leave and get around the tongue of the landslide before dark. He was doing that when he saw the boat approach the edge of the reef where Martin was diving. He saw someone throw what looked like an anchor off the back of the boat. He yelled at Bobbie, but she was underwater. He picked up a chunk of coral from the beach and threw it toward where he could see her snorkel. It landed in front of her, and she came out of the water furious. Sanele pointed out toward the boat. They watched the man in the back of the boat hauling in on the rope then throw the anchor thing again. Sanele called out. Bobbie, now standing on a coral head, called out to the boat. The man heard them, saw them. Sanele started running toward the water.

That was it. The next he remembered he was lying on a bed of banana leaves beneath a leaky makeshift roof of coconut fronds and more banana leaves. It was raining hard. He was all alone. His head felt huge and throbbed. It was dusk or dawn, gray light, he couldn't tell. He sat up and passed out again. The next time he came to someone was holding him in a sitting position and making him drink something warm and bitter. It was still raining. He was cold. It felt like he had a helmet on his head. He felt it. It was a helmet of leaves. He went to sleep again.

The next time he woke up Uncle Nu'upo was putting new banana leaves on the crude roof just three feet above his head. He had no idea where he was. He was very weak. Uncle Nu'upo gave him *poi* made of ripe bananas and other things and gave him more of the bitter tea to drink out of a coconut half-shell. Nu'upo had Sanele change his clothes, handing him a T-shirt and lava lava that Sanele had last seen in his pile of clean clothes in his room. The rain had stopped. He slept again. He ate and drank Uncle Nu'upo's concoctions.

"Uncle Nu'upo told me that it was a dangerous time just now and that I should stay there with him until things passed over. He said he had told you where I was. I couldn't believe you wouldn't come and get me. Uncle Nu'upo was gone for long stretches of time. He told me to stay there, that I wasn't yet strong enough to move. I obeyed him, thinking every time he left that he would be coming back with you to bring me home. But you never came. All Uncle Nu'upo would say was that it wasn't yet safe enough to move."

"Where were you?" Apelu asked.

"At first I didn't know. I didn't feel strong enough to leave the little hut. Then I had to piss real bad and I crawled outside and saw that we were in Nandiaka, up against the cliff among the boulders. I knew that if you were all right you would have come that far to get me, so I figured Uncle Nu'upo wasn't telling me something. That something had happened to you and he was trying to shield me from something. I didn't know where you were, Dad. I thought something bad had happened to you, too."

Apelu felt like a mirror with his son's image in it.

"So this morning when Uncle Nu'upo left, I came home. There was nobody at Bobbie's cabin, no truck, no one here. I didn't know what to think. It was like everyone was gone and I was left alone. I was scared, Dad."

"How's your head?"

"Still hurts, but not so bad. Uncle Nu'upo's crazy, isn't he, Dad?"

"Don't say that."

"No, I mean crazy in the way that you got to protect him."

"Like some endangered species with no one to replace him?"

"No. I guess just crazy, all alone in his world."

———— o ————

Sanele took the news of Bobbie's death with what seemed to Apelu a calmness and maturity beyond his years. He asked for details. He asked about Martin. Then he excused himself and walked off into the bush. A half hour later he returned. Apelu could tell from his eyes that he had been crying, but all he said was, "What do we have to do to catch who killed her?"

It was Martin who came up with the central idea of their plan. They decided to try it immediately before either *Manusina II* or *Dream World* could slip away.

———— o ————

Roketi's *Dream World* was moored closest to the dock. Apelu parked the Park Service truck at the edge of the dock and honked the horn a few times. Then he got out of the truck and hailed the boat. He could see Roketi on deck, fixing a piece of plywood to cover the broken glass door. Apelu waved to Roketi to come get him.

"What now, Soifua?" Roketi asked as he pulled the dinghy alongside the dock.

"Take me out to *Manusina II*."

"What am I? Some sort of water taxi?"

"No, I need your help. I've found my son."

At the *Manusina II* there was no answer to Apelu's calls, so he climbed aboard again over the engines. Through a cabin window he could see Ilmars asleep on a bunk. Apelu pounded on the window until he woke him up. By now Roketi was also on board, tying up the dinghy. The Ilmars who shuffled to open the cabin door was not the same bristling man he had encountered in the morning. He unlocked and slid open the door, then he returned to his bunk and sat down. He said nothing.

"Superintendent?

"Yes?"

"Are you all right?"

"Yes, just tired. What is it now?"

"I am going to have to commandeer this boat, sir."

"Oh, bloody hell. What are you talking about?" The superintendent's right hand was searching for something in a net bag attached to the side of the bunk. He pulled out a vial of prescription pills, looked at the label, and put it back. He pulled out another vial, looked at it, opened it, and took a pill, swallowing it with a gulp of bottled water.

"Just for the remainder of the day, sir. We should be back into the harbor by dark." Apelu had followed Ilmars into the cabin, and Roketi was now standing at the door.

"Why don't you commandeer his boat?" Ilmars asked, jerking his head toward Roketi.

"Well, sir, I've already arrested this boat, and it is the commissioner's boat, so I'm sure he would understand."

"What the hell for?" Ilmar's head was down as if he were studying his knees.

"Well, sir, I've found the body of my son." Apelu didn't have to act here, just saying the words he had spent days dreading to say brought a hitch to his voice and a gasp for breath. He looked away and paused. "In To'aga, washed up on the beach, drowned."

Roketi shifted nervously at the door, but Ilmars didn't move.

"The villagers refuse to go into To'aga to help me bring him out." Apelu brought his voice back to normal. "So, I am commandeering this boat to go and bring his body back."

"I am in no condition—" Ilmars began.

"Roketi and I will manage the boat and what has to be done."

"We will?" Roketi said.

"You just rest, sir," Apelu said, and he shut the cabin door as he backed out onto the deck.

"What do you mean, I will help you manage the boat? Am I being commandeered as well?"

"What if it was your son's body out there?" Apelu asked without turning to face him. "I can't do it alone."

———————— o ————————

Roketi took his dinghy out to untie them from the mooring, then together they got the anchor up and got underway, Roketi's dinghy bobbing behind them. They didn't talk. Ilmars stayed in the cabin, lying down again in the bunk. Once out of the harbor they turned east toward To'aga.

"He's not well?" Apelu asked after a while.

"I wouldn't know. He doesn't seem so."

"I thought perhaps you two knew one another better, through the Paradise Escape Resort deal."

Apelu was at the wheel. Roketi gave him a quick sidelong look. "We met once or twice. The superintendent isn't someone you get to know." After that Roketi went forward and sat in the bow.

Off To'aga, Apelu brought the boat in close, searching for his spot. The tide was high over the reef. He coasted farther eastward, then idled the engines. Roketi came back to the stern.

"I had to bury him in the beach," Apelu said, "near here. Would you see if the superintendent is well enough to take the wheel, keep her off the reef while we go in?" Apelu hadn't counted on Ilmars being out of commission, but the superintendent came out onto the deck, scowling, looking a bit more like himself.

"What is it?"

"If you could hold her pretty much in this location, sir, chief here and I will go in to get the body."

"You'll be paying me for all this fuel we're using up?"

The question didn't deserve an answer. Even Roketi shook his head. Apelu and Roketi got in the dinghy and headed for shore. There was an easy swell and plenty of clearance over the coral. The sundown shadow of the ridge was already over the beach.

"Your son, you found him yourself?" Roketi asked as he surfed the dinghy down the waves into the beach.

"Yes. Every day I've come looking, and today the sea returned him."

"Was he . . . ?"

"Yes, he was killed the same as Dr. Wentworth, a blow to the head then probably drowned unconscious. Look, I don't want to talk about it. Let's just get this over with."

"To'aga is an evil place. I don't know what the fuck I'm doing here. No one seems to get out of this place alive or sane. I'm dropping you off and going back. I'm not going up on the beach. This place is a killer."

"To'aga didn't kill my son. Some person did. And for some reason, Roketi, I think you know who that person is. That's why you will come with me, because you're a suspect."

Roketi cut the engine and tilted it up out of the water as the last swell pushed them up onto the hard. Apelu grabbed the bow line, jumped into the receding foam, and pulled the dinghy farther ashore.

"I think you had a part in all this, Roketi, because you wanted the resort to go through for your cut of the lease money, and I'm going to find that part, that connection. That's my son's body up on the beach."

Roketi got out of the dinghy and helped Apelu pull it clear of the surf. "You're crazy, Soifua. I have no idea what happened out here that day. I wasn't here. I was at home in Ofu. Don't try to find people to blame To'aga's sins on. Don't start now."

They tied the dinghy's painter around a sharp black rock outcrop on the beach.

"This place gives me the fucking creeps," Roketi said.

It was time for Apelu to take his chance and set the hook, trust his guesses as to what had happened here three days before. "Look, Roketi, I have an eyewitness as to what happened, the superintendent's crewman, who swam ashore when he came in. He's from the village." As a matter of fact Apelu had not had the time to identify or find the man. "I have part of his story that I have to corroborate, but he is cooperating, which means he probably won't get charged with anything. I am offering you that opportunity as well."

"I don't know what you're talking about, Soifua, and I'm not going up there." Roketi took a step backward into the surf.

"Yes you are, Roketi, because if you don't help me out now I will show you absolutely no mercy."

Roketi followed Apelu up the beach. The plan was for Martin to bury Sanele high on the beach then hide, and they would try to frighten some sort of confession out of Roketi when Apelu brought him there. It wasn't much of a plan. They were winging it, but To'aga had a powerful hold on the imagination of all the villagers, including Roketi. Maybe they could spook something out of him. Sanele was to wrap himself in the blue tarp. They had taken Bobbie's tube of zinc oxide and rubbed it into his face and hands and arms to give him a proper pallor.

Apelu found the grave site easily—the beach around it was disturbed and there was a raised mound of sand and coral rubble. Roketi stopped when he saw it and looked nervously up and down the beach and along the edge of the jungle. Apelu went back, took him by the arm, and pulled him up to the grave. "Three people died here, and I'm not going to blame it on To'aga and I'm not going to leave it a mystery." He crouched down at the side of the grave and started pulling the rubble and sand away from where he presumed Sanele's head would be. The mound was deeper than he thought it would be. God! If Martin had buried him too far down he couldn't breathe. Maybe his head was at the other end? He started digging more furiously. Roketi, sensing something was wrong, took a few steps back. Apelu found the blue tarp, dug some more to find a corner, then pulled it back. There was nothing. He pulled it back further and things started crawling out—sea eels and sea slugs and land crabs. He yanked the tarp further back. A large almost dead parrot fish with blood-red sides flopped in the midst of the other creatures, all of whom were trying to make their escape.

"He was buried here," Apelu said, standing up and glancing frantically back and forth at the border of the bush, not sure what to think.

The white owl streaked out of the bush at them maybe five feet above their heads. It startled Apelu enough so that he jumped and made some sort of noise. Roketi screamed a woman's scream. He turned and ran toward the dinghy.

"Sanele! Sanele!" Apelu called. No answer. The owl had vanished as quickly as it had appeared. He shouldn't let Roketi get away. He ran down the beach where Roketi in a panic was fumbling with the painter rope. Apelu again grabbed his arm, but Roketi yanked it away.

"You're not keeping me here. I'll tell you everything I know, but I'm not staying here." Roketi pushed Apelu away as he finally freed the line, and Apelu fell. He looked back over his shoulder at the grave site and the line of jungle. Nothing. He got up and followed Roketi into the surf.

"Okay, okay, let's go," Apelu said, helping Roketi turn the dinghy into the wash and off the beach. They both got in and Roketi started the tiny outboard. The dinghy labored against the on-shore swell but made headway. Apelu turned to face Roketi. "Okay, let's talk."

Roketi kept looking back at the beach as if he suspected they would be pursued. "I had no hand in it. I really don't know what happened, honest, Soifua. All I know is what I heard that thug Ace talk about, and I didn't even want to hear that."

As they rose and fell against the incoming surf Roketi told his story. He didn't exactly blurt it out. Apelu had to extract it from him piece by piece. As the darkening shore receded behind them Roketi became a less cooperative witness, and at one point Apelu had to reach out and push him aside, grab the outboard's handle, and turn the dinghy back toward the beach. In the scuffle that ensued Roketi got punched very hard.

"I'm going to leave you on the beach, Roketi. Maybe the *aitu* can get the truth out of you." The shadows were already deep on the beach. Apelu was afraid he had lost his son again, that this time To'aga had taken him.

Roketi pleaded with Apelu to stop and turn back. He would talk, he would talk. "It was him," he said, pointing out toward *Manusina II* still idling in bright last sunlight beyond the reef. "You should ask him. He knows."

"Knows what?" Apelu said, cutting the outboard engine and turning the dinghy sideways to the swell. He looked back at the beach where nothing moved, no one waved to him. He turned the dinghy back toward the beach. How could he leave without Sanele?

Roketi started shaking in the bottom of the dinghy. There was blood on his face. "Don't go back, don't go back. I'll tell you everything I know." It came out haltingly, and Apelu had to ask Roketi direct questions to fill in the gaps. Twice more he stopped to look back at the empty beach, and Roketi would start talking again.

The superintendent had first arrived in Ofu harbor on *Manusina II* three days before, on the weekend. Roketi said Ilmars was pissed off at this Martin guy. It had something to do with his trying to stop the resort. Ilmars went ashore and came back even more pissed, because he had called the Park Service cabin and no one was there. He came onto Roketi's boat *Dream World* and wasn't making much sense. Ace was there. Yes, Roketi admitted, Ace had been living on *Dream World* after his family had thrown him out. Anyway, Ace went with Ilmars to *Manusina II*, and they pulled up anchor and left.

"And then?" Apelu cut the engine to idle. They were closing on *Manusina II* too fast.

"They got back after dark, but separately," Roketi said. Ace had come back first and called from the dock for Roketi to come get him. He complained about having to walk all the way back from To`aga and sneak past the village on the beach. A little while later the *Manusina II* slipped back into the harbor and Ace swam out to it. End of story. "I was happy to have him off my boat. I went ashore. The next day was Sunday, and I spent it with my family. Monday morning when I came back, *Manusina II* was gone and so was Ace. All his gear was gone from *Dream World*. Good riddance."

Above them the last of the ocean terns were returning to their roosts above To`aga. The sundown on-shore breeze had a chill in it. They were closing on *Manusina II*.

"Now you are going to tell me what Ace told you," Apelu said.

"What do you mean, what Ace told me?"

"You said Ace told you things that you didn't want to hear. What things? You're still on the hook, Roketi."

"Okay, okay. When Ace came on board *Dream World*, he found a bottle of rum and downed half of it. He started bragging about how that *palangi* dude Ilmars owed him big time, how he had saved his ass. I told him to shut up, that I didn't want to hear about it, but he was so full of himself he couldn't shut up. He was all hyped up."

It turned out that Ace was prone to seasickness and he had gotten kind of green going around the point to To`aga, so he had the superintendent pull in close to shore near where the new landslide entered the ocean and he swam in from there. He would rather walk to To`aga. The superintendent had scraped the hull on a boulder going in there and got angry with Ace about it. Now Ace figured the superintendent could go fuck himself about the hull. The dude had fucked up, and he, Ace, had saved him.

"Meaning?" Apelu asked.

"Meaning I don't know what. The *Manusina II* came into the harbor. Ace swam over there, and that was the last I saw of him."

They came alongside of the *Manusina II* and Roketi climbed on board its stern with the bow line. Roketi hadn't told it all, but it was all Apelu had. He followed Roketi onto the deck.

---

o

"No body?" Ilmars asked, but neither Apelu nor Roketi answered him. Apelu was looking back toward the beach. Roketi was securing the dinghy's line to a stern cleat.

"What's that?" Roketi asked. Something had bumped up against the boat's hull. In the next swell it bumped again, slightly forward starboard side. Ilmars was leaving the deck, going back to the cabin. He was quite pale. Roketi moved forward, looking over the starboard rail. "Wait! Wait!" he called. "Is that . . . ?"

Apelu and Ilmars joined Roketi. There in the shadow of the hull something was floating. Part of it was shiny black, the rest was white. The swell bumped it again against the hull. They could see an arm and legs, the back of a head above a wetsuit top.

Suddenly Ilmars had a long gaff in his hands, and before Apelu or Roketi could stop him he pushed at the floating body. "Get away. Get away from my boat," he said. The body rolled over and sank, but before it disappeared they could see that the face, though white and lifeless, was Martin's. Apelu wrestled the gaff away from Ilmars. Roketi raced to the stern of the boat, untied his dinghy, jumped in, and was gone.

Ilmars held onto the starboard rail with both hands, holding himself upright. "You brought that with you, didn't you?" he said, looking into the water. "You brought that to scare me into confessing or something, like you scared Mr. Rocket. A cheap trick, Detective, and unnecessary. I'm not scared of the dead. I'm not spooked by To'aga. I'm almost dead myself. Why, I belong here in this godforsaken place, this hell hole, hell gate. It doesn't really matter. What's another body or two?"

The engines were at idle and the *Manusina II* swayed aimlessly in the conflicting currents of the outgoing tide and the onshore swell.

"So many bodies. That's all any of us really are, just bodies, pre-corpses. At least when they sink they don't stink. Have you noticed my smell? I've already begun to stink like a dead man. You and I are exactly alike, Detective, identical carbon-based potential compost. Don't you think it preferable to be eaten rather than to rot, more useful, back in the food chain faster? But then you just lost a son, so you can't be rational about this sort of thing. Martin was useless. It's good that he never reproduced himself." Ilmars turned to look at Apelu, who was just listening.

"You don't like me, Detective, and you—like me—don't believe in God. Do you? Without a god you've got no absolute good, so you can't have a measure of evil either. So I can't be evil. You just don't like me. It doesn't matter. Do you have a daughter, Detective? I have a daughter. She's twenty-eight years old and not doing well. Salt Lake City. Needs money. New start. If I can get the money the developers promised me to her before I die, no one can take it away from her. New start, get her kids back. I've never done much of anything right by her. Maybe this, she'll forgive me the rest. Do you see why you can't scare me?"

"Where's Ace?"

"He probably stopped swimming many hours ago."

"Long way to go?"

"Too far."

"He kill Bobbie and Sanele?"

"His turn to be To'aga's doorman, I guess. Nobody asked him to do it. He was an animal. He felt free to kill there. Afterward he thought I owed him something for clubbing a couple of innocent bystanders. I drowned him the way you would drown a mad dog."

"Or a witness."

Ilmars straightened, turned, and headed back toward the cabin. "A witness to what, Detective? All I did was your job. I saved you the trouble."

"The same way you drowned Martin?"

"I'm not sure how Martin died," Ilmars said, going into the cabin. "But I do know about Ace's end," he said, coming back out of the cabin with a small black automatic in his hand. "And yours will be similar. Stand over there." He wagged the gun in the direction of the cabin. "I'd rather give you a sporting chance and not have your blood all over your boss's boat. Just another drowning to add to To'aga's toll. It doesn't matter, remember?"

Apelu moved in the direction the gun's muzzle wagged. Ilmars moved to the wheel and nudged the port engine's throttle forward, pointing the boat toward the open sea, then he pushed both throttles forward. The boat shook in the water as the props found a grip and then headed out.

"A lot of loose ends, Ilmars."

"Not for me. This will sort of tie it all up, actually. You see, I don't like you either, Detective, just another uppity native, someone who thinks he's clever and important. No one is going to miss you, and you know there's no afterlife to welcome you."

The boat was picking up speed. Ilmars kept the gun trained on Apelu while his left hand held the wheel. They were going too fast against the chop. It was bound to happen. The boat took a sea swell on its shoulder and shuddered. The wheel spun out of Ilmars' single-handed grip and he instinctively grabbed for it with his other hand. It was three steps and a dive over the side for Apelu. He heard one shot before he hit the water. Three more shots banged out behind him after he resurfaced and started to swim, none of them close. The boat kept on toward the open sea, bouncing erratically under close to full throttle.

———————— o ————————

The three of them were waiting for Apelu on the beach. Sanele and Martin were still white as ghosts in their zinc oxide makeup. Sanele's skull had a new wrapping of leaves. Nu'upo, dressed just in an old lava lava tucked up like a loin cloth and his battered yellow Lands' End fanny pack, was pacing back and forth on the beach behind them. Again dusk was folding in on To'aga, the dark blanket of the ridge draping its protective shadow over the pillow of beach and blue sheet of sea.

Sanele met him in waist-deep water. "We heard the shots," he said, "and then for the longest time we couldn't see you swimming. Uncle Nu'upo saw you first. Is he gone?"

"Yes, son, the last of the bad guys is gone. How are you?"

"Okay, I guess." They were walking toward the beach, the retreating waves pulling at their legs. "We changed the burial thing."

"So I noticed," Apelu said.

As they came out of the water Martin met them. "You mean you let that asshole Ilmars, the man who tried to kill me, get away?"

"You make a better corpse than I do, Martin."

"I checked the hull. That's the boat. It was him, wasn't it?"

"Yes, I believe so."

"So, he gets just to sail off into the sunset?"

Nu'upo's turn was next. He did not stop pacing back and forth as he addressed Apelu, but he only spoke as he was walking toward him. "You idiot motherfucker." He paused as he walked past Apelu then turned. "You were going to bury my boy here at To'aga." He paused as he passed and turned. "After I had saved him from death at the very same spot." Pass, pause. "You have no respect, no idea of the danger, no common sense."

Nu`upo stopped in front of Apelu. "To`aga would never have given him up a second time. Don't you understand anything?"

"I think it's time we headed back," said Martin.

"You can't be trusted." Nu`upo was talking now into Apelu's face. "Can't you see the boy is not well, not fit to be buried alive?"

"Uncle Nu`upo," Sanele tried to intervene.

"No, rest, my son. Do not get involved," Nu`upo said as he led Sanele away and sat him down in the sand. He fussed with the vines of Sanele's green headdress. He went to the ocean and brought back a cupped double handful of seawater to sprinkle on Sanele's head. "You must keep it moist," he said. "You need more medicine. We'll go back to our little camp. Have you eaten? I'll feed you there. There is eel—many bones, you must be careful, Etuane, not to choke on them, they're small."

"No, not tonight, Father," Sanele said. "Tonight I will go home with Apelu and Martin. I must change my clothes, sleep in my bed, call my girlfriend."

"Your girlfriend Filemu?" Nu`upo asked.

"Yes, Filemu."

"Say hello to her for me." Nu`upo unzipped his fanny pack and pulled out a battered plastic water bottle and handed it to Sanele. "Here, drink this. I got it today especially for you. It will keep you smart for an hour or two, long enough to talk with Filemu. What thighs she has! Like brown wings opening." Nu`upo stepped away from Sanele, resting his hand once on Sanele's head. "Good luck," he said, and he disappeared into the bush.

———— o ————

The moon was full with the tide and rising. Martin, Sanele, and Apelu picked their way around the landslide tongue of boulders and back to the NPS cabin. Along the way Martin asked Apelu about Ilmars.

"Close to death," Apelu said.

"But free?"

"The opposite of free."

"How so?"

"He's out there alone in the open ocean at night with just enough gas to get him into the middle of nowhere, which is probably where he belongs. I saw what he had left in his tanks. By midnight he'll be adrift, out of gas."

"Full moon, anyway."

"I don't think that will help Ilmars much tonight."

Back at the cabin Martin cooked something, but long before it was ready Apelu and Sanele were asleep side by side on the cabin floor.

CHAPTER 16

———————— o ————————

SANELE WANTED APELU TO COME ALONG THIS TIME. APELU knew that when Sanele had disappeared over the past few weeks, he had been going up to see Nu`upo. Things were almost back to normal on the island. They'd fixed the interisland plane and it was flying again. They'd almost finished clearing the road to To`aga and Olosega. No one had asked Apelu again to sign anything that had to do with the resort. Martin was back in Pago Pago, acting park superintendent again.

Superintendent Ilmars had been rescued at sea, against his wishes, it would seem. When the commissioner found out what had happened to his boat, he called in air searches, and when the *Manusina II* was spotted adrift halfway between Ofu and Tutuila he arranged through the Coast Guard to have an albacore boat in the vicinity find it and tow it back to Pago Pago. Ilmars had fired the rest of the slugs in his handgun at his rescuers' boat, but to no effect. They brought him in anyway. The commissioner was so pissed about the damage to the *Manusina II*'s hull that he had Ilmars charged with the murder of Ace as well as the attempted murders of Martin and Apelu, though the Ace case would be hard to prove with no body and no witnesses. It didn't make

246

much difference. Ilmars was too sick to make even his preliminary hearing. The feds medevaced him up to Hawaii, though no one could help him.

Apelu and Sanele walked up together. Along the way up the ridge, Sanele had set bird traps here and there in the bush, perfecting a new design that never seemed to work. He came back every time empty-handed, shrugging his shoulders. It was not a day to be hiking up the ridge. There was barely a cloud in the sky, and it was very hot. When they reached the top, Sanele cut off on a trail to the right, not to Nu`upo's camp but along the cliff edge of the ridge above To`aga.

"Dad, do you believe in the past?"

"What a weird question, son. What part of the past are you talking about?"

"I mean the past when things were different than they are now."

"Yeah, I believe the past was different sometimes. Why?"

"Because Uncle Nu`upo doesn't. He says chaos doesn't change, that we're no different than what we came from, and that's the way it should remain."

"Too deep for me. What do you think?"

"I was hit on the head, remember?"

"But what do you want to believe?"

"He says the past and the afterlife are the same thing—the present."

"Pretty deep shit."

"But that's what he says."

"You like Uncle Nu`upo?"

"I'm important to him. He's cool to be around."

"But then, you were hit on the head."

"Dad!" Sanele turned around and punched Apelu playfully but hard on the arm.

"Just don't hit me in the head," Apelu said, raising his arms in front of his face. "Someone in this family has got to make sense."

Sanele laughed and threw another, softer, punch.

Nu'upo was sitting again on the edge of a cliff, this time looking out over To'aga back at Olosega. He was breathing heavily and sweat was dripping off of him.

"Uncle Nu'upo, are you all right?" Sanele asked as they walked up to him.

"She was after me again, son, but I'm still in better shape than she is. She'll never catch me. You brought the cops?"

"Just my dad. I wanted to show him what I've done."

"Your son does good work. He learns fast," Nu'upo said, squeegeeing the sweat from his face with the palm of his hand, "but he still doesn't bring enough food. What is wrong with kids these days?"

"May I?" Sanele asked.

"What am I going to do? Throw him off the cliff? Your dad is harmless, an outsider to meaningful chaos. So show him, show him."

Sanele led Apelu to a spot further along the cliff, at the very edge overlooking To'aga. He squatted down. "What do you think, Dad?" In front of him on a flattish piece of the top of the cliff was a cleared area of rock maybe three feet square into which had been cut ancient petroglyph designs—sea birds, turtles, sharks, and simple geometric patterns.

"See, I started here. Uncle Nu'upo showed me how and told me to just like doodle. Then I got into it and they got bigger. See?"

Next to Sanele's piece was another. This one had sailing ships and the vagina design.

"That's Uncle Nu'upo's new one. When we're both done, we're going to pry them loose and send them down into To'aga. Uncle Nu'upo says that chaos needs all the help it can get. You won't tell anyone, will you, Dad?"

"I won't tell a soul, son, not a soul."

ACKNOWLEDGMENTS

I WOULD LIKE TO ACKNOWLEDGE THE DEBT I OWE TO TERRY Goodman and Alison Dasho of Thomas & Mercer and to David Downing for their always professional guidance and especially to my agent, Peter Riva, for the faith and confidence he has shown in my work. Faafetai tele lava.

ABOUT THE AUTHOR

———— o ————

JOHN ENRIGHT WAS BORN in Buffalo, New York, in 1945. After serving stints in semi-pro baseball and the Lackawanna steel mills, he earned his degree from City College while working full-time at *Fortune, Time,* and *Newsweek* magazines. He later completed a master's degree in folklore at UC-Berkeley, before devoting the 1970s to the publishing industry in New York, San Francisco, and Hong Kong. In 1981, he left the United States to teach at the American Samoa Community College and spent the next twenty-six years living on the islands of the South Pacific. Over the past four decades, his essays, articles, short stories, and poems have appeared in more than seventy books, anthologies, journals, periodicals, and online magazines. His collection of poems from Samoa, *14 Degrees South,* won the University of the South Pacific Press's inaugural International Literature Competition. Today, he and his wife, ceramicist Connie Payne, live in Jamestown, Rhode Island.